WITHDRAWN

PATRICK GRIFFIN'S
LAST
BREAKFAST ON EARTH

PATRICK GRIFFIN'S
LAST
BREAKFAST on EARTH

NED RUST

ROARING BROOK PRESS
New York

Text copyright © 2016 by Ned Rust
Illustrations copyright © 2016 by Jake Parker

Published by Roaring Brook Press
Roaring Brook Press is a division of Holtzbrinck Publishing
Holdings Limited Partnership
175 Fifth Avenue, New York, New York 10010
mackids.com

Library of Congress Cataloging-in-Publication Data

Names: Rust, Ned. | Parker, Jake, 1977– illustrator.
Title: Patrick Griffin's last breakfast on earth / Ned Rust ; illustrations
  by Jake Parker.
Description: First edition. | New York : Roaring Brook Press, 2016. |
  Series: Patrick Griffin and the three worlds ; Book 1 | Summary: "A
  12-year-old boy sets out on a crazy adventure through parallel worlds
  and learns he and a giant bunny are the key to saving the universe"—
  Provided by publisher.
Identifiers: LCCN 2015017843 | ISBN 9781626723429 (hardback) |
  ISBN 9781626723436 (e-book)
Subjects: | CYAC: Fantasy. | Space and time—Fiction. | Heroes—
  Fiction. | BISAC: JUVENILE FICTION / Action & Adventure /
  General. | JUVENILE FICTION / Humorous Stories. | JUVENILE
  FICTION / Fantasy & Magic.
Classification: LCC PZ7.1.R875 Pat 2016 | DDC [Fic]—dc23
LC record available at http://lccn.loc.gov/2015017843

Our books may be purchased in bulk for promotional, educational, or
business use. Please contact your local bookseller or the Macmillan
Corporate and Premium Sales Department at (800) 221-7945 ext. 5442
or by email at MacmillanSpecialMarkets@macmillan.com.

First edition 2016
Book design by Elizabeth H. Clark
Printed in the United States of America

1 3 5 7 9 10 8 6 4 2

For Ruth

CONTENTS

PART I: INNOCENTS

1. THE BETTER PART OF NEGLECT 3
2. CAT'S AWAY 8
3. WAFFLES REDUX 13
4. FIRST DAWNINGS 17
5. OBSERVABLE PHENOMENA 20
6. UNIQUE QUALIFICATIONS 25
7. A DIFFERENT SORT OF HOMECOMING 30
8. A PLACE OF SENSE 32
9. SORRY, WRONG HOUSE 39
10. SECOND THOUGHTS 45
11. SERVICE OUTAGE 49
12. KEEPING UP APPEARANCES 58
13. DAUGHTERLY SUPPORT 64
14. MASSIVE MULTIPLAYER 69
15. HOUSEHOLD ODORS 82
16. TWINNING 86

PART II: INTERLOPERS

17. MAPS & ANTS 91
18. ADEPT INTERCEPT 100
19. INTRO TO MODERN CHEMISTRY 102
20. LIFE & DEATH IN THE BUSH 115
21. THE FIRST OF LASTERS 120

22.	CRACKIN' UP	136
23.	PAIN IN THE GRASS	144
24.	FOUR-CHILD GARAGE	156
25.	SANNYTATION	159
26.	ROADSIDE ASSISTANCE	176
27.	WHAT MEETS THE EYE	183
28.	SUNSHOWER	194
29.	THE HISTORY OF ITH, V. 12.17	197
30.	FIELD OPERATIONS	205
31.	THE COLOR CRIMSON	208
32.	IXNAY ON THE ODENTRAYS	219
33.	BASELINE CONDITIONS	226
34.	LOCO PARENTIS	232
35.	TALKING TO GIRLS	235

PART III: IMPRESARIOS

36.	SITUATIONAL ASSESSMENT	241
37.	A SPY IN THE HOUSE OF PUBER	244
38.	YOUTHFUL FOLLOWINGS	253
39.	ATTITUDES ON GRATITUDE	256
40.	CHILDREN AND FOOLS	265
41.	TO SLEEP, PERCHANCE TO DREAM	270
42.	BACKUP DRIVER	276
43.	BIGGY PACKING	282
44.	COURSE CORRECTION	290
45.	TO DREAM, PERCHANCE TO SLEEP	295
46.	EXECUTIONAL ASSESSMENT	297

47. UNDERGROUND MOVEMENTS 306

48. STAY CLOSE 313

49. HANGING ON THE LINE 326

50. PROVING GROUND 329

51. SIBLING RELATIONS 336

52. SITE SEEING 342

53. TWIN TAILINGS 348

54. THE DREAMER'S DODGE 350

55. POINT OF SOME RETURN 359

56. FOSSE AUX LIONS 362

57. SURREPTITIOUS RETURNS 365

58. REMOTE CONTROL 375

59. MOMMA DON'T PLAY NO GAMES 377

60. LONG-DISTANCE COMMUNICATIONS 380

61. A FLOCK OF GRIFFINS 383

62. SHORT-DISTANCE COMMUNICATIONS 386

63. FOOL ME ONCE 390

64. WAKEY WAKEY 394

For me, O Partha, there is naught to do in the three worlds, nothing worth gaining that I have not gained; yet I am ever in action.

—BHAGAVAD GITA

PART I: INNOCENTS

Q: Let me put it another way. What, of your own experiences, have been the most frightening?
A: Betrayals. Abandonments.

—TRUMAN CAPOTE, *Nocturnal Turnings,*
bcp §81¶1987

CHAPTER 1

The Better Part of Neglect

AS FAR AS PATRICK GRIFFIN COULD TELL, THE ONLY good thing about being the middle-most of seven children was that he tended to get ignored. Getting ignored meant he could *sometimes* have time, toys, and thoughts to himself—things that were otherwise pretty hard to find in the bustling, helter-skelter Griffin home.

The rest of it, of course, was that being one of *seven* Griffin kids meant he had all the problems that came with receiving only *one-seventh* of his parents' attention and resources. And, in reality, he figured he got less than that.

But to his mind not a single piece of neglect had ever

come close to that rainy Saturday morning in March—the morning of the day he disappeared—when he arrived downstairs to find there were no waffles.

There had been an eighteen-pack yesterday. He'd pulled it out of the freezer case at Kroger himself. Friday afternoons, while most of his siblings were at sports, Patrick would go shopping with Mom and the Twins, and they would pick out a treat for Saturday breakfast: coffee cakes, sticky buns, bagels, sometimes even a big box of some sugar-crusted cereal.

Yesterday, the four of them had decided on toaster-ready waffles.

If you counted Mom and Dad, there were nine people in the family. Divide eighteen waffles by nine people and you get two waffles per person—two waffles; not three, not four, not one, and definitely not *zero* waffles.

"Mom!"

He padded to the top of the basement stairs, yelled her name another time, then went to the den. Annoying Neil would probably be in there holding a game controller—or

Dad the universal remote—and would know where she was. But neither Neil nor Dad was there. Nobody was there. He observed the rain pattering on the casement window and decided there was no point checking the yard.

"Mom!!!" he yelled up the front-hall stairs. "Somebody ate my waffles!"

For the third time there was no reply. And something was strange. This was different from those rare moments when the Twins weren't awake, Neil wasn't getting yelled at, Carly wasn't throwing a fit, Mom wasn't on someone's case, Dad wasn't trying to find something, and Eva wasn't laughing at somebody. No, it was more than quiet right then at 96 Morningside Drive; it was *silent*.

He took the stairs, two at a time, to the second floor. His parents' bedroom, and the rooms of his younger siblings, Carly and the Twins, were all vacant. And neither was there anybody in the bedrooms or bathrooms on the third floor. Which left only one place to check: he drew a deep breath and climbed the steep, creaky fourth-floor stairs to the attic, and the lair of his oldest sister, Lucie.

"Lucie!?" he asked from the wooden landing. "Lucie—are you there?"

He knocked loudly four times before turning the handle. It was risky enough touching something of Lucie's she'd left on the kitchen counter; entering her room without permission . . .

Every one of Patrick's siblings terrified him on some level—the Twins for their control over his parents, Carly for her eardrum-splitting temper, Neil for his inability to leave any other human (and especially Patrick) at peace, and his second-oldest sister, Eva, for her sarcastic and confidence-shattering putdowns—but nobody scared Patrick like his eldest sibling, seventeen-year-old Lucie. Lucie who lived in the attic. Lucie who wore a black leather jacket even when it was hot out. Lucie who painted weird paintings. Lucie who listened to heavy electronic music that made Patrick feel seasick. Lucie who gloomed in and out of the house as if she were a gothic priestess renting an apartment that—to everybody's discomfort—didn't have a private entrance.

Patrick stepped into the shag-carpeted, incense-smelling room and, just to be safe, called her name once more. But she clearly wasn't there. The easel in the middle of the room held a charcoal sketch of a squirrel with its head twisted around the wrong way. Above, in harsh, dripping letters, it read, "LOOK FORWARD TO THINGS, IT'S BETTER FOR YOUR POSTURE."

He shivered and went to the window. It happened to be the only place in the house with a good view of the driveway.

He stood a moment, resting his cheek against the pane, his breath fogging the glass and obscuring his view of the wet blacktop where his parents' cars would have been parked, had they been home.

· · · · ·

Patrick pulled his face from the window and blinked hard, reassuring himself that this really wasn't such a bad situation. Was it not one of his most frequent, if not heartfelt, wishes that they all just leave him alone? And, if he was now here in the house all by himself, was that not exactly what was happening?

There in fact was right now *nobody* around to tell him what to do or, for that matter, what *not* to do. He could go pick what he wanted to watch on the TV and even turn the volume up too loud. He could go play one of Neil's treasured PlayStation 4 games. He could go search through Carly's room and find the *Westing Game* book she claimed not to have stolen. He could go take back his Legos Mom had given to the Twins. He could go to his parents' room and eat some of the candy that Dad kept hidden in his sock drawer. Or he could stay right here and look for evidence that Lucie smoked cigarettes like the kids at school said she did.

Patrick bolted from the room, a crooked grin on his face. He knew exactly what to do about the missing waffles.

CHAPTER 2

Cat's Away

PATRICK LONG-STEPPED HIS WAY DOWN THE stairs—two at a time—which he wasn't supposed to do because it was dangerous (and noisy), and then, on the third floor, opted for the back stairwell and another prohibited method of household descent: the wooden banister to the mud room.

The banister was both steep and long and, unless you went down feetfirst on your belly, braking with your hands, you came off so fast you either had to hit the ground running or fall flat on your face.

Patrick squatted, peering down the stairwell for any

obstacles. The mud room, as his mother often complained, was the family's dumping ground, most always strewn with pieces of clothing, shoes, slippers (his mother forbade the wearing of "outdoor shoes" inside the house), school books, umbrellas, backpacks, and other random items that had come across the threshold without enough momentum to make it to their proper places.

From here at the top of the stairs he could already see a reusable grocery bag and one of Carly's soccer cleats. He'd have no trouble with those. The real challenge, as always, would come with objects that lay out of sight, past where the stairwell ceiling cut off the view.

He pulled off his socks, stood, shook his arms like a sprinter, drew a deep breath, and mounted the railing sidesaddle-style.

"Three, two, one," he said, and let go.

There was something white—a shin guard, probably— off to the left, and a gray sock near it, and then a broom up against the radiator on the right—no problem there— and then something dark a little farther along—something dark and furry: Carly's greasy-haired old alley cat was napping in the middle of the floor.

"SHOOOO!" yelled Patrick as he shot off the railing, landing his first step almost two yards past the bottom stair. The unpleasant animal—Neil had nicknamed it Balrog after a cave monster in *The Lord of the Rings*—now startled awake and sprang to its arthritic feet. But it was too late; Patrick was either going to have to purposely crash into the wall to avoid hitting it or—

"Three!" he yelled in triumph as he stuck the landing on just his third step. The cat, meantime, managed an impressive burst of speed, reaching the end of the hall and scrambling three-quarters of the way up the screen door. It hissed like a punctured tire, glaring hatefully at Patrick—baleful yellow eyes narrowed to demonic slits, greasy hackles raised from its dandruffy pelt, and veiny ears flattened against its wedge-shaped head.

"You want out?" he asked.

A neighborhood Scottish terrier had been taken by a coyote that summer, and this past fall a wandering bear had caused a park closure a dozen miles away in Peekskill. Carly may not have lavished much care or attention on her pet—most of the time it was Mr. Griffin who filled its food bowl, and as far as Patrick could tell, nobody but Dad had ever emptied its litter box, either—but Carly apparently enjoyed the feeling she was keeping the creature from certain doom, and so the cat was never allowed outside.

"Seriously," said Patrick, nodding at the green brightness beyond the door. "You want to go out? Carly only lives *here*, you know. If you get a good head start—"

The cat's growls devolved into an otherworldly moan, the sort of sound you'd indeed expect to hear from some leathery, hobbit-eating cave monster. It now climbed to the very top of the screen, its freakishly triangular head somehow aimed at him the whole way.

Patrick took a step back, grabbed the plastic-bristled broom leaning against the radiator, and said, "Let's do each other a favor, okay?"

The cat uttered a new sort of hiss that raised goose pimples up and down his arms.

"Deal," said Patrick. He angled the broom ahead of him like a lance, stepped to the front edge of the "Bless This Mess" entryway mat, judged his mark, and charged.

The tip of the broom handle caught the latch, flinging the door wide and dislodging the animal, which—seemingly in slow motion—sailed out over the flagstone walkway. Like some mangy, waddle-bellied high-diver, it corkscrewed in midair, somehow got its legs beneath it, and disappeared with a dull thump among the Christmas ferns along the side of the house.

The creature then periscoped its bony head above the foliage, gave Patrick the briefest devil-eyed stare, and torpedoed away through the plants, across the lawn, and through the thirteen-foot-high hedges of Mr. Coffin's mansion next door.

"Don't do anything I wouldn't do," he said softly. It was one of Dad's more annoying fuddy-duddy expressions but Patrick figured it was actually kind of funny in this case. He pulled shut the screen door and headed into the kitchen. He was past starving.

CHAPTER 3
Waffles Redux

ONE THING PATRICK HAD ALWAYS BEEN VERY GOOD at was cooking. Mom said it was because he had an organized mind—just like hers—at least when he chose to use it. But Patrick knew the biggest reason he was good at cooking was that he *wanted* to be good at cooking. And the principal reason for this was that Uncle Andrew had told Patrick that cooking was a lot like chemistry.

If there was one person in the whole world Patrick wanted to emulate, it was his Uncle Andrew. Uncle Andrew didn't talk about baseball or golf or politics. Uncle Andrew didn't get on Patrick's case about grades. Uncle

Andrew didn't compare Patrick to his brothers and sisters. Uncle Andrew brought Patrick cool gifts like *Calvin and Hobbes* books. Uncle Andrew told jokes and stories—like the one about the farmer, the pig, the cork, and the monkey—that Patrick would never in a million years have heard from his parents or from any other adult he knew.

And Uncle Andrew had a job Uncle Andrew loved, which was not something Patrick could say for any other grown-ups he knew. A car ride home from school usually involved his mother complaining about a client meeting, her schedule, her co-workers, or her commute. A dinner seldom went by without his father saying something gloomy about the prospects of the book publishing company for which he was a sales rep.

Patrick climbed onto a stool, retrieved the seldom-used waffle maker from the top cabinet, grabbed some Fluffy Clouds pancake mix from the pantry, logged into the kitchen computer, converted the back-of-box recipe into metric units, and typed up a proper experimental protocol.

And, from there—and in a matter of only thirteen minutes—he managed to produce twelve perfectly cooked waffles.

Uncle Andrew, he was certain, would have been proud.

• • • • •

Patrick felt a little queasy after the seventh waffle, but it was okay. It was nice for once: his own stomach letting him know he was full rather than—as was generally the case—somebody else telling him he'd had enough, and that he should go put his plate in the dishwasher. Plus, they had been the best waffles he'd ever eaten.

He burped into the back of his hand and went to the bathroom for some vitamins and some of his dad's fruit-flavored antacid pills. The latter were a good source of calcium and he tried to eat a few every week.

Patrick didn't get bullied or teased at school for being small—he was pretty much average for his class—but Neil had taken to calling him Patty Shortstockings, and one of his greatest wishes in life was to one day become taller, and stronger, than his thirteen-months-older brother.

Patrick chewed down a third chalky tablet—this one was "berry" flavored and hurt his mouth slightly less than the "lime" ones—and wondered if he'd ever in his life heard himself chew like this.

The quiet was almost alarming. He reassured himself that everything so far this morning had only been good. He'd broken his banister-slide landing record, he'd liberated his sister's evil cat, and he'd made the best waffles of his life. In fact, bad stuff—getting yelled at, punched, tackled, breaking something, spilling something, having to talk about something boring, having something stolen from him, getting laughed at, getting teased, getting forced to run errands or to do chores—all of that was obviously way more likely to happen when he *hadn't* been forgotten all alone at home.

Plus, if something actually were to happen, he could always call Mom or Dad on their cells.

No, the only thing he should be worrying about now was wasting what little time he had left. He regarded the tubes and bottles on the medicine cabinet shelves in front of him and—in a flash—what to do next became abundantly clear.

CHAPTER 4
First Dawnings

MARY MEYER GRIFFIN, PATRICK'S MOTHER, JOLTED as if she'd heard a gunshot. Her memo tone—a few bars from the theme to *Jeopardy*—had just gone off, prompting her to glance at her iPhone. The reminder read,

Crly sccr

This was so she wouldn't forget to take Carly to her soccer clinic. She'd already done this. The next was

Mouth grd 4 Neil

This was so she wouldn't forget to pick up a new mouth-guard for Neil's lacrosse game that afternoon, which was why she was now standing in the checkout line at Cap'n'Jock's Sporting Supply Company. It was her eldest son's third mouthguard already this season. He chewed them to pieces, much as he'd done with pacifiers and then plastic toys as a small child. She and her husband some-times joked that he was one-quarter Labrador retriever.

Ptrk b-day: Andrew

This third was not so that she didn't forget Patrick's birth-day on Thursday—she liked to think she was incapable of being quite that negligent—but, rather, a reminder to take some extra care picking out his gift.

Her otherwise reserved middle son was openly crazy for chemistry, so for this past Christmas she'd gone on-line, done some research, and ordered him the J. G. Bal-lard Junior Laboratory Experiment Kit. It had been in the right age range, had received positive customer reviews (four and a half stars), and had only cost $54.99, with free shipping.

Patrick had of course been very polite about receiv-ing it. Much like her brother Andrew, Patrick was the quintessential middle child—seldom if ever throwing the sorts of tantrums or succumbing to the emotional outbursts of his older and younger siblings. But she'd known the instant he'd unwrapped the gift and forced himself to smile (and later, when he'd managed to solve every experiment it contained in under an hour and had neatly put its box away in the playroom closet) that the kit had been beneath both his abilities and his interest. This coming birthday she was resolved to make it up to him.

And so this memo was to ask Patrick's favorite uncle, Andrew, for some guidance.

But now, as she stuck Neil's unpurchased mouthguard into a trading card display and apologized her way past the customers standing behind her in line, she realized she might be responsible for something a lot worse than a disappointing Christmas gift.

"Rick!" she screamed her husband's name into her iPhone as she ran through the crowded, rainy Saturday-morning strip-mall parking lot toward her silver SUV. *Please tell me you brought Patrick with you this morning!?*

CHAPTER 5
Observable Phenomena

HALF A BOTTLE OF CLOG-B-GON DRAIN CLEANER, two liberal shots of Summer Shine dishwasher gel, a quarter bottle of Shopmark cooking oil, ten drops of Dr. Rainbow's food coloring, a quarter bottle of Healthy Nailz nail polish remover, thirteen sprays of Today's Gent cologne, the remnants of a long-expired bottle of Borominic cough syrup, ten Clarity Organics window cleaner squirts, three caps of O'Connell's Pore-Reducing Cleanser, one dusty bottle of Miracle Klear eye drops, half a bar of Scottish Dingle soap, one quarter tube of Magic Tuba toothpaste, two Calcicon antacid tablets, two peppermint-flavored Agree mints, a few dashes of Toru's Patented Super Hot Chili Sauce, half a cup of ammonia, and various sprinkles and dashes of other household liquids and powders didn't—Patrick soon concluded—make for the world's most active chemical reaction.

Despite the food dye, the concoction was a boring gray. And, despite the cologne, it smelled really, really bad— kind of like the men's room at a highway rest stop.

He scowled down into the bland-looking soup. All his mixing and careful considerations had been for nothing. Here he'd had his first chance to cause a spontaneous reaction—bubbling, smoke, solid precipitates, anything— and it had been, as Neil would say, an *epic fail*.

Of course he hadn't exactly had ideal laboratory conditions. So as not to press his luck, he'd chosen ingredients as much based upon the unlikelihood of anybody noticing they were missing as upon their likely reactive properties. And there weren't any Bunsen burners, distillation tubes, graduated cylinders, Rotovaps, or Erlenmeyer flasks in the Griffin kitchen; he'd had to make do with the stainless steel sink, some measuring cups, and a whisk.

But Mom was always saying beggars couldn't be choosers, and when would he ever have another chance like this? She would probably be back in a matter of minutes, and after this he was sure he'd not be left alone in the house again, ever.

He found some dishwashing gloves under the sink, wedged next to a box of copper pot-scrubbers, and, reaching for them, bumped the inside of his arm against the elbow-joint drainpipe.

"Ouch!" he yelled, falling back on his butt.

"What the—?!"

As he watched, the letters YA-WAY rose up on his skin.

Wincing but too startled and excited to cry, Patrick went back into the cabinet, grabbed the flashlight, and found the source of his red-lettered burn: the manufacturer's name, JACKYAW-AYERS FOUNDRY, was stamped along the length of the pipe. It and the underside of the sink were hot as a teakettle.

He leapt to his feet and examined his concoction, now bubbling vigorously and giving off a milky, slightly greenish gas.

"Oh, yeah!" he exclaimed, reaching across the frothing sink to slide open the kitchen window. He should have thought to do it earlier—he wasn't working in a fume hood, after all—but then he hadn't been expecting a reaction quite *this* powerful. The heat, the bubbles, the gas . . . despite the lame selection of ingredients and equipment, he had touched off a seriously exothermic reaction!

As he grappled with the latch some of the stinging vapor reached his nose and he paused, trying to decide if he was going to sneeze or cough. *Cough*, his throat and lungs quickly made clear—it was definitely going to be a cough. His shoulders hunched forward and he brought the crook of his elbow to his mouth as a searing whiteness marched in from the edges of his vision.

He stumbled back from the sink, nose and lips burning like he'd bitten into the world's hottest chili pepper. And then the cough came—a single, deep, rib-bruising bark that dropped him to his knees.

And no sooner had it subsided than another started to come on, and this was a problem because he couldn't conceive of drawing enough breath to possibly let it happen. A keening tone filled his ears, and his eyes seemed to have been dropped inside a fluorescent bulb—everything was a swirling, brilliant, blue-tinged white.

And then—as if a magician had snapped his fingers—it all went away. His vision came back, he could breathe, and he felt strong and healthy and happy like he'd just had a great night's sleep and it was either his birthday or Christmas morning.

He laughed with relief and decided to sit down on the floor. But somehow it seemed like gravity had weakened and, rather than taking the time to unfold his knees and tuck his legs, he chose to just sort of lean backward. The kitchen phone began to ring as he slowly toppled back to the floor. He wondered if he'd accidentally made chlorine gas . . . or cyanide . . . or some sort of powerful neuro-toxin? He realized that would be bad . . . although still, pretty freaking cool to have done it in a kitchen sink . . .

The phone rang again and it occurred to him that he should answer it—perhaps it was Mom—but he was really busy sitting down right now, and anyhow, it was *way* too far away.

A brilliant green light filled the room as he fell backward toward the polished split-bamboo planks of the kitchen floor. It was the green of a late-spring field day, the shade of a Pentecostal chasuble.

His head bounced on the floor once, twice, three times. The light soon subsided, but the ceiling, the counter ledge, the window over the sink, the wooden-handled cabinets, the plastic-seated kitchen stools—everything around him—was turning green and slightly fuzzy, as if the entire room was growing a coat of Astroturf.

Then the phone rang a third time and Patrick closed his eyes, and kept them that way.

CHAPTER 6

Unique Qualifications

THE HEAVY STONE DOOR SLAMMED SHUT WITH A floor-shaking thud. Mr. BunBun shivered and turned on the censer, placing it inside the carved stone bowl of the font. He waited to see the first puff of smoke and then laid his furry brown body down on the straw-covered floor. He would soon be on his way.

He had expected to be more excited. This was, after all, the brink of one of the world's most (if things worked out) historic journeys. He and so many other soldiers for the Commonplace, the book of the Minder's wisdom, had worked so hard—and risked so much—to get here.

But rather than feeling like the hero of some poem about to embark upon an epic journey, he was starting to worry he was more a guinea pig about to be embarked on a laboratory experiment. Or, if not a guinea pig, at least a rabbit. He still wasn't entirely comfortable with his BunBun nickname—weighing more than forty kilograms, gifted with the ability to speak, and possessed of a pair of antlers that would make a young deer green with envy—he was hardly a *bunny*. But his protests had only strengthened his friends' insistence on the nickname; and what did he really care, anyhow? He was a grownup; he could take a joke.

What he wasn't so sure he could take—at least any longer—was this particular situation. None of his friends and co-conspirators, after all, had ever *done this*. None of them had ever (except perhaps in dreams) even *laid eyes on* his destination.

Earth. It was supposed to be a world where poetry, art, and music still flourished—a world not yet enslaved by Deacons. But it was also a place where untold *millions* suffered from oppression, famine, and war. And it was where Rex Abraham, Decimator of Worlds, was even now plotting another apocalypse.

Which was why he was undertaking this mission.

But a lot of good it did him to have misgivings now. Now, after he had *volunteered* to wake up the people of poor, disconnected Earth to the massive threat at their door. Now, as he sat on the brink. Now, after he had said his goodbyes to all his friends and entered the nave. Now, as the heavy stone door had been sealed. Now, as the vaporous tendrils of transcense were beginning to flow over the lip of the ceremonial font.

He pressed down hard on his whiskered lip and blinked his rabbity eyes.

"Well, you've really gotten yourself into it this time, BunBun," he said to himself. And then, thinking of his leaders, "I sure hope this is not another classic case of them not knowing what it is they do."

Checking the time upon the device strapped to his furry wrist, he put back down his antlered head, closed his eyes, and went through the preparations from *The Book of Commonplace*. Preparations he had rehearsed a hundred times in the past week alone:

One: Lie down on your back.
Two: Hold close any items you wish to bring with you.
Three: Close your eyes and relax.
Four: Do not struggle—let your impulses run free.

This last one meant that if his lungs wanted to cough, he should cough. If his eyes wanted to cry, he should let them cry. If his gut wanted to belch or fart, he should let it belch or fart.

Mr. BunBun didn't quite do either of the latter, but as the first acrid wisps of smoke reached his face, he did cough: a single, rib-bruising bark that caused his antlers to scratch along the floor and his legs to kick straight out in the air. A keening tone filled his ears now and a swirling white—as brilliant and unnatural as fluorescent light—crept in from the edges of his vision.

He kept his eyes clenched shut as bouts of vertigo rocked his world. He was barely able to recall the last preparation:

Five: Keep your mind on your mantra.

His mantra! He scoured his dissipating memory. How could he possibly no longer remember it? How many times had he recited the thing—a thousand? Ten thousand?

And then—just like somebody pressed a button—it all stopped. The searing whiteness lifted and he could breathe, and he felt strong and healthy and happy like the morning of a festival day.

Had it happened? Was he there, on the other side?

His eyes fluttered open.

No. No, he was still in the smoky transubstantiation chamber. But a verdant light was gathering. He'd been told of this. Everything in the room—the stone pillars, the vaulted ceiling, the dais, the single-columned font—they all were becoming greener, and greener, and greener. It soon was as if everything was made of golf-course grass.

And then his Commonplace mantra came back,

"Ears are for Earth
 Eyes are for Ith
 And both in their way
 Help the true become Truth!"

He closed his eyes and said it again. And again. And again. And then—finally—it happened.

CHAPTER 7

A Different Sort of Homecoming

A **FLAT-FACED FIRE ENGINE DOPPLERED BY AS LUCIE**
Griffin reached the entrance to the empty, rain-soaked playground between Lexington and Sunset.

She was returning from the public library with a book on George Grosz, an old German painter whose cartoonish depictions of bloated, hypocritical adults had become her latest artistic fascination.

Propping the big flat book and the handle of her umbrella between her chin and shoulder to free her hands, she opened the gate in the chain-link fence. A police car roared by, headed toward Morningside, *her* street. Curiosity and a measure of something else seized her.

"There's no way—" she started to say, but even as she peered through the leafless maples at the back of the O'Donnells' yard, she could see the police car and also a fire engine—plus two other police cars and an ambulance—stopped in front of *her house*.

Lucie hated anything athletic and most especially the act of running, but she furled her umbrella, clutched her book to her chest, and sprinted harder than she had since she was a little kid.

CHAPTER 8

A Place of Sense

SOMETHING WAS NUZZLING PATRICK—SOME things, rather: things with whiskers, moist snouts, and malty breath. He opened his eyes and saw three collared sheep standing against a low gray sky. A donkey and a big brown cow, also wearing collars of blue seat belt–like fabric, stood a few paces behind. There was nothing the least bit threatening about any of them, but these were no ordinary barnyard animals. It took Patrick a moment to think it through, and then it came to him: the sheep, the donkey, the cow—their eyes were all too big, like manga characters brought to life.

Otherwise, he supposed, everything was normal enough. The wind was gusting, tousling his hair and the grass around him. But how, he asked himself, was the grass dry if it had just been raining?

And then it hit him—he was dreaming. He wasn't *really* outside with a bunch of freaky big-eyed animals. He clenched his eyes shut, hoping to move to the next dream or even to wake back up, but the sheep's nuzzlings were really starting to tickle. Giggling and lazily swiping at them, he rolled over to protect his belly.

"Hey you!" said a piercing, hooting voice.

Patrick opened his eyes and lifted his head from the grass. Standing just beyond the donkey, a big-eyed boy regarded him with rank disapproval.

"Who on Ith are you?"

Patrick considered whether the boy might have some sort of accent to be pronouncing the word *Earth* as *Ith*—like it rhymed with, well, *with*.

"And why are you in our yard, and why were you laughing—and why are your *ears so big*!?"

Patrick still didn't know quite how to respond. First, he really wasn't in the mood to speak. Second, he didn't have big ears. And, third, it struck him that if anybody should be asking questions about this entire situation, it should be him.

He pushed up on an elbow and looked around. He'd

assumed he was dreaming of a farm, or maybe a petting zoo. But this was somebody's front lawn, and not a somebody he ever remembered having visited. For one thing, most people he knew had houses with windows and didn't have plants growing on their roofs. It wasn't an ugly building, exactly. But Patrick had definitely never seen it, or any structure quite like it, in his entire life.

Similar slope-sided houses lined both sides of the street, some also with blue-collared farm animals standing in their well-kept yards . . . and even upon their gardened roofs.

He turned his attention back to the boy with the tiny ears and the ridiculously, impossibly big eyes. The kid was now aiming a fancy-looking cell phone at Patrick—presumably filming him.

"Well?" prompted the boy. "Do you intend to answer?"

The boy looked to be Carly's age—fifth grade or so—a pale, understuffed dumpling of a boy wearing brown corduroy pants and a too-big sweater vest squeezed up over his collarbones by his too-tight backpack.

Patrick also couldn't fail to observe that the boy was wearing makeup.

Dream or not, Patrick couldn't contain his surprise at that: "Are you wearing *lipstick*?" he blurted.

"I could have begun by asking why you *aren't* wearing any," said the kid, still aiming his smartphone at Patrick. "But frankly your *ears* are what demand the greatest explanation. I mean anybody, in theory, could have for-gotten to apply cosmetics in the morning; but most people don't wake up with fantastically large *ears*! Wait, is that a costume!? Are you an *Anarchist*!??"

"A what?"

"Don't play games with me!! I've just escalated my feed for review by the cops!"

"Wait. What?" said Patrick, trying to think things through. Was he trespassing on the kid's lawn or some-thing? "Where am I?"

"You're at 96 Eveningside Drive," said the boy. "Right in *my* front yard."

"96 Eveningside Drive?" asked Patrick. "That's funny. I live at 96 Morningside Drive."

"Yeah, hardy-har-har," said the boy, his pubescent voice dripping with sarcasm. "Great joke. Now, explain your-self and don't try any—"

The boy broke off. Clearly he'd just thought of some-thing and—judging from how he clasped his hands and did a little jump—it was a pleasing notion.

"Wait, are you an *Earth*ling?!"

"Umm," said Patrick. Wondering again if the boy had said *Earth* or *Ith* before, and also if maybe the boy was like Stephen Westrum, Jeff Hookey, or one of the other crazy Doctor Who–Heads from school, always obsessing about aliens and robots and mutant plagues.

"Holy flipping sight!" yelled the boy, looking down at his smartphone. He was bouncing up and down like he had to go to the bathroom. "I found one! I found one! I'm going to *mega-index*!"

"Found one *what*?" asked Patrick, standing up. Despite his now very concerted attempts to shoo them away, the sheep weren't budging, and he was becoming increasingly worried one might step upon his shoeless toes.

"An Earthling, stoop!" said the boy, looking intently into his phone. He glanced up suddenly, embarrassed. "Oops, sorry, I mean an Earthling, sir."

"O-kay," said Patrick.

"Wait—Rex—they say he didn't even know where he was at first. Am I the first person you've seen?"

"Seen? You mean in this yard?" asked Patrick. He wanted to ask who Rex was but the boy cut him off.

"Here on *Ith*, am I the first *Ith*ling you've seen?"

"I'm going to guess you like science fiction," said Patrick.

"Where were you before you got here?!" demanded the boy.

"Umm," said Patrick. "I was at the kitchen sink and then—"

"And then suddenly you just found yourself here—here, in front of me?"

"Something like that," admitted Patrick.

"That's why your ears are so freakishly big!" shouted the boy, smacking his palm against his cheek and spinning around. "I can be so *blind* sometimes. Of course!"

He observed the skeptical look on Patrick's face and broke into a nursery rhyme of sorts:

"Ears are for Earth
Eyes are for Ith
And both in their way
Help the true become Truth!"

"O-kay," said Patrick, crossing his arms and noticing the raised skin of his burn. He'd forgotten all about it—strangely, it didn't hurt at all.

"You're on Ith! *Ith!* You're on a whole 'nother world!"

Patrick looked at his arm. The letters, *YA-WAY*, were very clear—raised and bright red upon his light brown skin—but the thing was more like a healed scar than a fresh wound.

"What's that on your arm? A cut?"

"No. A burn, I guess."

"A burn?"

"Yeah, there was a hot pipe in the kitchen this morning."

"Why were you near a hot pipe?" asked the boy. "Are you an HVAC tech or something?"

"Um, no," said Patrick as a sheep came up and pressed

the surprisingly hard top of its head against his leg. "So what's the deal with all the farm animals?"

"Farm animals?"

"The sheep and cow and—" Patrick broke off, noticing a llama on the roof of the house next door.

"What do you mean what's the deal with them? They control plant growth, and provide milk, wool, and fertilizer for the municipality."

"What's going on, Kempton?!" demanded a woman's voice from behind Patrick. "With whom are you speaking?!"

"Mother! I found an Earthling! Didn't you see my feed?!"

Patrick looked up as a blond woman, hands on her wide hips, came down the path from the house. She was wearing a neatly ironed flower-patterned dress and had on even more makeup than the boy. Her ears were similarly tiny and her eyes enormous—and they got even larger as she looked up from her own fancy smartphone, regarded Patrick, and began to scream.

CHAPTER 9

Sorry, Wrong House

CHABOD COFFIN WAS NOT HAPPY. ULTRAVIVID dreams—including one in which some very strange people had moved next door and taken to throwing loud parties—had kept him tossing and turning all night long, causing his back to seize up and forcing him to seek relief in the massage chair down in the den.

He was still in the motorized chair—his reading glasses perched at the tip of his parrot-beak nose, his MacBook Pro centered in his flannel-robed lap—as the sun cleared the pine trees in the backyard and cast an annoying glare upon his newsfeed.

Watching people on Facebook had become one of his favorite pastimes of late. The idea of actively joining—commenting, sharing, telling people about his own life, etc.—seemed crazy to him, but he did occasionally feel pressure to be a part of the community and would sometimes press the Like button to show his approval of, or at least his amusement at, other people's posts. He somehow was fascinated to see other people show off their kids, their puppies, their cats, their cars, their gardens, their meals, their deluded impressions of what was politically important . . . They were all so alarmingly stupid and spoiled—and this whole braggy social-media thing was to his mind another sign of civilization's demise—but, at the same time, it was utterly riveting.

And he would have watched longer this particular morning despite the sun's glare, but at 9:33 a.m. a flash of green issued from the hallway, together with an enormous, floor-shaking thud that caused dishes to chime and tinkle in the kitchen, and he broke off.

His mind flailed for explanations. It couldn't be Consuela. His Ecuadoran live-in housekeeper had left last night to visit her daughter in North Carolina. Had an appliance or a lightbulb exploded? Maybe those new high-efficiency LED bulbs he'd installed weren't stable? But an exploding bulb couldn't possibly have made *that* much noise. And why would there have been *green* light? It had definitely been green.

He could call 911 but the police would take minutes to get here, and to talk right now might be to alert a home invader to his presence. He could run—flee through the front door in his bathrobe and bare feet—go to a neighbor's house. But what if there was an innocent explanation?

Clearly he should first figure out what was going on, and *then* decide what to do about it.

It had to be a burglar. Ichabod's great-grandfather had been a banking tycoon and, though no Coffin since had much grown the family fortune, the old man's inheritance had been managed well, and the eight-bedroom, timber-framed house still reeked of wealth.

But if anybody thought it was going to be an easy job to rob the Coffin estate, the low-life scumbag had another think coming.

Despite Hedgerow Heights' nearly nonexistent crime rate, Ichabod had installed tens of thousands of dollars' worth of silent alarms, motion detectors, panic buttons, and security cameras throughout the estate. And he'd taken other measures, too, including stockpiling self-defense items. In the coffee table right in front of him, for instance, was a Taser X3—the most advanced nonlethal self-defense item one could legally purchase over the Internet.

He pulled open the drawer and removed the black-and-yellow, pistol-like device. Holding the weapon out with both hands like a TV-show policeman, he crab-stepped his way out into the narrow hallway.

A faint but sickly sweet, smoky smell greeted his nose, and he could hear a low, regular rasping noise like somebody breathing, somebody with asthma. He quietly stalked to the end of the hallway and peered around the mahogany doorjamb. There on the floor next to the marble-topped counter, an *animal* was sprawled, apparently asleep, its furry gray-brown, puffy-tailed butt pointed right at him—there was a *bear* in his house!

But the creature appeared to be asleep. He immediately thought to retrieve one of the six cans of bear spray he'd ordered after the Peekskill sighting a few months back. One was stashed by the seldom-used front door. But he probably shouldn't be setting off bear spray inside a house and anyhow it wasn't a very large bear—probably just a cub, not much bigger than a large dog—and certainly a good deal smaller than a full-grown criminal.

He considered the weapon in his hand, leveled his arm, and placed the red laser-sight dot right in the middle of the animal's fluffy rump. There was a terrific *pop!* and a series of clicks, and the next thing he knew the animal was flopping on the floor, its claws clacking noisily on the polished hardwood.

It was a disturbing sight, not that he spent much time watching. He dropped the still-discharging weapon and ran—or at least tottered—back down the hall as fast as his knob-kneed old legs would take him.

He didn't get very far. As he crossed the dining room he was nearly dropped to his knees by a terrifying pain in his chest. He gasped and placed his right hand on his left breast. An image of a trout flopping in the bottom of a rowboat came to him and he did his best not to panic. He needed to stay calm. He needed to think rationally. He needed to slow his pulse and be clearheaded. And especially he needed to avoid having a heart attack while there was a *bear* in his kitchen.

Putting his free hand on the back of the nearest chair, he dropped his head and concentrated on his breathing. Just breathing, like he did for his weekly calisthenics: *In. Hold. Out. Hold. In. Hold. Out.*

The tingling in his arms, and the ringing in his ears, began to fade. He raised his head and listened. No sounds were coming from the kitchen. Maybe he'd killed the animal or—better yet—maybe it had fled back outside the way it had come in? Had it entered through an open window? Had Consuela left the back door unlatched?

"A bear," he whispered to himself. "A *bear* in my kitchen!"

And a strangely colored one at that. It had to have been

43

a black—there were no grizzlies east of the Rockies, thank God. But this one had been grayish brown in color. Perhaps sometimes black bears weren't entirely dark, or maybe their young sometimes were lighter colored.

But it had definitely been a bear. Its legs had been thicker than a dog's, and most dogs didn't have puffy tails. But . . . did bears have puffy tails?

He drew a deep breath, held it, let it out, and tried letting go of the chair.

He was fine. He could walk. He—

"What kind of greeting was *that* for a world-weary traveler?!"

The servant's door was being held wide by a relatively short furry animal standing on its hind legs.

As Ichabod Coffin's eyes nearly bugged out of his head, the creature craned its antlered head over its shoulder.

"Gah!" it exclaimed as it yanked one of the electrodes from its rump. "These things have *barbs* on them!"

"O-oh-a-o-eh!" replied Ichabod, collapsing back against the dining table, his heart once again flip-flopping in his chest, his lungs aching for breath, and his mind—as he lost consciousness—busy trying to decide if the police sirens he was hearing were real, or figments of his imagination.

CHAPTER 10

Second Thoughts

MOTHER!" YELLED THE BIG-EYED BOY NAMED Kempton. "Cut it out. It's okay. This is a *good* thing! It's an *Earth*ling!"

Kempton's mother kept right on screaming. Patrick wondered if, beyond the obviously large eyes, she might have outsized lungs, too.

A big-eyed businessman rushed out of the house, button-down shirt untucked, a white streak of cream cheese or something on his rouged cheek, and a torn edamame pod in his hand.

"Darling, darling!" he yelled as he stumbled down the path, startling the animals into the neighbor's yard. "What's the matter!?"

A dark-haired girl about Patrick's age trailed after the man. She had the same big eyes and was dressed all in black except for some silver rings on her fingers and an Egyptian ankh pendant hanging from her neck. Of everyone there, she had on the least makeup.

Kempton's mother buried her head in her husband's chest and began to sob.

"Is it Kempton? What's he done?!" blurted the man. He gave his wife a one-armed embrace and squinted down the path.

"Kempton Chappaqua Puber! Come here right now and apologize to your mother!"

"But, Father—didn't you see my vid-feed?—it's an *Earth*ling!"

"I'll make you wish *you* were an Earthling if you don't get here in two quints!"

Kempton's mother was blubbering words including *sick, inconsiderate, imp, horrid, ungrateful,* and *apologize* at her husband.

"Wait right here," said Kempton.

"I wouldn't know where else to go," said Patrick softly, and stuck his hands in his pockets.

Kempton stomped away toward his parents.

The dark-haired girl regarded Patrick from the flagstone walkway. "So, how's your day going?" she asked.

"Um. Okay," said Patrick, a little flustered. She was quite pretty and he found himself dropping his eyes to the ground, whereupon he noticed her shoes were like gloves—the fronts were indented around her individual toes. He looked up the path and now noticed the same was true of the father's, the mother's, and the boy's, too.

"Just kind of found yourself on our lawn?" she asked.

"Um, yeah," said Patrick.

She nodded as if this were what she had been expecting him to say. "What's your shirt all about?" she asked.

"Umm," said Patrick. He was wearing Neil's They Might Be Giants shirt with the giant squid on it—a hand-me-down. He'd slept in it last night because his pajama drawer had been empty. "Umm, they're called They Might Be Giants—they're sort of a rock band," he said.

"Rock band? What's that?"

"Umm," said Patrick again, wondering if she was making fun of him. "You know, they play music."

"Cool," she said. "I like the lettering."

Patrick looked down at the shirt again.

"Hey, Earthling!" yelled the boy from up the walkway.

"I'll handle this, Kempton!" said the boy's father, turning and beckoning Patrick with his soybean-holding hand. "Come here, son, I want a word with you."

47

"I'm Oma, by the way, Oma Puber."

"I'm Patrick," he replied, fascinated as a gust of wind set her crow-black hair whipping about her shoulders, "Patrick Griffin."

She offered him a Mona-Lisa smile as he turned and headed up the path.

"What on the Minder's green Ith—" said the father as his eyes settled on Patrick's face, and ears.

Patrick stopped at hand-shaking distance and tried to smile.

"Father, there's tofu whip on your cheek," said Kempton.

The big-eyed man handed his bean pod to his wife and absently wiped at his cheek.

"Allow me, son," he said, reaching out and gently grabbing both of Patrick's ears.

"They're *real*," he gasped.

Patrick shrugged.

"See?" said Kempton, offering his father what looked to be a bottle of hand sanitizer. "I told you so."

The woman tentatively stopped crying. *"Really?"*

After wiping his hands, the man waved at a security camera atop a polished aluminum street pole and stumbled back up the path toward the house. "Wait here, everybody. I must have left my binky in the kitchen."

CHAPTER 11
Service Outage

GRUNTING AND GASPING LIKE HE WAS GETTING into a way-too-hot bath, Ichabod Coffin rolled onto his back and immediately wished he hadn't—the back of his head felt like he'd been smacked with a board, and his wrists ached, too. Perhaps he'd tried to stop himself from falling? Perhaps he'd tried to fend off—

The creature with the antlers!

He felt up and down his body and, failing to find any torn fabric or gaping wounds, raised his hands to his face. There didn't seem to be any blood—clearly he hadn't been mauled.

Had he had a stroke or a heart attack? If so, he felt pretty okay. Well, okay other than for questioning his own sanity. Had the creature—whatever it was—actually spoken to him? Had he hallucinated?

He rolled over and sat up. At which point he noticed a water glass and a small card on the floor next to him. He picked up the latter and squinted at the large, handwritten block letters.

FORGIVENESS IS THE CALLING CARD
OF THE BRAVE. -BCP §3079404

He flipped the card over and—with some difficulty—read,

JOHN ANDERSON PERTOLOPE, ESQ.
a.k.a. Mr. BunBun
Trans-World Consultant and Fomenter

He clucked his tongue in anger. What was going on here? Some sort of prank? It made him furious to consider this, but at the same time, it was some reassurance: clearly he hadn't lost his mind. Obviously it *couldn't* have been a talking bear or a giant antlered rabbit, or really, an animal of any sort. It had been somebody—a person, a criminal— in costume. It made perfect sense. Criminals, of course, often wear disguises.

He replaced the card and looked at the water glass. He was quite thirsty but it obviously had been put there by whoever had left the card and he shouldn't disturb the crime scene. The police could dust it for fibers and finger-prints.

He stood and, steadying himself on a chair, reached for his iPhone. It was clearly time to call 911.

But the smartphone wasn't in the pocket of his robe where it should have been. He let loose a torrent of very bad words as he bent and looked under the dining room table, where it wasn't, either. The hooligan had clearly *taken* it.

Running his hand along the wall for support, he headed back to the den and saw, with some measure of relief, his Macbook Pro still on the coffee table. What *was* missing, however, was the house's cordless phone.

He considered why a burglar would steal a thirty-dollar phone when a three-thousand-dollar lamp and a two-thousand-dollar computer were right there in plain sight. Probably they had taken it precisely to prevent his calling 911.

He shuffled to the kitchen where he found the parquet floor under a half inch of water. Letting loose another tor-rent of bad words, he kicked off his slippers and splashed to the overflowing sink to shut off the tap. The drowned carcasses of his iPhone and apparently every other phone in the house were at the bottom of the stainless steel basin. Another business card was propped on the window-sill behind the faucet. The message written upon it read,

BINKIES ARE FOR BABIES -BCP §1401917

"What on Earth is *that* supposed to mean?!" he wondered aloud.

The bird clock on the wall said it was almost nine forty-five a.m. He'd assumed it was later. The person had taken the time to write two notes, pour a glass of water, collect and drown all the phones in the house. That alone could have taken twenty minutes, and if he'd only been passed out for ten or fifteen . . .

Perhaps the malefactor was right now upstairs cracking Mother's jewelry safe, or down in the basement searching for the false panel behind which the Eau Clair silverware was hidden?!

The Taser clearly hadn't worked that well.

"The bear spray!" he said aloud. Wasn't it guaranteed to be powerful enough to stop a seven-hundred-pound bear!? The closest can was stashed in the broom closet by the back door. He quickly sploshed across the kitchen and removed it from the top shelf, breaking off the safety tab and giving enough of a read to the directions to realize they were a silly restatement of common sense ("Use only in case of impending attack," "Hold can perpendicular to the ground," "Do not use indoors," "Do not spray upwind," etc.). Then he noticed movement through the back door's four-paned window. The costumed burglar was out in his backyard demolishing the bird feeders!

"You good-for-nothing vandal!" the old man screamed as he burst out the back door and stumbled down the brick path. "Look what you've done! Are you *eating* my birdseed?!"

"Oh, I'm so sorry, is it yours?" replied Mr. BunBun, slowly swallowing a last mouthful of seeds as he sized up the angry man. "I assumed since it was out here and otherwise the birds would eat it all up—"

Two things dawned on Mr. Coffin. The first was that animal costumes had come a long way in the dozen years since he'd last opened the door for a trick-or-treater (the mask was so lifelike—the shiny black eyes, the intricately molded teeth, the glistening mouth and snout, the multi-textured fur . . .), and, second, that no sober burglar would be out in the yard ransacking somebody's birdfeeders.

"Are you a *druggie*?!"

"Druggie?" asked Mr. BunBun. "I'm not familiar with that word."

"You're a disgusting, filthy drug addict, aren't you?! That's why you were asleep on the floor of my kitchen, that's why you're out here in an animal suit *eating birdseed*! You're higher than a kite!"

"Kite? What? I—"

"You picked the wrong house to mess with, you reprobate!"

"Reprobate? Mess with? Sorry? I'm afraid I don't have the foggiest notion—you seem to be angry—perhaps we should back up and—" BunBun broke off, bemused suddenly. He'd been worried the object the old man was holding was another weapon like the one with which he'd first electrocuted him. But now he'd had a better look at it. "Is that can you're holding labeled 'bear spray'? Do you think I'm a bear?"

"I know you're not a bear!!" screamed Mr. Coffin. *"Bears can't talk!"*

"No, not unless they're Mindthling bears, I don't suppose."

Mr. Coffin looked at him dumbfounded.

"You know it's kind of funny—back on Ith the natives thought I was a giant rabbit, which is ridiculous because lagomorphs don't have antlers. In fact, that's how I got the name Mr. BunBun. I don't really mind, of course; I mean, I'm not a child. I don't mind a little fun. But for a moment there I thought maybe you thought I was a bear! Imagine if I'd come to Earth before I went to Ith and I'd been given a bear nickname. I wonder if it would have been something like Mr. BearBear, or a play on—"

"So what is it?" interrupted Mr. Coffin. "Uppers? Downers? Speed? Horse? Reefer?"

"Sorry—again our vocabularies diverge. Or are you being poetic? I've heard of Earth's poems!"

"Shut up or I will spray you so hard you'll wish you were dead!"

"With the bear spray? Again, I'm not sure I understand. What is this 'bear spray'? A deodorant?"

The old man's eyes looked like they might entirely bug out of his head. "I am not joking around here."

"I'm thoroughly confused," said Mr. BunBun. "Or is it *from* rather than *for* bears—like skunk spray? Do bears on Earth have scent glands?"

"What are you talking about? Of course it's not spray *from* a bear—it's spray *to stop* a bear!"

"But I'm not a bear. And why would you wish to stop one? Shouldn't one just let a bear go about its business? I mean you might make it mad if you interrup—"

"I know you're not a bear; you're a *drug-addicted burglar*!!!"

"What?" asked Mr. BunBun.

"Are you trying to distract me?! Get me to drop my guard?!"

"Sir, I am certain that we are simply misunderstanding each other."

"Listen up, you costume-wearing psycho—we're going over to the neighbors' to call the cops and I don't want to hear another peep."

"KOPs?" said Mr. BunBun, horrified. "You have them here on Earth, too? Already!?"

"I mean it! Just one more peep!"

"Peep?" asked Mr. BunBun.

"What?!"

"You said peep. I don't know what that means. It sounds like an onomatopoetic construction?"

"You're a dead man if you say just *one* more word," said Mr. Coffin, gesturing with the can. "Now, *move!*"

"Oh, really, I'd love to join you but I'm afraid I can't—I have places to go, people to see. Speaking of which, can you kindly point me toward the nearest metropolis?"

"Shut *up!*" screamed the man, and shook his arms at Mr. BunBun with the unintended effect that he accidentally depressed the spray can's trigger. There was a terrific hissing noise as a jet of the powerful repellent arced out a dozen yards to Mr. BunBun's left.

"Jesus Christ on a stick!" screamed Mr. Coffin as he fumbled to control the stream and, in his panic, dropped the can to the damp ground. In less than a second he found himself deep inside a caustic cloud of bear repellent. His eyes swelled shut, and his nostrils and mouth exploded with pain.

Mr. BunBun was safely a few paces upwind but his acute sense of smell, coupled with his extensive chemical training, told him that the horrible compound the old man had just sprayed would have much the same effect on him. On the bright side, he could also tell that the man's physiological reaction to the spray—while terrible—was transitory. Capsaicin, the principal irritant in hot peppers—while highly painful—tends not to inflict permanent physical damage.

BunBun sympathetically regarded the fog-shrouded man as Mr. Coffin sank to his knees and wailed like a small, if very loud, child.

"I wonder if all the humans here are so volatile," BunBun said, backing away as the man fell forward on his belly, passing out for the second time that morning.

BunBun stood a moment, observing the slowly dissipating vapor. His binky beeped and he looked down at the screen on his wrist to see that several RF transmissions were closing on him. He quickly surmised they must belong to the uniformed people he'd seen gathering around the light-flashing vehicles parked in front of the house to the west—the ones that had been making so much noise earlier when the man had been unconscious the first time.

The device indicated these nearby signals were not Ith protocol, but it had also picked up some distant ones that were. They might not yet be close, but Rex and his aspiring Deacons knew he was here. And they would surely be coming.

CHAPTER 12

Keeping Up Appearances

ON REFLECTION, THE MOST SURPRISING THING WAS
how calm and reasonable everybody was being.

If the tables had been turned and a big-eyed, small-eared,
makeup-wearing Kempton had arrived on the sidewalk in
front of the Griffin home back in Hedgerow Heights, Patrick was certain there would have been a code-red freak-out.

Police departments, fire departments, and—if they'd
suspected Kempton really was an alien—scientists in
yellow biohazard suits would have been all over the place.
Humvees bristling with antennae, quarantine tents, satellite news trucks, helicopters, protest marches . . .

Patrick reminded himself this was a dream and so logic was probably at least a little bit out the window.

The father reemerged from the house and stumbled down the front steps.

"It's okay," he yelled, waving his cell phone at them, "I've got my binky!"

"And," he said as he got near, "I've received a message from the admins that we should introduce ourselves to our guest!"

"Some of us already did," corrected Oma.

Mr. Puber regarded his daughter. It seemed to Patrick like he might be considering a list of potential replies and wasn't finding any suitable to say out loud. He cleared his throat and turned his attention back to Patrick.

"Well, we're the Pubers and this—" he said, gesturing behind him at the windowless house, "is our home. So, of course, I'm Mr. Puber, this is Mrs. Puber, and these are our children, Kempton and Oma. And *your* name is?"

"I'm Patrick," said Patrick. "Patrick Griffin."

"Well," said the man, beaming with pride or, at least, self-importance, "welcome to Ith, Patrick Griffin!"

"Thanks, uh, for having me."

"Tell us, honey," said Mrs. Puber to her husband, "what do the admins wish us to do next?"

"Oh, umm, well they wish for us to—" The man's phone made a note like an electric cricket and he broke off, eyes widening and face turning scarlet even through his makeup.

"What's happened, dear?" said his wife. "You seem flustered!"

"Well, I should say I'm flustered!" the man spluttered. "I've just gotten a direct SMS from Deacon Sabrina Kim herself!"

"WHAT!!!??" shouted Kempton.

"And she has given us an additional and quite *wonderful* job ticket!"

"FROM DEACON SABRINA KIM—FOR *YOU*?!" asked Kempton. "A PERSONALLY DIRECTED SMS?!!? AND A *JOB TICKET*?!!!"

"Yes indeed," said the man, beaming again. "Here, allow me to read:

Family unit coordinator at 96 Eveningside Drive, The Ministry of Awareness is aware of the arrival of a trans-world emissary at or near your residence. In the interest of full transparency, and to be entirely mindful of the comfort of this distinguished personage, you are hereby granted the profound privilege of providing board, shelter, and entertainment to our visitor. To the purpose of his orientation and greater comfort, you are to provide him a fully immersive experience.

• Today, Sixday, Dodecuary 24th, you will entertain him at your residence so that on-boarding preparations can be made in the wider community. You are to keep him indoors and acquaint him with any and all residential systems and technologies.

• Tomorrow, Sevensday, Dodecuary 25th, you will have him join your own similarly aged children in any and all previously scheduled school and extracurricular activities.

The term of this request shall hold until superseding notice is delivered to you by an official of rank seven or higher.

"But what does that mean, dear?!" asked Mrs. Puber.

"Yeah, Dad—does that mean he's *staying with us?*"

"Yes—we are to show him all about life here on Ith, and the best way to do that is to give him immersive, on-site experience!"

"Wait, does that mean tomorrow—"

"Yes, he will be accompanying you and Oma to school for Lasters Day."

"That's so totally awesome—my feed's going to go *viral!*" Kempton shouted, pumping his fists at the sky.

A windowless six-wheeled vehicle shaped like a giant brick—though bright green and bristling with antennae—trundled up the street and stopped in front of the house. A small-wheeled robot emerged from a hatch in its side and scooted up the front path. Kempton reached into a hopper on its back and removed a pair of purple five-toed shoes.

"What a wonderful color!" exclaimed Mrs. Puber.

"Yes, they'll go very nicely with your blue pants," said Mr. Puber, referring to Patrick's jeans.

"And with your, umm, black-and-orange shirt," said Kempton. "Now, here's your binky," he said, handing him a fancy cell phone just like everybody else's.

Patrick examined its shiny, keyless surface. Letters and strange symbols wobbled across its wrap-around screen, and a large-eyed smiley-face emoticon lit up at the top.

"And here's your binky belt," said Kempton, handing him a case for his phone attached to a shiny cloth belt. The garment was the same purple as his new foot-gloves.

"Thank you," said Patrick, a little distractedly. He hoped wearing it was optional.

Kempton smiled contentedly as he lathered his hands with a fresh dollop of sanitizing gel.

"So now," said Mrs. Puber, "we have to just take care of one other thing."

"What other thing?" asked Patrick.

Oma broke into a musical laugh.

"Well, you need to reapply your cosmetics," said Mr. Puber.

"What!?" asked Patrick. "I mean, I'd rather not—"

"You really *are* an Earthling, aren't you?" said Mrs. Puber. "Here on Ith, one simply doesn't go out in public with a naked face."

"You might as well not wear any pants!" said Kempton.

The donkey happened to bray just then, and everybody but Patrick laughed; Patrick was busy pinching his arm and wondering what else he could try to wake himself up.

CHAPTER 13
Daughterly Support

MRS. GRIFFIN, OBLIVIOUS TO THE DRIZZLING RAIN, was out in the yard pulling at her hair with one hand, pressing her phone to her ear with the other, and screaming hysterically. Firemen in rain-beaded face masks and elephant-trunk respirators were trooping in through the front door.

"Mom!" yelled Lucie, running up to her mother.

"He's gone, he's gone, he's gone, HE'S GONE!" her mother was screaming. "Rick—THEY CAN'T FIND HIM!"

The emergency vehicles had by now shut off their sirens, leaving the damp, still air nothing to hold but the chugging of their diesels and the crackling of fuzzy-voiced dispatches. Lucie could hear her father's placating voice on the phone: it was going to be okay, he'd be there in forty minutes—he and Neil were driving back from Paramus already—there had to be a reasonable explanation.

"But THERE IS NO reasonable explanation!" Mrs. Griffin screamed. Lucie had a feeling like she was on the backside of a roller coaster incline.

"Somebody used POISON GAS and PATRICK IS *GONE!*"

"What?!" said Lucie, dropping her book and umbrella and grabbing her mother's free hand.

Mrs. Griffin looked down at her teenage daughter.

"Oh Lucie, Lucie!" she cried, dropping the phone to the grass, fresh tears spilling from her eyes. "What have I done?"

"Mom!? What happened to Patrick?"

Mary Griffin buried her face in her daughter's black hair. "I left him all alone," she blubbered. "And he's gone. They used gas to abduct him—I'm not being hysterical—*terrorists* have taken him!"

"Mom," said Lucie, somehow reassured by what her mother had said. There was no way terrorists had shown up in Hedgerow Heights and taken her favorite little brother, Patrick. Although it wasn't exactly like him—her brother Neil was the one more apt to do something epically moronic—he'd clearly taken advantage of getting left alone in the house and done something, well, weird. But there was no way he'd been abducted by terrorists. Probably he had burned something in the toaster oven and was now hiding, hoping to avoid trouble. Only, of course, with a fire engine, two police cars, and an ambulance—to say nothing of an emotionally traumatized mother—it was a little late for that.

"Calm down, Mom," she said, grabbing her mother's rain- and tear-streaked face with both hands. "Patrick's totally fine. You and Dad are going to ground him for the rest of his life, I'm sure, but I promise he's perfectly safe."

A firefighter emerged from the front door, mask tilted up over his forehead. "I think we've found a clue," he said. "Looks like somebody did a chemistry experiment in the kitchen. Sink was full of some concoction—there were spray bottles, soaps, window cleaner, you name it, all out on the counter. So that's what set off your smoke alarm. Your son into science projects by any chance, ma'am?"

Mrs. Griffin stifled a sob and nodded.

"You see, Mom? No terrorist poison gas attack," said Lucie. It made sense Patrick had been messing around with chemicals.

"It's true. Patrick wants to be a chemist just like his Uncle Andrew," said Mrs. Griffin.

"Well, then," continued the firefighter, "the little

Einstein's probably hiding someplace—none of us likes trouble, do we?" The man smiled kindly and strolled off to his truck.

"You see, Mom?" asked Lucie. "That's what happened."

"But it's not like Patrick—"

"Ma'am," said an approaching police officer. "You left your son home at what time? Eight forty-five? It's ten twenty-five now. Give us a call if he isn't back in a couple hours, okay? Is this yours?" He retrieved her iPhone from the wet grass. It appeared to still be working.

"Thank you," said Mrs. Griffin, taking the phone. "But something *has* happened to him, I *know* it. I can *feel* it."

"Mom, the officer's right," said Lucie. "Patrick just went off to Dexter's or is hiding inside someplace. I'll look for him, okay? And Dad and everybody can help when they get back."

"Meantime we'll keep our eyes peeled and—" said the policeman.

He was interrupted by a piercing wail, a horrible scream that brought goose bumps to Lucie's arms.

"What the f-f-f—" the officer started to say.

"That isn't *Patrick*, is it!?" interrupted Mrs. Griffin, her voice cracking under the weight of her fear.

The scream trailed off. It seemed to have been coming from behind the Coffin mansion next door.

"No, that was *definitely* not Patrick," said Lucie.

"Stay right here!" said the policeman. He began shouting instructions into his handset and took off running toward the old house.

Lucie took her mother's trembling hand.

"How do you *know* it's not Patrick, Lucie?"

"Mom, for one thing, that was clearly a *woman*'s voice."

"I guess it was."

"And, for another, in your whole life, have you ever heard Patrick actually scream?"

Mrs. Griffin gave a grateful squeeze to her daughter's hand.

It was true—neither of them could remember Patrick screaming in his whole life—sure he'd cried as a baby, but even then he'd never really screamed. Unlike the other Griffin children, he somehow just wasn't wired for drama.

CHAPTER 14

Massive Multiplayer

AFTER APPLYING PATRICK'S MAKEUP—AND another dose of hand sanitizer—Kempton strapped himself into the contoured chair in the middle of the cornerless gray room and began barking commands: "Join formation, config seven, passkey November-Echo-Romeo-Delta!"

A moment later he—together with Patrick and Oma, standing behind his control chair—were skimming like a jet plane above the canopy of a canyon-fractured rain forest.

If Patrick hadn't been told it was a game, he'd have sworn that somehow the entire room had turned to glass and gone airborne. The vibrations, the detail of the trees, the clouds, the brightness of the sun—

"You're late, ABK-96," said a nasal voice. Patrick guessed it must belong to the pilot of one of the other four slate-gray, disc-like vehicles flying in formation with them.

"You clearly haven't been checking your soash feed, D-Con Soldja," said Kempton.

"Why would anybody be checking soash feeds during Arse-Five-Oh?"

"You going soft on us, ABK?"

Patrick wondered what the heck they were talking about—every third word they said he'd never heard before—but they were taking this all very seriously and he decided he shouldn't interrupt.

"We'll see who's going soft," retorted Kempton. "First I'll kick all your butts and then—while you're waiting to respawn—you'll learn that the reason I was late was that my feed happened to go *viral*."

"Wha-at?" said one incredulous voice.

"Ri-ight," said another.

"The only reason," said a third, "that your feed will ever go viral, ABK, is if you have such an epic fail that it rips a hole in the fabric of the universe."

"Whatever you belties say," replied Kempton.

A bat-winged, eagle-headed, lion-bodied creature with reptilian forelegs exploded from the forest canopy like a

70

shark leaping from the ocean—a shark that could fly at what looked to be two hundred miles per hour.

With one, two, three powerful wing strokes, it launched itself at the underbelly of the nearest slate-gray sky-car, raking the craft with scimitar-like claws. The eviscerated vehicle angled toward the left horizon with a trail of smoke and a tapering scream.

Patrick inserted his index fingers into his ears as the hideous creature let out a blood-curdling shriek and plunged back into the forest canopy.

A series of interlocking metal hoops now emerged from the floor around Kempton's chair, enabling it to detach from its pedestal and pitch, roll, and spin with his piloted surroundings.

"What *is* this?" Patrick said to Oma.

"I think it's called Abomination Redress Squad 5D."

The room slanted violently as Kempton dove. Instinctively Patrick shifted to his left foot and found himself waving his arms for balance. With a gentle laugh, Oma grabbed his shoulder to steady him.

Kempton meantime landed his sky-car in the forest. The game view shifted abruptly to third person—his helmeted, flight-suited avatar appeared before them, exiting the sky-car as the real-world Kempton undid his safety harness and climbed out of his chair. The pivoting rings folded themselves back down into the floor.

"Are *all* games like this?" Patrick asked Oma.

"Well," she whispered into his ear, "for Kempton's demographic, most are actually pretty much *exactly* like this. The chance for young males to safely indulge in senseless acts of violence has been a wonderful boon to worldwide order and not a small part of the Deacons' success. Keeps young men off the streets and, at the same time, ensures the government a constantly renewing crop of well-trained young soldiers. Should they ever need them."

Patrick looked at Oma to see if she was being serious. She certainly seemed to be.

Kempton's muscle-bound character was now running through the forest at superhuman speed—veering left, dodging right, jumping rocks, ducking limbs. Blue vector lines blinked ahead, and a shimmering yellow-orange-red series of blotches began to grow.

"I got him on Mo-Rez!" he shouted as the blotches coalesced into what was shortly recognizable as a four-legged, two-winged lion-shaped creature bounding, banking, and generally sprinting for its life through the vine-draped forest.

"S-R-Sitzen, D-Con Soldja, get ready—keep that trash locked down. I'm going hot!"

Kempton's gun exploded to life, mowing down the vegetation as he closed in on the fleeing monster.

Torn leaves swirled, and widening shafts of smoke-filled sunlight opened all around.

"I feel carsick," said Patrick to Oma.

"Try to keep an eye on the horizon."

Patrick couldn't see any horizon, just churning forest. It was like being inside a salad spinner.

The creature's digitized orange shape had been growing increasingly yellow, and now nearly white as Kempton closed in.

"All. Most. There," Kempton said, and then: "Disengage Mo-Rez!" The blotchy shapes disappeared and they could now see—maybe fifty yards distant—actual glimpses of the creature as it madly scrambled through the forest, banging into trees, leaping ditches, plowing through thickets.

And then it was gone.

"What the heck?! Any of you got him?! Where'd he go?"

"I dunno," said a particularly twerpy voice. "Sensors are dark."

"Engage Residual-Sensitivity I.R.!" Kempton screamed.

The world around them became a green-gray realm inhabited by spots of blue, purple, red, orange, and yellow—most of which seemed to be on the ground. Patrick realized these must be the creature's paw- and claw-prints.

Kempton inclined his head toward the glowing footprints and, the room's view bobbing as he walked, followed them right up to where they disappeared in a quivering thicket of brambles.

A waist-high, violet-streaked black area appeared on his sensors.

"There's a cave behind these bushes!" yelled Kempton.

"Could be a trap!" shouted one of his buddies.

"Could be a full-on lair!" shouted another.

"There could be dozens of them down there—wait for backup!" yelled a third.

"And give you guys point-share?" snorted Kempton. "Yeah, I'll just sit and eat a BLK till you catch up."

"Don't be stupid, ABK-96, wait for us—"

Kempton didn't wait.

· · · · ·

The only other time in his life Patrick had seen something that had actually, physically made him want to throw up had been the day Neil and his friends had taken him to see a road-killed fawn on Old Post Road.

Neil and especially his six-foot-tall, chinless friend Andrew Shandler were kings of gross-out—forever flicking boogers at each other, making jokes about dead nuns, reveling in their ability to turn enemy soldiers into clouds of "pink mist" in Call of Duty and the other military video games they played. So it probably wasn't surprising that they had shown great interest in the rapidly bloating carcass. Still, the worst any of them had done was poke the animal's eye with a stick.

Patrick reminded himself this was just a video game—and a video game within a dream at that—but the realization didn't stop the cloying taste of maple syrup from creeping up into his throat.

Kempton, having tracked down and single-handedly killed the monster—*the abomination*, as they called it—had just finished using his combat knife to saw off one of the creature's clawed toes for a trophy. His friends wanted more.

"Stick a frag in its mouth!" yelled one.

"Yeah, that'll open it up!" observed another.

"That'll only explode its head," said Kempton.

"Try its anus!"

"You are sick in the head, D-Con," replied Kempton, placing his boot on the edge of the creature's gaping neck wound.

"Do it!" said the others, and then they began to chant.

"You want to do the honors, Patrick Griffin?" asked Kempton, turning to Patrick.

"Uh, no thanks," said Patrick.

"Okay, but don't say I didn't offer."

Kempton's avatar carefully placed the grenade on the edge of the wound and then, with his foot, he pushed the grenade inside the creature's throat cavity.

"Set fuse five quats! Mark!" he commanded, then turned, jogged, crouched, and re-exited the cave.

The ground shook and another dust cloud billowed from the cavern's mouth, this time suffused with a slightly pink hue.

Glowing point totals cascaded around the scene as Kempton and his friends hooted and cheered.

"Lovely, right?" said Oma as she took Patrick by the hand and led him from the room.

"You know the joke about cave mushrooms and gamers?" asked Oma as they emerged into a bright, beach-themed hallway.

Patrick blinked at the brightness and shook his head.

"What's the difference between them?"

"A cave mushroom and a gamer?"

"The cave mushroom is a better conversationalist."

A portion of Patrick's brain got the joke but he was preoccupied by the fact that she had just let go of his hand. She had grabbed it in the first place in order to lead him out of a fairly dark room. That had to be all there was to it.

"Let's see if Mother needs any help with dinner," she said. "Are you hungry?"

Patrick shrugged. He was still feeling a bit queasy from the game.

They turned a corner and stepped through a doorway

into what—judging from the small steel-topped island and four chrome-legged stools—appeared to be a kitchen. There was no sink and no visible blenders, mixers, dishwashers, ovens, range-tops, coffee grinders, toasters, or any of the other appliances Patrick was used to seeing. Also, there didn't seem to be any conventional cabinets or drawers; the featureless electronic walls were displaying an ultra-realistic summer meadow.

Mrs. Puber, rouge-cheeked and oblivious to their arrival, stood against the island wearing a metallic blindfold. The rest of her face was a churning sea of emotion—smiling one moment, disapproving the next, horrified the one after that.

"Is that some sort of, umm, binky on her face?" Patrick asked Oma.

"Yes, it's her binky," said Oma.

"It's, like, some special model?"

"You don't have binkies on Earth, do you?" she asked.

Patrick shook his head.

"Visor config," she said to her own device, causing it to fold open into two eye-covering panels, complete with elastic headband. It was now identical to her mother's.

"Oh," said Patrick.

"You'll have learned all its features soon enough," said Oma, and then turned to her mom. "Mother! Oh, Mother! Sorry to interrupt!"

"Oh," said Mrs. Puber, turning to them with her device still attached to her face.

"Almost dinnertime, right?" asked Oma. "Anything we can do?"

"No, the pod just arrived and the prepbots are at work. We should be ready to begin in—let's see—*five terts*. Go sit with your father and I'll be right there."

"Sure thing, Mother."

"Her favorite dysma's in its first release window," Oma explained to Patrick as they left the kitchen, "so she's a little out of it right now."

"Dysma?"

"No dysmas on Earth, either?" she asked.

Patrick shook his head.

"I think I might like Earth," said Oma. "A dysma's a video entertainment produced in Silicon City. There's a new episode every day and they're basically about these people in a made-up town that doesn't have the benefit of the Seer's oversight, so there's scandal, murder, theft, and treachery and all kinds of deep stuff like that going on. You see, they're *dys*topia and dra*ma* rolled into one badly acted package, hence, dysmas."

"Oh," said Patrick.

"Yeah, another advance in social sedative technology, brought to you by the Deacons."

"What does that mean?"

"Think about it. How do you keep people from thinking their own thoughts? How do you keep people from figuring out that they might want things to be different? How do you keep discontent from breaking out around the world like a bad disease?"

"By keeping people happy?" he suggested.

"That would be a logical choice. But think of all the empowerment that comes with happiness. Why cure a disease when you can prevent its symptoms with absolutely zero risk to the status quo?"

"The shows keep people in line?"

"Shows, games, online discussion forums, you name it. Keep them numb and self-satisfied, as opposed to open-eyed and curious. Make them expert at made-up stuff so they don't learn to be expert at real-world stuff."

"Oh," said Patrick, wondering if he should maybe not play so much Minecraft when he got back to his real life.

They stepped out of the summery kitchen and into what at first appeared to be a redwood forest. An obsidian-black table—at which Mr. Puber was sitting—and the fact of a polished wood floor beneath their feet (plus realizing that the Pubers probably couldn't fit an actual forest inside their home) made Patrick realize that once again he was experiencing an immersive holograph.

"Ah, there's our famous guest!" said Mr. Puber.

"Been snacking, Father?" asked Oma, gesturing at the side of her own face.

"What?! No. Wait. Umm." His forefinger found the moist brown paste on his cheek.

"Right," he sighed, realizing he couldn't deny the evidence. "I had a *very* light lunch, you see."

He wiped his finger on his red napkin and turned back to the display—about the size of a place mat—on the table in front of him. It showed an animated, three-dimensional map.

"Watching a hunt, Father?" asked Oma.

"Yes, this live-scene," he said, gesturing at the forest displayed around them, "is from the very area where a Class II was spotted last night."

"Father enjoys watching feeds from ARSO missions," explained Oma. "Next to watching the World Champions' League, it's his favorite entertainment."

"It's not entertainment," her father objected. "It's a citizen's right and responsibility to review ARSO feeds. 'Many eyes make right work,'" he quipped.

"Oh," said Patrick. "What are ARSO feeds?"

"ARSOs," said Oma, her voice dripping with mock formality, "are Abomination Redress Squad Operations."

"It's no joking matter," said Mr. Puber. "The Anarchists aren't content to interfere with human society; they want

80

to disrupt the planet's fundamental *natural* order! Have you been told of the abominations?"

"Oh, yeah," said Patrick. "Like in Kempton's game?"

"Precisely!" said Kempton, entering the dining room, rubbing hand sanitizer into his hands once again. "That one you saw me frag was a Class III—one of the very worst!"

"Yes," said Mr. Puber gravely. "The mission I'm contributing to now is on the trail of a Class II, a variety known as a Shambling Mound. Highly camouflaged, very hard for our sensors to detect."

"So. Wait. There are, like, real monsters out there?" asked Patrick, remembering anew that this was—it obviously had to be—all a dream.

"Real monsters!?" said Mr. Puber. "Quadrupeds with twelve-inch teeth and razor-sharp claws that live only to kill and maim! Flying chimeras that can pluck a child from a sidewalk on its way home from school! Humongous, hirsute humanoids that can tear a man limb-from-limb!"

"Are there *real monsters*?!" Kempton said with a snort.

"Why would anybody make such things up?" said Mr. Puber.

CHAPTER 15

Household Odors

MRS. GRIFFIN AND LUCIE WATCHED AS Mr. Coffin's unconscious body was loaded into the ambulance.

"Medics say he's going to be fine," said the returning policeman. "Had a little accident with some bear spray is all."

"*Bear spray?*" asked Mrs. Griffin.

"Yes, ma'am," said the officer. "That's the third accident with that stuff since the Peekskill sighting. People have been stocking up on it, and I guess getting a little trigger-happy. Just three weeks ago a guy over in Pleasantville sent two barbecue guests to the hospital because he thought it would be a good idea to test the stuff on his patio."

"That scream we heard was *Mr. Coffin*?" asked Lucie.

"Yep," said the officer, hooking his thumb at the ambulance. "Pretty high-pitched for an old guy, right? Like I said, stuff's very powerful. And, obviously, painful."

"And there was no actual bear?" asked Lucie's mother.

"No bear. The old man was actually babbling about rabbits and deer before he passed out. I shouldn't speculate, but it's possible he was under the influence of something or other. You notice anything odd about him lately?"

"He never comes outside except to complain about the noise of my husband's lawn mower. He's basically a hermit," Mrs. Griffin replied.

"He doesn't even answer the door on Halloween, even though we know he's in there," added Lucie.

"Yeah, well," said the officer, taking off his hat and mopping his brow with a coffee-stained paper napkin. "Anyhow, why don't you go back in the house and check for any hiding spots we may have missed. We've alerted the entire force, so if anybody sees him around the neighborhood, they'll know to call it in. But I'm sure he's fine, ma'am. Just give him a couple hours. Boys will be boys."

A silver Mercedes sedan with tinted windows slowed down in front of the house just then.

"Neighbor?" asked the policeman.

"I don't know *whose* car that is," said Mrs. Griffin.

The car sped away.

"Probably just a looky-loo," he replied. "You know how people are—they see flashing lights and they gotta go stick their noses in it. All right, we're going back to the station but give us a call as soon as he turns up, okay?"

"Thank you, officer," said Mrs. Griffin.

As she and Lucie watched the policeman return to his car, she began to sob.

"Mom, don't cry. You heard the policeman. Everything's fine."

Mary Griffin looked at her daughter. "I see why what you're saying makes sense, but I'm just—I'm just . . . I have this terrible *feeling*. It's not a *regular* feeling, Lucie."

"You've had a scare, Mom. That's all," said Lucie, squeezing her hand.

"What kind of mother *am* I leaving him all alone like that? He must have been scared to death waking up in an empty house."

"Patrick's the least likely person in our family to be scared. Plus, he's twelve, Mom. If he'd had a real problem, he would have called, right?"

Mrs. Griffin tapped in her password and examined her call history.

"I didn't miss any calls."

"You see?" said Lucie. "He was okay. And he *is* okay—he

just went off someplace or is hiding because he knows he's in big trouble."

"I'm a terrible mom."

"You're a great mom," said Lucie, surprised at herself for feeling so concerned about her mother's feelings.

"You don't mean that, but thank you, Lucie," she said, squeezing her daughter's hand. "What if there *was* a bear?"

"A bear didn't come into the house and eat Patrick, Mom. That's crazy."

Mrs. Griffin smiled at her daughter. "You're right."

"Come on," said Lucie, pulling her mom toward the open front door and thinking to herself it was almost as if she were helping her *own* kid. "You check the basement and first floor closets and I'll check the upper floors. And if that little creep went into my room, well, *then* you can worry about his safety."

"No jokes now," said Mrs. Griffin as they stepped inside. "Please."

"Gosh, I *know* that smell," said Lucie.

"I do, too."

"It smells like, like—is it?"

"Incense," whispered Mrs. Griffin. "It smells like Easter Sunday in here."

CHAPTER 16
Twinning

THERE WAS DEFINITELY SOME RESEMBLANCE between the four-year-old Griffin twins, Cassie and Paul—the thin-lipped mouths, the sharp points of their noses, the spacing of their fierce brown eyes—but that was about it. Cassie was black-haired, slight, and olive-skinned like their mom. Paul, meantime, was beefy, blond, and as pale as milk.

But where they differed in appearance, they were purely identical in their interests and activities. Everything they did—and thought and tried and said—they did *together*. They ate together, slept together, bathed together, played together, wandered off together, and had playdates together.

Today's playdate was with the only other twins they knew, Phoebe and Chloe Tondorf-Schnittman. Every other Saturday the Griffins dropped Paul and Cassie at the Tondorf-Schnittmans' at nine a.m., and then picked them up at one thirty p.m. And on the alternate weeks, the Tondorf-Schnittmans dropped their twins with the Griffins.

The Saturday of Patrick's disappearance, the Twinfest—as Mr. and Mrs. Griffin called it—was being held at the Tondorf-Schnittman residence.

The four children had so far spent the entire morning down in the playroom in front of the sixty-four-inch HDTV engaged in a game that entailed emptying three chests and two closets of the Duplo blocks, baby dolls, plastic cars, VTech appliances, dollhouses, baby strollers, folding tunnels, and all other toys and pieces of play furniture, and then stacking it all into a series of unstable towers, which they hoped might reach the eight-foot-high sound-proofed ceiling. The room basically looked as if a giant had upended a toy store.

Mrs. Tondorf-Schnittman had so far failed to notice the project, partly because she had become preoccupied with a slew of urgent telephone, Facebook, and text-message communications. For starters, Jenna Michaels had put out a request for daycare help in coming weeks because she was separating from her husband. No great surprise there, but still a hot item. And *then* she saw Gail Munson's message about Mary Griffin's son going missing.

Everybody knew what an organized, competent mother Mary was, and the majority of the back-and-forth messages either posited or affirmed that it was all some innocent misunderstanding. But, still, this was a very serious matter, and one that called for immediate response.

She was unable to get Mary on her phone, but she e-mailed, texted, and posted that she was happy to watch Paul and Cassie for the entire day if it was any help, and "not to worry about picking them up at 1:30!!!!"

And then, she called Rachel MacDonald, texted Georgia Dolan, and Skyped Helen Heinz about the situation. It was important to let people know that she was going to be watching Mary's kids during this crisis. Which—as the activities taking place outside her house would soon prove—she obviously wasn't.

PART II: INTERLOPERS

Earth? No, I have no idea why
it's spelled that way.

—Ivan Dunn,
bcp §70¶1290

CHAPTER 17

Maps & Ants

THE SCHOOL RECEPTIONIST—A NERVOUS, KHAKI-uniformed woman, hair hard and shiny as a mahogany sideboard—seated Patrick and Kempton on a cushioned, lumbar-contoured bench in the Reception Rotunda, a bubble-shaped structure attached to the front end of the sprawling, semicircular Educational Complex. The building basically reminded Patrick of a modern airport terminal, although one with no windows and a lot more hand-sanitizing stations.

"Is there anything you, umm, require?" she asked.

"Not that we know of," said Kempton, somewhat rudely thought Patrick.

"Okay then, umm, your sixth-echelon magister will retrieve you shortly."

"What's a magister?" Patrick asked Kempton as he watched the woman's uniformed figure recede down the hall.

Patrick knew that echelons were what they called grades, thanks to a conversation the family had had yesterday when deciding whether he should go to school with Oma or Kempton. Oma was thirteen years (or *yies* as they called them here) old, Patrick was twelve, and Kempton eleven. So it had been decided—so that nothing was too academically challenging for Patrick—that he should go with Kempton. Who was in the sixth echelon.

"A magister is an academic instructor," said Kempton.

"We call them teachers, I think," replied Patrick.

Kempton forced a smile. "That's interesting," he said. "Now, I've got to finish a level." He'd been playing some game on his binky all morning. "I'll be right back." He again pulled the retractable strap from the backside of his binky and put it over his eyes in the same configuration that his mother had used last night for her show.

His disinterest in talking today, Patrick reflected, was a

big turnaround from last night when he'd been unable to get Kempton to *stop* talking. All the excitement Kempton had shown yesterday about being his host seemed to have disappeared. Maybe he just wasn't a morning person, but Patrick also had the sense that Kempton had been hoping he would get more special attention than he had been for being Patrick's chaperone. He'd kept talking about how he was going to "mega-index" and "go viral" online, and how the kids at school were going to freak out. But so far, other than for having been kept home yesterday, and for having been sent here to reception rather than straight to class today, there didn't seem to be any special attention coming Kempton's—much less Patrick's—way.

Patrick was feeling a little disappointed this morning himself, but for another reason. He'd been hoping that by falling asleep when you were already asleep, maybe you would fall *awake*. Obviously this was not the case.

The dream appeared to be very much the same as it had the night before. He'd woken up in the guest bed in Kempton's room and eaten a rather unappetizing breakfast of oats, some unidentifiable (and very hard) nuts, and chalky yogurt. Patrick didn't pry, but he gathered from this—and from last night's dinner of eggplant mash, kale salad, and seed-filled pita bread—that the Pubers were vegetarian, like his parents' friends the Nagars.

Not that it really mattered. So far, at least, he hadn't felt hungry in the slightest.

The only discomfort he was experiencing—despite the overall strangeness of this dream—was a certain sensation of confinement, like he was being expected to sit still through an epically boring church service. Though it wasn't that interesting stuff wasn't going on; it's just that he felt like he didn't really have any control over any of it. Which, since it was his dream, he guessed meant there was nobody to blame but himself.

Patrick glanced at Kempton. The light from the boy's game was playing out on his cheeks.

He hadn't gotten a very good look at it but, from when they'd been walking and Kempton hadn't had it strapped to his face, he'd seen that it involved spheres, cubes, and gelatinous blobs that grew, shrank, pulsed, and zipped around.

He had a couple questions he'd have liked to ask—about what they'd be studying at school today, about what this "Lasters" thing was that he'd heard Kempton's parents mention, about where Oma's classroom was relative to Kempton's—but he figured it would be rude, or at least pointless, to interrupt and instead turned his attention to the room's central exhibit: a hovering, slowly rotating globe of the world. It was really big—you could have fit a small car inside it—and its textured surface was animated with swirling cloud masses and blinking temperature and weather conditions.

Other than being unable to determine how they got it to hover and spin as it did—maybe there was an elaborate system of magnets under the floor?—he was most intrigued by how it was labeled. Iraq was ɪ**rak**. England was **ɪngɪənd**. The Pacific was **pəsifik oʃun**. France was **frans**. Luxembourg was **ɪuxəmbōrg**. Australia was **ostrᴀʟɛə**.

Kempton moaned and unstrapped his device from his face.

"Hard level?" Patrick asked.

Kempton nodded glumly.

"So that's the storm you mentioned?" asked Patrick, gesturing at the churning red-and-yellow squiggle moving east across the North American continent.

"Yeah," said Kempton. "It's meeting all the models so

far, should be a real record-setter. Lucky thing we live in AR 50 or it might really knock things for a loop."

"What's AR 50, this area?"

"No," said Kempton. "AR 50 is the yie. I was talking about our state of technological development."

"Oh," said Patrick. He regarded the big three-dimensional icon, **ið**, hovering above the North Pole. "And what's that?"

"What do you mean, 'What's that?'"

Patrick pointed. "The thing that looks like a backward six with a line through it."

"The 'eth' in Ith, you mean?" asked Kempton incredulously.

"I guess so. That's a letter? What'd you call it? *Eth?*"

"Uh, hello? How else would you write *Ith*?"

"I don't know, I mean, we spell *Earth* E-A-R-T-H," said Patrick.

"What?"

"E-A-R-T-H."

"O-*kay*," said Kempton, widening his eyes and turning back to his binky.

"Hey," said Patrick, leaning forward as he noticed other strangenesses: "And does that say Antarctica there?" The tribble-shaped island in the North Atlantic was labeled **antarktikǝ**. "Isn't that Iceland?"

"What are you talking about? Antarctica is Antarctica and Iceland is Iceland."

"But, on Earth," said Patrick, bending down and observing the continent at the bottom of the globe was labeled ısland, "it's the other way 'round."

"Huh," said Kempton, clearly wanting to get back to his game.

Patrick glanced up at a large, black-tinted camera bubble in the ceiling. He thought he could make out something moving inside, presumably the camera itself, but just then a strange, stiff-backed man in a bright blue uniform came stumbling down the hallway, leaning forward almost as if walking into a gale.

"Hello, Kempton!" hailed the man.

"Good morning, Magister Dorkenlaffer!" said Kempton, standing and tugging on Patrick's T-shirt.

"And you must be, umm, Patrick Cudahy Griffin of Earth!" said the man.

Patrick stood and tried not to gawk at the ribbons and ornaments up and down the man's chest and arms. Some were traditional medals—gold stars, eagle wings, lightning bolts, and things like that—and some sparkled and even contained blinking lights. A particularly eye-catching one on his shoulder resembled a spider carrying a stop sign:

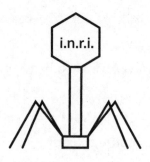

The letters on it refracted the hallway lights like the surface of a DVD.

"Just Patrick's fine," said Patrick, steering his eyes to the official's homely, wide-jowled, heavily made-up face. The man, pleased by this reply, had broken into a fit of laughter that made Patrick think of a drowning person gasping for air.

"Shall we go to class now, Magister Dorkenlaffer?" asked Kempton.

"Of course, of course!" He regained his breath and gestured for the boys to follow. Patrick noticed that in addition to the man's peculiar habit of leaning forward, when he turned, his shoulders and head all moved together—like he had a board strapped to his back.

"What's wrong with him?" whispered Patrick as the teacher lurched sideways, pushing open a door that creaked as if its hinges hadn't been oiled in twenty years.

"What?" asked Kempton.

"What's wrong with him?" repeated Patrick. "He, um, walks a little funny."

"Freak triking accident," replied Kempton a little too loudly for Patrick's comfort. "Broke his back. He's still partially paralyzed from the waist up."

Patrick followed Kempton and the teacher into a dimly lit classroom. He was pretty certain you couldn't be paralyzed from the waist *up* and made a mental note to raise the issue when there was a better opportunity to talk. Now clearly wasn't the time—far too many people were staring.

CHAPTER 18

Adept Intercept

NOVITIATE FRANK KYLE, ONE OF THE 120 REMAINING candidates for Earth's coming Deaconry, slowed his Mercedes to observe the activity at 96 and 102 Morningside Drive.

His dash-mounted BNK-E continued to scroll texts and to squawk calls from emergency responders regarding the missing child at the first house and the old man with the heart attack (exactly three hundred cubits away) at the next.

"Microparticle detection app, tau setting," he said to the air.

"Transcense levels approaching three parts per million," replied a female-inflected voice.

He smiled and pounded his fist on the goat-leather steering wheel: he was first-to-scene, which meant the mission was *his*. All he had to do now was execute the operational orders to eliminate the visitor, and do so discreetly. And that shouldn't be a problem. A single enemy combatant operating here without any support network didn't stand much of a chance.

He punched the accelerator pedal and—without breaking the speed limit—drove off. All he had to do was spiral outward from this location. Now that he'd found the insertion point, the trailhead, he had just to keep an eye on his chemical detectors and he'd find the creature's path. The residue from the transcense—the unique, unstable substance that had fueled the enemy combatant's journey here—would leave a faint but detectable trail for the next two dunts (about five "hours" as the locals would say).

He would find it and kill it and, in so doing, achieve a significant piece of mission experience to separate himself from the other 119 novitiates and boost his chances of becoming one of the final twelve, the new leaders of Earth. None of his peers would be able to deny that—however easy this mission proved to be—he'd have been the one who had put an end to the enemy's first known attempt to disrupt Earth's coming Purge, and the glorious Reboot to come.

CHAPTER 19

Intro to Modern Chemistry

FROM BEHIND FIFTEEN NEATLY ARRANGED DESKS, fifteen pairs of luminous eyes studied Patrick as if he were some sort of space alien although, of course, it was they who more resembled bug-eyed Martians.

"Class," said Magister Dorkenlaffer. "As you know, we have a very special guest today. For only the second instance in Ith's history, an *Earthling* is among us, and *our* class has the profound privilege of hosting him!"

Fifteen hands shot into the air as Patrick tried to keep his face from going any redder than it already was.

"I need not remind you to be on your very best behavior

and to accord him—*Patrick Cudahy Griffin*—every courtesy. He is a stranger and deserves your alpha-level interpersonal protocols at all times. Now, questions, and— Nevis! Do you require a time-out? You know there is no personal videography permitted in classrooms! Shocking!"

A slight, towheaded boy in the third row dropped his binky to the desk and slumped down in his seat, eyes lowered as he received the big-eyed staring treatment from his peers.

"Yes, Timar?" said Magister Dorkenlaffer, pointing to a copper-skinned boy in the front row.

"Is he related to Rex?"

Magister Dorkenlaffer turned to Patrick. "Are you related to Rex?"

"Who's Rex?" asked Patrick.

"He doesn't know who Rex is!" a girl yelled from the back of the room.

"Oh, dear," said Magister Dorkenlaffer, adjusting his brass-buttoned shirt collar. "Umm, Rex was, you know, the first Earthling, umm, emissary . . . Surely you are familiar with *Doctor Rex Abraham*?"

"He arrived here on Ith fifty yies ago," offered Kempton.

Patrick shook his head.

Magister Dorkenlaffer cleared his throat. "Of course there are differences between Patrick's world and ours.

Now, Kempton Puber, would you please show our guest to his seat?"

Patrick followed Kempton to two vacant desks in the first row.

"The important thing at this juncture," said the teacher, reading from his handheld screen, "is that we all recognize the significance of our Earth brother's arrival and are eager for him to become an integral member of society. To that end," he said, "Patrick Cudahy Griffin, you will please let us know if there's anything we can do to help you in *any* way, or—on the other hand—if there is anything we are doing that makes you uncomfortable that we should therefore *stop* doing."

"Does this mean there will be another Pandemic?" blurted a girl with the most elaborately bejeweled corn-rows Patrick had ever seen.

"Bilma!" said Magister Dorkenlaffer. "I don't believe you were called on to ask a question and *of course* there is not going to be another Pandemic. You know modern science has made such a thing *statistically* impossible."

The girl seemed somewhat abashed but fired off another question anyhow.

"And will he die before very long, like Rex did?"

"Bilma, I *still* haven't authorized you to ask a question, much less one even more patently ridiculous than your first! Don't make me put a note out to the Admins!"

Bilma promptly sat down and closed her mouth.

Magister Dorkenlaffer meantime turned back to Patrick and, seeing the confusion on his face, hastened to explain: "Rex died in the Pandemic."

"Yeah, when he saved the Seer!" yelled the same boy who'd asked if Patrick was related to Rex.

"Class!" Magister Dorkenlaffer yelled. "Remember the Twelfth Tenet: Patrick is an *emissary*; he is not a paid performer here for your amusement!" He coughed into the forest of wiry gray hairs on the back of his hand before adding, "I'm certain the Seer is right now entirely *appalled* at your behavior."

The students did not seem to like this thought and fidgeted uncomfortably.

"Umm, who's the Seer?" asked Patrick.

Everybody gasped except for Magister Dorkenlaffer, who gurgled.

"She's, umm," said Magister Dorkenlaffer, again adjusting his shirt collar, "you know, err, much like your Hearer."

"My hearer?" asked Patrick.

"Yes," said Dorkenlaffer. "The leader of your sense, the ruler of your world."

"You mean the President of the United States?"

"The resident of what? No, I do not mean—"

Kempton turned to Patrick and hissed. "Are you making

105

a joke? The *Hearer*—your world's representative to the *Minder*!"

"I have no idea what you guys are talking about."

Dorkenlaffer made a frantic beckoning gesture at a security camera in the ceiling and the children began to chatter among themselves. Patrick overheard somebody speculating that this must be some sort of drill.

"Ah, never mind," said the teacher, seeing something on his binky. "Eyes forward. *Quiet now!*"

Patrick looked down at his binky, which, at the moment, was showing a title menu for "ᴀ **fōkusd** revü uv ᴅe **pᴇrᴇodic** **ᴇʟəmənts**."

"What does this say?" asked Patrick.

"What?" asked Kempton.

"Let's see, 'A focused, rev-uh—' "

" 'A Focused Review of the Periodic Elements,' you mean?"

"Oh," said Patrick.

"Yeah," replied Kempton.

"So this is a chemistry class?" asked Patrick.

"Look around," replied Kempton, gesturing behind them.

Patrick turned around. Maybe he hadn't noticed before because the back of the room was so poorly lit, but he could now discern it contained lab benches, faucets, equipment clamps, sinks, Bunsen burners, insulated dry ice buckets, and fume hoods.

"We're on chapter eighty-six," said Kempton. "Optical properties of the noble gases. So just skip to that section and process along with the rest of us, okay?"

Patrick rubbed his eyes and looked back to the front of the room, also now noticing a periodic table of the elements on the wall and a ball-and-stick model of glucose on the teacher's desk.

"And stop touching your face," whispered Kempton. "You're smearing your mascara."

Patrick studied his new binky. He hadn't spent much time on it yet, but it seemed fairly intuitive. The screen resolved, swiped side to side, magnified, brought images and text forward and backward in three dimensions with amazing ease, and—before he figured out it was controlled by the natural movements of his eyes—he had the eerie sensation it was reading his mind.

He played a holographic video showing how a stream of electrons could cause neon atoms to give off light. It was very cool, but the captions were pretty confusing. With a little concentration he was able to figure out at least most of the words (like **at<u>om</u>ik** he assumed meant *atomic*) but quite a few were harder than that.

"Is there some way to have it show regular words? A

settings menu? What's this big red eye symbol in the corner?"

"That's the Inform icon! Only select that in case of suspected malefaction!!!"

"Oh," said Patrick.

Kempton leaned over and studied Patrick's binky. "And what do you mean, 'regular words'? They look fine to me."

"Well, I mean, the writing's just not, well, English."

"English?"

"Well, this word right here is supposed to be *light*, right?" he said, pointing his finger at a word that read LIT.

"Uh, yeah?"

"Well, on Earth, that spells *lit*. The way you guys write I think is kind of how they show pronunciations in dictionaries."

Kempton regarded him as if he'd just spoken a foreign language.

"It's not how we write on Earth is all I'm trying to say."

Kempton turned and yelled, "Magister Dorkenlaffer! Patrick can't read!"

"Great," muttered Patrick as, once again, the entire class was staring.

"Oh, dear," said Magister Dorkenlaffer. "Well, Mr. Griffin, why don't you come up here"—he gestured for Patrick to come up to his desk—"and we'll see what accommodations can be made?"

"It's not that I can't read," he said as he took the chair next to the teacher. "It's just that your writing's different and we read in lines, not like with the words coming one by one like that."

"Fascinating. Do you not have screens on Earth?" Magister Dorkenlaffer said, gesturing at the binky.

"Yeah, I mean, sure we do. But we also read from books a lot."

"I have seen *books*," said the man in a hushed voice. "They are *so* beautiful."

Patrick couldn't figure out why the man was whispering and thought that *beautiful* was taking things a little far.

"Anyhow," continued the teacher more loudly as he looked at, or read, something on his own binky, "it sounds like we've un-ithed another fascinating difference between your world and ours. Not to worry—I believe your binky can easily translate to your written language. Let's try this—'Binky, default settings: please translate to Pre-Pandemic Written English,'" he said to the device. Instantly, all the words became readable.

"Cool," said Patrick.

The teacher smiled. "The Interverse is a multi-splendored thing, is it not?"

Patrick agreed, but before he could appreciate any more of the Interverse's wonders, the classroom door creaked loudly open and Magister Dorkenlaffer—together with every kid in the room—sprang from his seat and saluted.

"Provost Bostrel!" exclaimed Magister Dorkenlaffer.

Patrick got to his feet but the visitor in the elaborate gray military uniform stopped him before he could salute.

"Emissary Griffin," said the man. "It's an *honor* to meet you."

"Umm, it's an honor to meet you, too, sir," said Patrick as he tried not to stare at the man's nose. He supposed he'd seen bigger ones, but it was still a whopper.

"I was just going down the hallway and thought I'd check in," said the man.

Patrick dropped his eyes to the man's uniform. It had same **i.n.r.i.** spider logo on the left shoulder as Magister Dorkenlaffer's, but the rest of it was adorned—if possible—with even more jewels, ribbons, and spangles.

"Patrick's taking to the syllabus like a duck to water," said Magister Dorkenlaffer, "but he did give us a little scare—he said he *didn't know who Rex was*!"

"Well, that's not all that surprising. Studies show that memory issues are a fairly common side effect of interworld relocation," said the provost.

"Ah," said the magister, sighing like an expiring can of spray paint. "Of course."

"Patrick Griffin," continued the big-nosed man, "do please forgive our disorganization. I'm afraid you've caught us on one of the busiest days of the yie and, on top of everything else, I'm stuck in meetings for most of the day. But we should have a quick chat. Do you think you can have your escort lead you to the main office at four dunts?"

"Sir, yes, sir!" shouted Kempton from where he was standing by his desk.

"Very good then," said Provost Bostrel, extending his right elbow at Patrick.

"Umm," said Patrick, looking at the man's elbow.

The man nodded encouragingly, then raised a neatly tweezed eyebrow and somehow made clear to Patrick that he was supposed to extend his own elbow, which he did, and the man promptly bumped it with his own. Perhaps, Patrick considered, this was how they shook hands.

Everybody remained quiet as the provost left the room and Patrick and Magister Dorkenlaffer locked eyes a moment.

"Pah!" spluttered the magister, releasing his breath and smiling brightly. "You are *such* a lucky fellow to have a *personal interview* with the *provost!*"

He turned to the other students and waved them to sit down. "Kempton!" he said. "You and Patrick are to leave the field at three-eight. No dillydallying at games. Straight to your lockers. Alpha protocols, boys. You are to be *clean* and *presentable*; I do *not* want any reports of two boys showing up at the main office trailing Lasters mud from their sneakers."

"Uh, what exactly *is* Lasters?" asked Patrick.

"It's today—the best day of the entire school year!" said Kempton.

"It's the last day of the academic year," said Magister Dorkenlaffer.

"And there are oat snacks and smoothies!"

"And mud, did you say?" asked Patrick.

"Yes, from the games," said Kempton.

"On the playing fields," explained Magister Dorkenlaffer. "Which is why I asked that you boys make sure you are clean and presentable for the provost."

"Oh," said Patrick, guessing that all made sense: Lasters must basically be like Field Day back home. "And so Provost Bostrel, he's like the school principal?"

Magister Dorkenlaffer raised a shaggy eyebrow.

"I mean, his uniform—" Patrick started to say.

"Bostrel the Nostril!" somebody yelled from the back of the room.

Magister Dorkenlaffer tried to look angry at the remark, but couldn't. "That's not—" he said, clutching his belly and dissolving into laughter.

"Who said—" he tried again.

A bell rang and Patrick reflexively put his hands over his ears. It was among the loudest noises he'd heard in his life, and yet he seemed to be the only one in any kind of discomfort; the other kids were jubilant.

Magister Dorkenlaffer collapsed in his chair and, still failing to control himself, covered his brow with one hand as he waved at the door with the other.

"Go," he managed to pant as the bell stopped ringing. "Go out to Lasters! Have a restful and rejuvenative break. And don't forget to check the assportal!" Then he exclaimed "Nostril!" to himself and began shaking with laughter all over again.

"Did he say assportal?" Patrick asked Kempton.

"Yes, what else would he have said?"

"What is it?"

"An assignment portal? It's where we get our home-work, of course."

"Oh," said Patrick, following Kempton toward the door as he considered that this was not something his brother Neil would have accepted nearly as calmly as he just had.

Magister Dorkenlaffer stood and gave Patrick a kindly wink.

"It's been a pleasure meeting you, young man. And I'm so sorry we didn't have more time for chemistry."

"Me, too," said Patrick.

Most of the class had filed through the door by now and, as Kempton turned to get some more hand sanitizer, the teacher leaned forward, shook Patrick's hand, and whispered, with a distinct note of secrecy, "Despite how strange this must all seem to you, I hope you find the coming day's events *have a certain commonplace aspect to them.*"

Before Patrick could think what to say Kempton was back at his side, ushering him through the door and out into the boisterous throng of students coursing down the hall.

CHAPTER 20

Life & Death in the Bush

CARLY'S CAT—THE ONE PATRICK HAD LET OUTSIDE
earlier that day—had at one point been a formidable
hunter. Dozens upon dozens of birds, rodents, and even
snakes had met their untimely end in its hook-shaped
claws and sharp-toothed jaws.

But since the unfortunate day when it had been captured by a Westchester County Animal Control agent in
the lot behind the Hedgerow Heights Library, its natural
calling had fallen into terrible disuse. Captivity had trans-
formed it from fearless predator into fearful prey. The only
thing it had caught in the past six months had been a

single moth that had, like it, had the misfortune to become imprisoned in the Griffin house.

But already it all seemed just a passing nightmare. Here again was the life it had been born to live—the sun glinting through the clouds, the buzz of early-spring insects, the birds chirping so tantalizingly close by—

The cat dropped its chest to within an inch of the ground, raised its ears, and commanded its tail to rigid quietude. Upwind, a sleek gray squirrel was obliviously rooting around the base of a tree.

It was true that squirrels like this one—safe from the wild predators of prehuman North America and largely dependent on free food sources like birdseed—were generally slower, fatter, and duller than their forebears. But stalking even the most suburban of squirrels was still a dangerous undertaking.

Squirrels have massive teeth—teeth that shatter nuts and chew through branches, teeth that can remove a talon from the foot of an uncareful hawk, teeth that can inflict deep and grievous wounds in the flesh of a less-than-expert predator. Squirrels have long, curved, wicked-sharp claws that allow them to cling upside down, even on the stone-smooth bark of beech trees. And squirrels, gray squirrels in particular, are big—easily half the size of an average cat.

But no creature embodies the expression "nothing

ventured, nothing gained" like a predator, and especially a predator that has just escaped six months of domestic confinement.

The cat instinctively knew the key would be to grab the soft underside of the rodent's neck. This was where to find the blood-filled arteries and the breath-carrying windpipe. This was the way to make the kill shorter and safer, rather than longer and more dangerous. It waited through one, two, then three gusts of wind till the squirrel— digging for nuts in the winter-tired leaves—turned and exposed its flank.

Then the cat pounced, but not stealthily enough. The squirrel flinched, and the cat's teeth, instead of circling up under the chin, closed on the rodent's shoulder.

Desperately grappling and scratching, the cat pushed the squirrel's sleekly strong body out and away. Ideally he would have shifted his grip—let go and quickly bitten again closer to the throat—but the risk was too great. The flailing prey might wrench free and find opportunity to use its sharp-toothed mouth to do more than scream.

"Chh-chh-chh-chh-EEEEEEEEEE! CHH-chhh-chhh-chh-EEEEEEEEEEE!" chattered the stricken animal as they rolled, writhed, flipped, and flopped across the forest floor, their furry shapes blurring together.

Till now the cat had kept his ears flattened to his head and his eyes firmly shut. Millions of years of selective pressure had hardwired the habit. When you have a flailing animal in your mouth, an open eye invites poking, an extended ear invites shredding, and both pairs of organs are important, if not vital, to a hunter's survival in the wild.

But sometimes instinct has to be put in the backseat and, as the two animals rolled again—the squirrel chatter-screaming the whole way—the cat opened an eye and looked around for something to stop their aimless tumbling. It quickly spied an old timber crucifix, erected by Agnes Coffin in the 1970s, the focal point of a long-abandoned woodland shrine.

The cat then began to shift its weight so that each tussle brought them closer to the cross. Soon, they were up against it and, from that moment—gifted with the leverage to exert his superior strength—things became much easier for the cat. The squirrel soon stopped chattering and, a few off-kilter heartbeats later, its body went entirely limp.

Before the victory could be savored, however, there was a terrific thump. Something very heavy had landed on the ground right behind the cat.

It dropped the squirrel and turned to see—standing on its hind legs, tall as a human—an enormous, white-bellied, short-eared rabbit. With antlers on its head.

· · · · ·

BunBun furrowed his woolly brow as the cat streaked off into the woods, then stooped to examine the dead squirrel.

"How barbaric," he concluded, and clucked his tongue for good measure.

His impulse was to dig a quick grave but just then he spotted an alabaster face through the curtain of vines ahead of him. It was the downward-looking face of Jesus Christ upon an overgrown cross.

"Oh, hello!" he said and—heart in his throat as he regarded one the most famous Commonplace contributors in all the three worlds—bowed low to the ground. "I've read *so* much about you."

CHAPTER 21

The First of Lasters

IT PROBABLY WOULD HAVE BEEN NICE TO BE AS excited as the rest of the yelling, laughing, squealing, jostling students, but Patrick didn't envy them. He simply wished he were someplace else, someplace quieter, someplace he could experiment on ways to wake himself up.

So far he'd only figured out that pinching oneself awake was a load of bull. He'd pinched every part of his body he politely could and none of it had changed a thing other than causing momentary doses of pain.

It came as no surprise, really. He'd never known anybody to say they had complete control over what happened in their dreams, and pinching oneself must be one of those expressions—like blessing a person who's sneezed or knocking wood for luck—that were just old pieces of superstition people repeated because they were something to say, and people are always scrambling for easy words, especially at times when they have the least idea what to think.

The entire situation was all starting to make its own sort of sense to Patrick: clearly everybody forgot nearly everything about their dreams. Probably, over the years, he'd dreamed himself in hundreds or thousands of other places just as weird as this and so this strange dream wasn't very strange at all; it's just that he tended to forget all of the other freaky things his sleeping brain cooked up. And this was probably good because he had enough trouble concentrating in school as it was.

But the other part of it was that it being a dream really didn't change anything: What difference was there even realizing it was all in his head? Was he supposed to act like somebody other than himself? Should he throw a fit and sulk in the corner like his sister Eva probably would? Take advantage of there being no adult supervision and do something annoying like Neil? Scream at the top of his lungs like Carly? Lock himself in a room and avoid everybody like Lucie? Sit on the ground and stick things in his mouth that he probably shouldn't stick in his mouth like the Twins?

Of course he *could* act any way he wanted; but still, why go to the trouble? Why make things harder when they could be easier?

He considered all this as they were jostled to the end of the hallway, across a playing field, and up into an enormous grandstand.

Kempton took his arm and led him to the very top row.

"This is some stadium," said Patrick, glancing down through the safety railing at the back side. They had to be seven stories up at least. He suffered a twinge of vertigo and remembered that he'd woken from dreams in which he'd fallen out of buildings and airplanes, or off a cliff or out of a tree. Of course, at least to his memory, those falls had always been by accident. Actually jumping off these bleachers on purpose seemed just as crazy and scary a proposition as it would have in real life. But—if he stood here awhile—maybe something would happen? Perhaps his dream would decide to give him a little accident? He gave a test shove to the safety railing but it seemed pretty solid.

"Admiring our grounds fauna?" asked Kempton.

"Your what?" asked Patrick, gauging Kempton's glance. A few hundred yards distant a large flock of blue-collared sheep, cows, goats, and llamas was milling about.

"Oh, like the animals in your yard, right? They're for mowing the ball fields?"

"Of course," said Kempton.

"And what's the deal with the trench?" asked Patrick. Past the animals was a long, shallow concrete depression.

"The manure culvert?"

Patrick raised an eyebrow.

"Come on," said Kempton, sitting down and gesturing for Patrick to join him. The green fields down below and off to the sides were flanked by jumbotrons. For the moment, they all seemed to be showing the same shimmering spider-stop-sign symbol that had been on Magister Dorkenlaffer's and Bostrel the Nostril's uniforms:

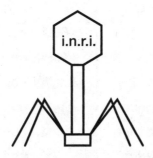

"So," he said to Kempton. "Are we going to be watching a game?"

"We'll be *playing* a game," said Kempton. "But, first—in a couple terts—there's going to be the commencement address from the provost."

"Oh," said Patrick. "What are terts?"

"Umm," he said, looking suspiciously at Patrick, "you know, ten quats?"

"What are quats?"

"You don't measure time in quints, quats, terts, deuces, and dunts?"

Patrick shook his head and Kempton, sighing like he was being forced to explain things to a not-very-bright kindergartner, held up his screen with what appeared to be a Wikipedia entry. The subject heading read, "tɪmkɛping."

1 quint	0.864	sec
1 quint	0.0144	min
1 quat	8.64	sec
1 quat	0.144	min
1 tert	86.4	sec
1 tert	1.44	min
1 tert	0.024	hour
1 deuce	14.4	min
1 deuce	0.24	hour
1 dunt	2.4	hour
1 dunt	0.1	day

"So," continued Kempton, "a *quint* is the smallest common increment of time measurement, right? One one-hundred-thousandth of a day. You know, count, 'one-Missouri, two-Missouri, three-Missouri'—and each of those is about a quint. And a quint is a tenth of a quat, so count ten quints and—" He broke off and stood up, exclaiming, "There he is!"

Patrick looked down to the field even as the world

exploded around them. He reflexively dropped down in front of his seat and covered his ears. The initial blast was followed by a series of rumbling notes that kind of sounded like a man—or a giant—talking. Another noise assaulted him next, a noise like a cresting tidal wave of applause and human voices and—

Patrick cautiously opened one eye, then the other. Everybody in the bleachers was jumping and cheering. He removed his hands from his ears, stood, and saw—down on the field at a podium and simultaneously playing upon the massive 3D jumbotrons—Bostrel the Nostril. The man was red-faced and fierce-eyed now, the cords on his neck standing out like cables under a tent canopy.

"We have a problem!" said the big-nosed man, waving impatiently for the crowd to sit. To Patrick, the problem was obvious: they had the volume up about fifty times too high. He clamped his hands back on his ears and looked around, astonished that nobody else seemed to even be flinching. A person in the next town could easily have made out every word.

The provost continued, "Your achievements this yie deserve recognition and, I daresay, real praise.

"But I'm not here to just pat you on the head and send you to the next term."

The man's eyebrows descended on his face and his fist on the lectern.

"Now is *not* the time for congratulations. Now is *not* the time for self-satisfaction.

"GRAVE PERIL is at our door!

"A menace like none we have ever known threatens to upend all the assiduous work of the Minder, the Seer, Rex, your parents, and all of us. The approaching new yie, the springtime of our birthright, can assuredly become a *waking nightmare*!

"You know the menace of which I speak?"

The kids around Patrick quivered in their seats.

"ANARCHISTS!!!" he screamed as the jumbotrons projected images of monsters like the one from Kempton's game.

Patrick winced at the pain in his ears.

"The Deacons inform us that these filthy scum, these degenerate solipsists, these *haters* of order and Nature and peace, these self-serving *monsters*, these agents of *entropy* have chosen this moment to wage an all-out campaign of terror!

"Our resolve must be like titanium-ceramic alloy!" he screamed. The images showed cities on fire, people running scared, soot-stained children crying in open fields.

"We MUST NOT waver, we MUST NOT flinch, we MUST NOT abandon our responsibilities, we MUST NOT question or doubt our course, and what they have done to us we MUST NEVER FORGET!

"To do so," he added solemnly as the screens went blank and then filled with the image of a middle-aged man in a black turtleneck.

Kempton elbowed Patrick to get his attention. "That's Rex," he said solicitously. "Do you recognize him now?"

Patrick shook his head. The man somehow looked like a cross between Steve Jobs and The Rock.

"To *forget*," the Provost repeated for emphasis, "would be to fail the Seer and the Minder himself.

"*'Why did they do it?'* we wonder. And why are those that remain continuing to flout Rex's Tenets? Why are they maliciously hacking our networks? Why are they impeding effective governance? Why are they tampering with the Minder-given order of Nature and turning genetic abominations loose upon us? Why are they attempting to disrupt the visit of our first emissary from Earth since Rex himself? Tell me now!!!"

"They're Evil!" screamed every student in the grandstand.

"I can't HEAR you!" the provost screamed back.

"THEY'RE EVIL!"

There was a thunderclap as he again pounded his fist on the lectern. "And, so, what quality must we embrace—on a daily basis, for every waking dunt—to ensure they don't carry off their nefarious plots!? What is our greatest weapon?!!"

"Vigilance!" shouted the students.

"And what do we do if we *see something* unusual?! We—"

"INFORM!!" screamed the crowd as the screens projected the eye symbol Patrick had seen on his binky.

"Louder!" screamed the man. "If you see something, you—"

"INFORM!!!!!"

"With your attention, with your focus, with your courage to observe and, yes, *inform* officials of any unusual occurrences, any potential malfeasances, we *will* be victorious. We *will* root them out and we *will* fulfill the Seer's vision . . . and the Minder's plan. We have withstood the worst plague in all of humanity's history—and we can finally triumph over the enemy!

"Now," said the big-nosed man, suddenly smiling brightly as the screens filled with images of streaking military aircraft and exploding rockets, "let's take a measure of this moment's importance and apply it toward our opponents on the playing fields of this fine institution of learning: *Let the games begin!*"

· · · · ·

"Kill the carrier? Like where one guy carries the ball?" asked Patrick. He was a little surprised. He'd seen it played—and played some himself—in backyards and neighborhood playgrounds, but he'd never heard of it being played as a legitimate sport. Somehow it seemed pretty dangerous for a school to ever approve, much less a school for a bunch of people who didn't even seem to like to shake hands.

"Really?" he asked.

Kempton cocked his head. "What do you mean? Don't you have kill the carrier on Earth?"

"Well, we do, but not at schools."

"Just a pro league, then? But why not at schools? What better place is there to memorialize the Pandemic?"

"The Pandemic? Is this what that kid mentioned in your class?"

"Yes, where the Anarchists killed more than 99 percent of the population."

"Oh," said Patrick, a little shocked. "When did that happen?"

"Fifty yies ago."

"Oh, wow," said Patrick, his head spinning. Could it be true? Ninety-nine percent of the entire world had died? And the people who made it, these Anarchists, were still around? No wonder Bostrel had been so worked up in his speech just now.

"So you didn't have a Pandemic on Earth?" asked Kempton.

"I don't think so," said Patrick.

"But you have the sport? What does the carrier symbolize for you, then?"

"Symbolize?" asked Patrick.

"It's symbolism, you know—the person carrying the ball is the one carrying the virus. That's why they must be stopped!"

"Oh," said Patrick. "I think the ball's just the ball on Earth."

"Well, you see, here on Ith, playing the sport helps make sure we'll *never forget*."

"That makes sense."

"Plus"—Kempton brightened—"it's *awesome* fun! Here, let's go get picked!"

They had come to the edge of the boys' echelon-six crowd, just then divvying itself up into teams. The two captains were tall, broad-chested, and—despite the heavy lipstick and purple eye shadow they wore—were obviously handsome and self-confident. Also, the only difference between them appeared to be the color of their shirts. One wore blue, the other red.

"Twins?" Patrick asked Kempton as they attached themselves to the line of still-unpicked kids.

"Yes, Breeden and Carl Luntz. Either would be the most athletic and popular boy in the class but there are two of them! Can you believe it?!"

Patrick had seen harder-to-believe things even in the past ten minutes but figured there wasn't much point saying so.

"Say," he said, "where are all the adults?"

Now that the provost was no longer at the podium, it struck Patrick there wasn't a single coach, referee, or teacher outside with them.

"Inside doing work, of course," said Kempton.

"But who's going to keep an eye on things?"

"What do you mean?"

"What if there's a fight or something?"

"A fight?"

"Sure, or bullying."

"What?"

"What if somebody gets hurt?"

"Then responders will come," said Kempton, raising his binky.

"They really let you do sports and stuff without *any* grownups around?"

"Why not?"

"Your team gets Kempton, we get Patrick Griffin," interrupted the red-shirted twin.

"No way, Breeden," said the blue-shirted one. "*Your* team gets Kempton."

"Those guys," whispered Kempton to Patrick. "They're trying to make you feel welcome."

"Tell you what," said Patrick, a little put off at how they were treating Kempton and realizing that here was a place where he could take advantage of this being a dream—and *his* dream at that.

"How about," he said, "*I* get to pick which team I join?"

The two boys—and every other sixth-echelon student—looked at Patrick with surprise.

"Who's got a coin?" asked Patrick.

"A coin?" replied Kempton.

"You know—a quarter, a dime, a penny . . ." Patrick's voice trailed off as he absorbed the looks of bewilderment around him. A few kids unholstered and began examining their binkies.

"Don't you guys have any change?"

"Change?" asked the blue-shirted twin. "You mean, like, alter the rules?"

"Money," said Patrick.

"Like pirates' doubloons?" asked a kid.

"He means coin money from the dark ages," said another, looking up from his screen.

"You guys don't have money at all?" asked Patrick.

"Umm," said the blue-shirted twin.

"No-o," said the red-shirted twin.

"'Money,'" said Kempton, reading from his binky, "'is an archaic system used to measure and mete out power in many suboptimized, nontransparent social organizations.'"

"Nerd!" said somebody.

"All right," said Patrick, realizing that this conversation was going no place fast. He stooped and plucked a blade of grass. "I've got a piece of grass and I'm going to put my hands behind my back and whoever picks the hand with it gets me on their team. And Kempton goes to the other. That's fair, right?"

Most of them seemed to agree. Patrick put his hands together behind his back and—so nobody could see—transferred the blade to his left hand, and then back to his right.

"Who gets to pick?" asked Kempton.

"It doesn't matter—you guys decide."

"You pick, Carl," said the red-shirted twin to the blue-shirted twin.

"Fine by me, Breeden," said Carl.

"All right," said Patrick. "Right or left?"

"*Your* right or left, or *his* right or left?" asked Kempton.

Patrick sighed and looked to Carl. "How about *your* right or left. Or, why don't you just *point*?"

"Don't let me down and give me Kempton, 'kay?" the jock replied with a mascaraed wink.

Somebody started chanting "Poo-ber! Poo-ber! Poo-ber!" and soon pretty much the whole crowd had joined in.

Three things became clear to Patrick in that moment. First, he might not be Kempton's biggest fan, but he didn't quite hate him, either. Second, the playgrounds of Ith were not much different from those of Earth—if he'd seen one, he'd easily seen a hundred jocks-laughing-at-wimps moments like this. And, third, if Breeden and Carl were to move to Hedgerow Heights, they'd probably become instant best friends with Neil and his idiot lacrosse-playing friends.

When the chanting and laughing had somewhat subsided, Carl reached out and tapped Patrick's right shoulder.

And then Patrick did something he'd never have done in a million years in real life: he raised his arm toward Carl and, instead of opening his fist and revealing the blade of grass it contained, he gave him a hand gesture that, had a teacher back home seen, would have earned Patrick detention. Here and now on the dreamed-up fields of the Educational Complex, however, his raised finger didn't seem to cause anything but confusion.

"Does that mean he didn't pick the grass?" asked Breeden.

Patrick felt his face flush hot.

"He seems upset," said Carl.

"I guess he didn't want to be on your team," said Breeden.

"I guess you didn't *not* want to be a dillhole," said Carl to his twin brother.

"Look—Patrick Griffin's ears are turning red!" shouted

a small boy, pointing. Kids began oohing and ahing, and taking videos with their binkies.

"They're like big, purple *seashells*!" said a flat-faced boy.

Patrick turned and aimed his finger at him.

"You really don't know what this means?"

" 'You're number one'?" guessed the boy.

"No," said Patrick.

"Does it mean 'no grass'?" asked Carl.

"No, it doesn't mean 'no grass,' Jock-o."

"What's 'jock-o' mean?" asked Kempton.

"Forget it," said Patrick, opening his fist to reveal the grass. "Let's just play."

"In that case, your team is up," said Kempton, gesturing for Patrick to follow Carl and the other boys onto the field.

"Here," said Patrick, starting to undo his binky belt, "where do we put these?"

"What are you *doing*?" asked Kempton.

"You wear these even when you play kill the carrier?"

"Why would you take it off?"

Patrick guessed binkies must be more rugged than the cell phones he knew from Earth.

It seemed like a good theory at the time.

CHAPTER 22

Crackin' Up

PATRICK'S FATHER AND OLDER BROTHER, NEIL, were on their way back from the Tool Town Super-store in Paramus where an investigation of hose gaskets had been cut short by a call from Mrs. Griffin. Mr. Griffin wasn't saying what was going on beyond "Your brother's done something stupid," but that was good enough for Neil. Patrick *never* got in trouble, so between that and the fact that they'd only had to spend five minutes inside that monumentally boring hardware megastore, the morning could have been going a lot worse.

But while the prospect of some justice coming down on

his little brother was pretty cool, what he'd just heard on the radio almost made him forget the entire situation: the news dude had just said the first interesting thing in his entire droning, epically boring life.

Neil reached for the volume knob so he could better hear over the squeaky wipers.

"What do you think you're doing, Neil?"

"Shhh! *Architeuthis*, Dad, *Architeuthis*!"

"What?"

"*Architeuthis*," repeated Neil impatiently, "the giant squid, Dad! Shhh!"

Scientists from Branledore University have rescued a juvenile Architeuthis sanctipauli, *the legendary giant squid, from a fishing net near the Comoros Islands. The creature was alive and has been placed in a high-pressure tank aboard the research vessel* Christy Jenkins. *Mission leaders hope to transport the cephalopod—the first giant squid successfully kept alive in captivity—back to a permanent facility in Corpus Christi, Texas, for study and public display.*

The largest invertebrate creatures on the planet, giant squids have been known to grow more than forty feet in length. They are believed to range throughout the deeper portions of the world's major

oceans. This specimen, it is reported, is just over fif-
teen feet in length.

And now the weekend weather: it looks as if a
high—

"They're going to kill it," said Neil, turning down the volume.

"Would you believe this joker?" asked his dad, gesturing at the tricked-out Range Rover in front of them. The big SUV had stopped just shy of the intersection. "That is known as a *yellow light,* not a *red light!*" he yelled at the windshield.

"Can I borrow your phone?" asked Neil.

"My phone, why?" said Mr. Griffin.

"I want to look up about this squid."

"Not right now, Neil," replied his father, sucking air through his lower teeth like he did whenever he was feeling impatient.

"The pressure only matters somewhat—it has more to do with the environment," said Neil. "And there's no way they're going to get that right in an *aquarium.*"

"So what's the big deal with this squid, kiddo?"

"It's a *giant* squid, Dad."

"Ah," said Mr. Griffin, drumming his thumbs on the steering wheel and glancing over at his son. "Okay, so how giant is giant?"

"Well, this one's a juvenile so it's not humongous. They said fifteen feet, and that's got to mean including the tentacles so, really, its body's probably just five or six feet long."

"That's still pretty decent, I guess," said Mr. Griffin, pausing to make his leaking-bicycle-tire noise again. "How big do the grownups get?"

"With tentacles extended, probably more than fifty feet."

"That's a lotta calamari!"

"Might as well be," said Neil, frowning. "Those idiots are going to kill it."

"That's too bad, buddy," said his father, his attention migrating back out the windshield.

"Can I go to Texas to see it?" asked Neil.

"Sure, whatever you want," said his father, *really* not paying attention to his eldest son now as he stared up at the light, trying to see if it had turned yellow for the cross street. "If this bobo doesn't get moving, I'm going to lay so much horn on him he's going to think he's been stomped by a moose."

"Antlers, Dad."

"What?"

"A moose has antlers; a bull has horns."

"Right," said his dad. "Stomped by a *bull*."

"Anyhow, it's probably not worth bothering," said Neil. "I bet they don't keep it alive more than a week."

Neil sat back and tried to calculate his odds of being able to swipe the phone from its cradle without his dad noticing.

The light changed and the Range Rover's left signal began to blink.

"Are you turning?!" yelled Neil's dad. "You conspicuously consumptive piece of nouveau riche, resource-hogging, impractical, humanity-hating soulless yuppie garbage!?"

The car behind began to honk.

"You have got to be kidding me," said Mr. Griffin, looking in the mirror. "A freaking Prius? Honking at me? Do you not see the mountain of waste ahead of us, my green little self-righteous, tailgating friend!?"

"Chill, Dad," said Neil.

"Yeah, I'll chill when people in this world stop being stark raving hypocritical entacks."

"What are entacks, Dad?"

"Never mind—forget I said it, buddy."

Neil shrugged and continued to obsess about his father's phone.

"Holy frack! Would you look at this bonehead! Want to give me just half an inch to get around you maybe?"

Sensing his father's distraction, Neil—with cobra-like quickness—snatched the phone from its cradle.

"What a donkey pit," said Mr. Griffin as he accelerated out through the intersection onto Benedict.

Neil nodded absently and tried to enter search terms into the smartphone hidden in the crook of his arm.

"Neil!" yelled his father. "What the heck, buddy?!"

"Dad, I just need it a minute, seriously, it's not like I'm going to blow out your plan by Googling a couple things, jeez."

"And you know how I feel about you using *jeez*, you smart aleck—seriously, put it down."

"What?" said Neil, hurriedly trying to finish swiping *texas aquarium squid* into the screen. "It's not like I'm going to *break* it—" But just then his hand—seemingly of its own volition—shot out and whipped the phone against the windshield.

There was a screaming sound as Neil's father stomped on the brakes and threw a protective arm across his son's chest.

The truck came to a dead stop and everything was silent as if time itself had ceased. Neil looked out the windshield and saw a large animal bound across the other lane and through a hedge. They must have missed the thing by inches. There had been something very strange about it. It didn't quite seem like a deer or a dog, and it had been carrying something in its front paws, almost like it was a person and—

There was a new squealing noise. "Sit back!" his father shouted, looking into the rearview mirror. He moved his foot from the brake pedal and pressed Neil firmly into his seat while he threw his own head back against the headrest.

The Prius behind them, after braking too late, now plowed into the back of Mr. Griffin's pickup, causing the airbags to deploy and sending the vehicle on a leftward-tilted twenty-foot skid down the rain-slick boulevard.

"*Stupid mother*-um . . ." said Neil's dad, pushing down the airbags and reaching for his insurance card in the glove box. "What was that idiot doing!? Did I miss a memo? Is it Incompetent Driver Day out there!!!?"

"What *was* that thing?" asked Neil.

"Dog clearly not on its leash like it's supposed to be by law," said his father. "This is *textbook* no-fault."

"Dad, are you sure that was a dog?"

"Of course it was a dog. You ever see a cat that big?"

"But wasn't there something weird about it?"

"I dunno," said Mr. Griffin. "I guess it was pretty chubby. Maybe it was one of those long-haired sheepdogs."

"It didn't have long hair, Dad."

"So maybe it was a short-haired sheepdog," said Mr. Griffin. "Look, stay in the truck and keep your seat belt on, kiddo. I'm going to go put flares out."

"But, Dad," said Neil, trying to think through the least insane way to describe what he knew he'd seen. "The dog—wasn't it carrying something in its arms?"

"What are you talking about—it was a *dog*."

"And didn't it have something on its head?"

"On its head?"

"You know, like *antlers*?"

Mr. Griffin stepped down out of the truck and looked at his son, a degree of distance in his eyes. He really hadn't gotten a good look but the animal had been too stocky to possibly have been a deer.

"Dogs have ears, you know," he said, and slammed the door.

"That was *no* dog," said Neil to himself. But he didn't say what he thought it was. *Giant antlered rabbit wearing a wristwatch and carrying a cross* just wasn't one of those things you said out loud, even when you were by yourself.

CHAPTER 23

Pain in the Grass

BREEDEN, THE RED-SHIRTED TWIN, REACHED THE ball first, scooping it up without breaking stride and—after scaring two boys out of his way with an aggressive lunge—broke out into the open field.

Patrick shook his head and started to jog after the pursuing pack. His new glove-like shoes felt pretty good. It was a strange sensation having his toes impact the ground separately, but they seemed to give his steps some extra spring. He quickly caught up with a thick-calved, blond boy at the back of the chase pack.

"So, how's it work? Anything illegal?"

"Wha—?" asked the boy, slowing down and looking at Patrick with big-eyed apprehension.

"Yeah, you know, probably no punching or kicking, but it's kill the carrier, right, so basically anything goes? Nothing around the neck or going for the face or the nuts, and no hair-pulling, right?"

"R-right," said the boy. "But, umm, you know—" he replied as Patrick took off in a purposeful sprint to get to the front of the pack.

Breeden meantime had feinted left and sprinted right toward an opening along the boundary line. The scrum followed but the lead boys were stretching out now—not so much as part of a flanking strategy, but simply because the faster boys, including Patrick, were making better progress than the slower ones. But even the speediest wasn't quick enough and Breeden again broke free. Patrick groaned in frustration.

Safely in the clear, the red-shirted boy held the ball aloft, high-stepping like a touchdown-scoring NFL player.

Cheers went up from the sideline. Patrick was reminded of the popularity of the lacrosse-team jerks—the Lax Bros as they were commonly known—at his own school, and felt a degree of anger welling up inside him.

He had never much liked being the center of attention. The thought of lots of people thinking their own thoughts about what he was doing just kind of made him queasy. But in this particular moment—perhaps because it was a dream—what other people thought seemed suddenly a very silly thing. As long as *he* really knew what he was doing, what did the opinions of these dreamed-up kids even matter?

He lowered his head and sprinted for all he was worth—quickly breaking free from the chase-pack and earning himself a collective chorus of *Ooh*s and *Oh*s.

Breeden noticed his effort, too, but rather than picking up his pace, dodging to one side, or betraying any annoyance, the big red-shirted jock—huge smile on his big-eyed, square-jawed face—stopped and faced Patrick.

"Come on, Big Ears, let's see what you've got!" he yelled, and began to run right *at* Patrick.

As will happen when two people—much less two reasonably fast young men—run at each other, they closed quickly. Neither boy slowed, flinched, or veered until they were maybe just a yard apart, at which point Patrick dove shoulder-first and a surprised Breeden—with split-second reflexes—leapt into the air.

But the leap wasn't quick or high enough. Patrick somehow kept his eyes locked on the boy's knees and managed to intercept his airborne opponent, receiving in reward something very hard—he wasn't sure if it was shoe, shinbone, or kneecap—right in the nose. All he knew was it felt like a hammer blow. His vision went white and he felt his body flop backward with all the grace of a rag doll.

He seemed to hang in the air awhile—long enough to realize he was still airborne and to vaguely wish he weren't—and then, suddenly, without feeling any impact, he was lying on the ground with his eyes closed. The pain was pretty intense but somehow he wasn't any more preoccupied by it than he was by the grass tickling at the back of his neck.

He could hear people gasping, and this sound somehow energized him. He opened his eyes, rolled over, and got to his feet. An ashen-faced Kempton was staring at him from the sideline.

"Where's the ball?!" yelled Patrick.

Kempton, his little jaw hanging open, limply pointed down the field. The shiny black object was sitting unattended by the far boundary line. Patrick noticed the other players on the field were standing just like Kempton: their lipsticked mouths wide and their outsized eyes staring in disbelief. A few appeared to be taking videos with their binkies.

Patrick noticed Breeden still sprawled in the grass.

"You okay, chief?" he asked.

Breeden grunted.

"Glad to hear it," said Patrick, and, stooping down, added, "Jock-o." Then he started jogging toward the ball.

But he didn't get very far before the most appallingly loud siren he'd ever experienced—easily ten times more deafening than the starter's signal, the class closing bell, or even Bostrel's speech—dropped him to his knees.

He jammed his fingers in his ears but it was no use. His eyes watered, his teeth rattled, his T-shirt flagged under the force of the sonic blast. He felt like an ant trapped inside an air horn.

He tried to stand and run—he didn't know how much more he could take. Tears welled up behind his eyes as he wished with all his might to wake up from this stupid dream already.

And then—for no obvious reason—the siren stopped.

A silence like crashing surf followed, and then a new sound began: a sound like thunder.

Patrick had never been crazy for science fiction, though he knew plenty of people who were—Stephen Westrum and Jeff Hookey from advanced math class, for instance, would go on and on about aliens and space weapons and were forever trying to get him to role-play in little games they'd set up. Lately they'd started calling him Rory, a character in the *Doctor Who* TV show. Not that he was hoping to be very popular at school anyhow, but those two sure didn't help.

But watching the white sky-ambulance streak across the sky toward them now, Patrick almost second-guessed his science-fiction stance. Was it possible he'd been missing out? Setting aside the appalling noise of its engines—which wasn't so easy to do—this was possibly the single coolest thing he'd seen in his entire life or, at least, that he'd ever dreamed.

The craft was white except for the big red cross on its belly, and was roughly Frisbee-shaped—maybe thirty feet across—with a series of jet or turbofan nozzles embedded in the outer portions of its fuselage.

It stopped, came to a perfect hover, gently descended to the grass, and shut off its engines. A ramp then telescoped out the back end of the craft and two men and a woman in red-and-white jumpsuits disembarked.

The woman and the taller man hurried to Breeden's side while the shorter one began erecting an orange safety cordon.

Breeden began to push himself up—it was pretty clear to Patrick he was less than mortally wounded—but the two emergency medical technicians forced him back down and began to wave sensors along the length of his body.

The man with the safety cordon meantime had finished putting up signs that read "**mōbəʟ heʟð yunit at wurk / 50m maxəmum uprōc**," and was now strolling the perimeter, staring menacingly at the throngs of binky-holding students.

Kempton stole up next to Patrick.

"Why on Ith did you *do* that?" he asked.

"Do what?"

"Hit him!"

"He had the ball."

"He didn't have the ball!"

"He got rid of it?"

"At least a full quint before you hit him."

"Really?"

"You saw where it landed—he chucked it halfway across the field!"

"Oh. I thought it must have come out when I hit him."

"He got rid of it *on purpose*. And now, thanks to you, he may be *injured*."

"Aw, come on," said Patrick. He was starting to worry that maybe Ith people were more delicate than Earth people, although, he reassured himself, if that were the case, there was no way kill the carrier would be a premiere sport.

"Did he have some special condition or something?" asked Patrick.

"What do you mean?" said Kempton.

A year ahead of Patrick at Hedgerow Heights Middle School there was this kid Dirk Nixon who had hemophilia. Every time Dirk got a scratch or a bruise they'd rush him off to the hospital. And the whole situation was especially complicated because Dirk—who was keenly aware nobody was supposed to hit him back—was always chucking things (pencils, juice boxes, baseballs, tape dispensers, books, shoes, rocks) at people and starting fights.

"Well, what's the deal with the paramedics?" asked Patrick.

"What do you mean? There was a trauma. MHYs are always dispatched to assess and treat traumas."

"Trauma? He got *tackled*," said Patrick. "And how did they get here so fast? How could they have known so quickly?"

"POP."

"Who?"

"They saw what you did and dispatched a unit."

"But it's only kids out here," said Patrick.

"POP sees what happens at all times," Kempton said, pointing up at the sky.

"What are you talking about? What's POP?"

"The Public Operations Panel? Tell me you don't have POP on Earth!?" Kempton dropped his jaw in horror. "To spot problems and dispatch assistance?"

"They spotted me decking that kid?"

"Of course."

"But how?"

"Probably when everybody hit their Inform buttons, duh!"

Patrick looked at Kempton to see if he was kidding around. He didn't seem to be.

"Okay, so if I'd tackled him and nobody had reported it, they wouldn't have known?"

"Well, a video algorithm probably would have picked it

up." He pointed at a nearby security pole topped with a black plastic bubble.

"Security cameras," said Patrick.

"And the drones, too," Kempton said, nodding up at the sky.

"Drones?"

"You don't have drones on Earth?"

"We do, but, like, not over our schools and stuff."

"Why *wouldn't* you have them over your schools? Don't you care about the safety of children?"

"Well," said Patrick, looking up. "So there are drones up there right now?"

"Why would the drones *not* be there!? You don't have a PSN on Earth!?"

"What's—"

"The Public Safety Network? You don't have one?"

"They have drones flying all the time watching everything you guys do? So, you have, like, zero privacy when you're outside?"

"What's privacy got to do with it?"

"Well, I mean—you're being watched all the time."

"We're not watched; we're *monitored*—for emergency responses just like this. And POP's data feeds also supply MA, whose algorithms and analytics suggest appropriate long-term development initiatives and organizational course corrections."

"MA?"

"The Ministry of Awareness."

"Oh," said Patrick.

"Anyhow," the boy continued, turning his attention back to the paramedics. "I'm frankly a little surprised MA only sent an MHY and didn't send cops, too."

Patrick shook his head. "The police?"

"O-M-S!" squealed Kempton, smacking his palm against his forehead. "What are you—from the dark ages? KOPs are Community Officers of the Peace. You know, to arrest you."

"Arrest me!? For what?!"

"For physical assault."

"What?"

"You *attacked* Breeden."

"Attacked? I *tackled* him."

"Which is a form of attack. Hello?"

"Look, I told you, I didn't know he'd gotten rid of the ball. And what's the big deal, anyhow? It's kill the carrier!"

"It's *not done*."

Patrick looked over at the sideline. The entire school seemed to be there. He spotted Oma standing a row back, smiling as if at an inside joke. He locked eyes with her long enough to feel a blush coming on.

The medics helped Breeden to his feet and the boy gave a celebrity-style half turn, giving his well-wishers a limp-wristed wave. The crowd, with a few exceptions—notably an amused-looking Oma—burst into cheers and applause as the medical technicians backed away.

"But, don't worry," said Kempton. "You're an emissary—you probably won't even get in any trouble for this."

"Puber!"

Kempton jumped with surprise.

A small man had come up behind him. He was thin-waisted, big-chested, had a fresh crew cut, and generally looked like a comic book superhero except that he was wearing gym shorts, a tank top, was a little on the short side, and—like everybody Patrick had met today—his face was covered with makeup.

"Hello, Kempton," said the man.

"Hello, Gymnasiarch Frayne," said Kempton.

"Erm," said the man to Patrick, and then, "Umm."

"I'm Patrick," said Patrick, offering his hand and then—as the man's eyes went wide—remembering to stick out his elbow instead. The man looked greatly relieved and quickly knocked elbows—rather harder than Patrick would have preferred—with him.

"There's been a change of plans," said the man as he turned back to Kempton. "Your appointment with Provost Bostrel has been moved to *two twenty-five*."

"But—but—" said Kempton, whipping out his binky and

confirming the update with a sigh, "well, maybe we'll *still* have time to grab smoothies and oat—"

"No time. Get cleaned up," said the man. He made an unconvincing effort at a smile and stalked back to the school building.

"But that's not—" said Kempton, but his words were drowned out as the ambulance roared into the sky, forcing Patrick to stick his fingers back into his ears.

"—and anyhow I don't see why we have to go in *now*," concluded Kempton as the aircraft disappeared over the trees. "I mean there are still three full deuces to kill before our meeting with the provost. But getting you cleaned up will only take a few terts."

"What does he mean by 'cleaned up'?" asked Patrick.

"Look at yourself!"

Patrick looked down at the grass and dirt stains on his jeans and T-shirt.

"Oh," he said. "But I didn't bring other clothes."

"Why would you need other clothes?"

"But . . . what am I supposed to wear while we wash these ones?"

"What?"

"Am I supposed to sit around in my underpants while they get washed?"

"You don't wash your underpants on Earth?"

CHAPTER 24
Four-Child Garage

THOUGH HIRED GARDENERS AND MAINTENANCE MEN did the bulk of the groundskeeping, the Tondorf-Schnittman garage held a decent collection of power tools—a WeedWacker, a hedge trimmer, a cordless power drill, a leaf blower, and a reciprocating saw. And, though these implements perhaps held even less fascination for the children than they did for their father, Mrs. Tondorf-Schnittman was not one to take chances with her daughters' safety: she kept the door between the garage and the playroom locked at *all* times.

A lock best prevents passage when the latch is shut,

however, and on this particular Saturday, Mr. Tondorf-Schnittman, in his haste to get to tennis, had not quite secured the door behind him.

And so it happened that as the four twins became first bored and then frustrated with their tower-building project, Cassie Griffin noticed a shadow around the door's edge, went over to investigate, and casually pushed it open.

"Garage?" she asked Phoebe.

Phoebe nodded emphatically at this delicious observation.

Paul Griffin reached up high along the wall inside the dim doorway, feeling for the light switch but instead finding the button for the automatic garage door opener.

A grinding mechanical sound filled the room and a widening slit of light appeared on the floor, gradually revealing the glinting silhouettes of Mrs. Tondorf-Schnittman's Toyota Sequoia and Mr. Tondorf-Schnittman's beloved but never-driven-in-the-rain Maserati.

Like civilians staring into the glowing interior of a just-landed alien spacecraft, the four-year-olds gawked past the cars into the expanding brightness beyond.

Mrs. Tondorf-Schnittman, hands-free Bluetooth in one ear and the blender just then grinding up her morning's second kale-mango-supplement-powder breakfast smoothie, didn't hear the *thunk* as the door reached its apex and the motor disengaged. And she certainly didn't hear the four silent, wide-mouthed children descend the three steps to the concrete floor and then pad softly past the barely used power tools and out to the rain-dampened driveway.

CHAPTER 25
Sannytation

KEMPTON STEPPED INSIDE THE CLEAR CYLINDER he'd called a *sanny*. It basically resembled an airport security body-imager.

"How does it work?" Patrick asked.

"Wide-spectrum sonic agitation and hyperpolarizing antistatic fields, mostly. Some antibacterial ultraviolet, too."

The sanny's door slid shut as Kempton looked at his binky. Then he closed his eyes and the machine began to *whir* and *thunk*. His sweater vest billowed, his hair whipped about like he was standing in the teeth of a storm, a bright blue light bathed him from head to toe. A humming noise began, then stopped, there were a couple moments of silence, and then a dysphonic buzzer sounded.

Patrick had to admit he did look pretty clean after the process—not that he'd had any visible dirt on him to begin with.

"Your turn," said Kempton.

"What do I do?"

"When you're inside, just select Activate on your binky and follow the instructions. All you have to do is stand still and close your eyes. It won't start if you leave your eyes open. Safety feature."

Patrick stepped inside the capsule. He looked at his binky and saw a big green **aktəvʌt** cube in the center of the screen. The icon swelled and grew brighter, and then winked out of existence. The door slid shut. His binky's screen was now occupied by a countdown clock and the two instructions Kempton had mentioned: **klōz iz** and **bɛ stil**.

He obeyed both requests and a moment later the process began. His hair and clothes tousled and flagged, and his skin felt warm, kind of like he was taking a shower only he was completely dry. But then the center of his chest started to get a little too warm and he wondered if he should open his eyes or say stop or something because it was getting pretty uncomfortable—really starting to burn, actually—but before he could make up his mind, there was a ripping noise, a whiff of smoke, and a wheezy buzzer sounded.

The They Might Be Giants logo on his T-shirt—squid and all—was simply gone.

The decal had been fairly wide and both his nipples and his navel were now visible through the smoldering, black-ringed hole where it had been.

"What happened to your shirt!?" Kempton exclaimed as Patrick stepped outside.

"I have no idea."

"Well, we can't take you to the provost like that." He rubbed his chin as he thought aloud: "Where. To. Get. You. Another. Shirt . . . *Bing Steenslay!*"

"What?"

"Bing Steenslay got niched!"

"What got what?"

"Well, most of us have emptied our lockers for break, but Bing was niched last week and they won't have gone through his stuff yet."

"He was neeshed?"

"On-boarded," said Kempton as he led Patrick down a row of lockers. "He was granted his career niche last week."

"Oh," said Patrick. "So he, like, graduated early?"

"Yeah," said Kempton, stopping and opening a locker. "He's a publicity cadet, working for MuK."

"Who's Muck?"

"MuK's not a who; it's a *what*—M-uh-K, the Ministry of Communication."

"Oh," said Patrick as he tried to make sense of the hideous black-and-yellow garment Kempton had just passed him.

"As you might expect of a future publicist, Bing was *pretty* cleanly," Kempton said, nevertheless wiping his hands with a fresh dollop of sanitizer.

"Great," said Patrick, holding the garment out in front of him. It appeared to be a long-sleeved exercise shirt and he doubted it was going to fit. The label read, **x-L-sm**, which he took to mean *extra-long small*. At least it didn't smell bad. And he supposed he really couldn't go around all day with his chest bare. He took off his ruined T-shirt.

"What's up with this pattern, anyhow?" he asked. It looked like a bee costume.

"Awesome, right? Bing was *very* stylish."

Patrick looked down and saw the hideous, black-and-yellow fabric gathered across his chest in folds like the neck of a turtle with its head pulled in.

"I'm guessing he was pretty skinny."

"They didn't call him String Beansley for nothing," said Kempton, touching up his makeup in a locker-door mirror. "Kid was a total beanpole."

Kempton slammed shut the locker. "These mirrors are

ridonkulously small. Let's go stop at the grooming station and touch up. That'll kill a few terts anyhow."

"What?" said Patrick.

"Our cosmetics," said Kempton, pointing at his face in exasperation. "We're a mess after the game. You, in particular."

Patrick looked at himself in his binky mirror. The eyeliner Kempton had put on him had smudged in the corners so that he kind of looked like an Egyptian pharaoh. An Egyptian pharoah wearing an ill-fitting bee costume.

"You know," said Patrick, running a finger along his eyelid, "I think I'm just going to take this stuff off."

"Oh, no," said Kempton. "You *can't*."

"What? Why not?" said Patrick.

"You'd look, you know, impaired."

"Impaired?"

"Like a belty. Mentally challenged."

"In my opinion," said Patrick, "I look like I have issues right now. I mean, if anybody from my school saw me like this . . ."

"Well," said Kempton. "Maybe you need to spend more time thinking about what people in *this* school think."

"Look," said Patrick, a little fed up. "Some adult would have come and *told* me what to do if it were that important."

"You're the first Earth emissary since Rex," said Kempton. "Nobody will come and *tell* you to do anything.

163

Tenet Twelve says 'Disobey the Minder's emissaries in nothing.'"

"Who is this Minder, anyhow? Is he, like, your God?"

"A god? What are you, being funny?"

"Well, I don't know who he is and you guys talk about him like he's some big deal."

"Some big deal? The Minder is the Creator and Sustainer of Worlds!"

Patrick decided that sounded like God to him. "Anyhow," he said, "so—if I'm this Minder's *emissary*—and if you can't boss emissaries around—then why did your parents make me wear makeup?"

"They only *suggested* you wear makeup," said Kempton. "For your own comfort."

"They didn't quite make me, did they?" said Patrick, a smile stealing onto his face. "Where's a sink?"

"Wait," implored Kempton. "Really—"

"Tell the emissary where to find a sink, Citizen Puber," said Patrick, kind of enjoying his newfound power.

Kempton put a hand over his eyes and pointed off to his left with the other.

"Thank you," said Patrick. He walked past the boy and soon found himself in a large, bright, soapy-smelling locker room. Opposite a wall of toilet stalls, a row of sinks and sanitizer pumps was set in a large counter scattered with abandoned lip gloss, eyeshadow, and mascara containers.

Above it was an enormous mirror upon which, written in red lipstick, was a block-lettered message:

THE SEER LIVZ WELL
CUZ SHEEZ KWIK TO BE LED
DA HEARER DINT LISSEN
SO DA HEARER IZ DED

"Well, maybe that explains why I don't know anything about a Hearer," said Patrick. "Sounds like he got whacked."

"Oh-my-goodness-oh-my-goodness-oh-my-goodness," said Kempton.

"Should we get somebody?" asked Patrick.

Kempton, pale and shaking, glanced at his binky and nearly dropped it in surprise.

"Seer gone blind!" he exclaimed, thrusting the device at Patrick. The screen was bright blue except for a single white-lettered statement: **nō signəl**.

"The INTERVERSE is down," Kempton said in a terrified whisper.

"You guys don't lose service often, huh?" asked Patrick.

Kempton began to stutter a reply but was interrupted by a reedy, singsongy voice: "Aw, poor little baby lost the teat!"

There was movement in the mirror and the two boys wheeled around. A shadowy figure emerged from the toilet stall directly behind them. It was a slight girl in a skin-tight ninja outfit—though of mottled gray, rather than the usual black.

"Hi, I'm Squirrel," she said.

"Squirrel, like—" asked Patrick.

"It does sound like the name of the arboreal rodent but I think on Earth you'd probably spell it S-K-W-U-R-L."

"Oh," said Patrick.

"Whatcha holding there?" she asked.

Patrick looked down at Neil's ruined They Might Be Giants shirt.

"My shirt kinda didn't do so well in the, umm, cleaning machine," he said.

"Ah," said the girl.

Kempton, meantime, appeared to have forgotten how to breathe.

The hood of the girl's one-piece outfit was pulled back, exposing a shaved brown-haired scalp and a lean, big-eyed face streaked with black-and-gray face paint.

Patrick judged she was smaller than his sister Carly and, yet, somehow—from the way she moved, or her proportions, or the confidence in her voice—she seemed older, maybe even Eva's age.

"You're a girl!" shrieked Kempton.

"Ya think?" said the girl named Skwurl.

"This is a *boys'* locker room!"

She cocked her head and gave Kempton an expression somewhere between pity and annoyance.

"And what kind of makeup is that on your face!?"

Patrick put a hand on Kempton's shoulder to calm him down.

"Not that it's any of your business, but the makeup I'm wearing is far superior to the kind you employ." She gestured at the smudges on her face. "It's the difference between *purpose* and *programming*."

"That might as well be dirt!" shouted Kempton, shaking Patrick's hand off his shoulder.

"You should really try thinking your own thoughts one of these days. It's no fun growing up to be a puppet, Kempton Puber."

Kempton dropped his jaw. "How did you know my *name*?"

"Oh, I don't know. Is it possible you spend so much time on electronic devices that there's a database someplace that contains your name, your birthdate, your favorite color, your entire DNA map, the names of your best friends—or, sorry, it says *you don't have any best friends*—so sad."

Kempton waggled his jaw as if trying to say something, but no sound came out.

"Kempton, you are so obviously one of those people whose minds run along in the narrow little courses set by the hypocritical bullies in charge of this place. The ones who find profit in the fear and stupidity they harvest from people, like you, who are only too comfortable Not. To. Think. For. Themselves."

"You're one of the, one of the—" Kempton spluttered.

"Better-looking people you've ever met?"

"What?! No—"

"Least-deluded people you know?"

"Anarchists!" gasped Kempton at last.

"Ah," said the girl. "That's what the Muckers are still having you call us, isn't it? Such clever practitioners of the reputational sciences. Portray us like we're trying to destroy rather than save."

Patrick was confused. This girl seemed pretty weird for sure, but somehow he highly doubted she was in league with a bunch of flying monsters and some organization that had killed 99 percent of the people on the planet.

Kempton bolted for a red button mounted on a pedestal between two of the sinks and began to pound it with his fist.

"You'll find the panic buttons have been shut down along with all other ancillary informational systems in this subprefecture. You're welcome to keep banging at it all you want; just do me a favor and please try to work toward a rhythm of some kind? You're giving me a headache."

Kempton punched the button for a few more seconds and then—not having elicited anything other than a faint clicking noise—slumped in place, dropping his narrow shoulders like somebody had let half the air out of him.

"Well, what do *you* call yourselves?" asked Patrick, genuinely curious.

The girl named Skwurl turned to Patrick and, with a sparkle in her eye, said, "I know it sounds weird, but we like to refer to ourselves as Commonplacers. We're kind of an underground group whose chief mission right now is to *wake people up* to the warping influence of the Seer and the Deacons, to help people see that this *isn't* the real world around them and that they're being kept in a glass cage. I'm sorry to be abrupt. I realize much of what I'm saying may seem rude and hypocritical—especially without you yet knowing the wider context here—but we don't have much time. It is a supreme thrill to meet you, Patrick of Earth," she said, dropping a mock curtsy. "But the Powers That Be will soon reactivate their panic buttons and precious security cameras and I really can't afford to have the Peepers get my image."

Mostly he followed what she was saying. Could all that Kempton and Bostrel and Mr. Puber and others have been saying be a bunch of propaganda? And was this why Oma had seemed a little cynical about things? "What are Peepers?" he asked.

"Employees of what they call POP," said the girl. "Peepers, Oglers, and Perverts."

"POP is the Public Operations Panel!" screamed Kempton.

"Public operations? More like proletariat *oversight* panel. And it also comprises undersight, around-the-corner-sight, through-the-wall-sight, secret-camera-in-your-restroom-sight—"

"There are no secret cameras in lavatories!" yelled Kempton. "Every POP camera on Ith is plainly visible and identifiable via the Camera Locator App!"

"Oh yeah?" asked Skwurl, pointing at the message on the mirror.

"What!?" demanded Kempton.

"One-way mirror," said Skwurl. "With a *camera* behind it."

"That's a lie!" yelled Kempton. "They don't put cameras in a locker room. That would be an Invasion of Privacy."

"Yeah, privacy's a *huge* concern of the Peepers'," sneered the girl.

"There are no—" Kempton started to say but then a wild look came across his face and he ran—arms outstretched—straight at Skwurl.

"Kempton!" shouted Patrick.

Skwurl sidestepped the charging boy, leaving him to crash with a *Whang!* into the stainless steel stall partition.

"Take it easy, Kempton," said Patrick as the red-faced boy regained his balance.

"I'm undertaking a citizen's arrest," roared Kempton. "Help me apprehend her, Patrick Griffin!"

The girl gave Patrick an amused eye roll and offered him her upturned wrists. It was a gesture, Patrick suspected, a real terrorist would never have risked.

"In the name of the Seer—" said Kempton, rushing the girl once more.

"Kempton!" shouted Patrick, now more than a little embarrassed by his host.

Skwurl ducked and swung out her left leg, knocking the charging boy's feet from under him. Then she pounced upon his fallen body and hog-tied his wrists and ankles with some black tape.

"Help me, help me!" screamed Kempton.

"Don't be a baby," said the girl, brandishing the roll of tape. "And stop interrupting or I'll seal your mouth shut and give you a wedgie!"

Kempton gave her a slow nod, genuine fear glinting in his oversized eyes.

"Well, I'm glad for at least *that* much consideration," said the girl. "Even if it's only yielded under duress.

"And now," she continued, "I suppose we have just a moment to get to the bottom of our previous disagreement about cameras."

Reaching over her shoulder, she produced a ten-inch baton. With a quick wrist-snap, she extended it into a vicious fifteen-foot-long metal whip that she flicked against the mirror. The glass shattered into a thousand pieces to reveal a cramped cavity containing a turret-mounted, fat-lensed camera.

"It's a plant!" shouted Kempton. "You must have put it there! This is a private area—there's no way the Deacons would have allowed a camera in here!"

"You think not?" said the girl. "And what did we just say about interrupting?"

Kempton clamped his mouth shut.

"Listen," she said to Patrick. "I've got to go, but I'm supposed to give you a message, and that message is this: 'The Minder is slipping, and the worlds are falling into a Tyranny of the Senses.'"

"Worlds?" asked Patrick. He'd been following her up to now but that last bit hadn't made much sense—had almost sounded religious or something.

"Yes, the three worlds," said the girl.

"You mean, like Earth, Ith, and . . ."

"And Mindth," said Skwurl.

"Mindth," said Patrick. "So, let me guess—people have big ears like me on Earth, they have big eyes like you on Ith, and they have big giant brains on Mindth."

Skwurl laughed.

"No, Mindth is a place unlike the two Sense Worlds. Eyes are for Ith, Ears are for Earth, and Dreams are for

Mindth. The people there—Mindthlings—come in all shapes and sizes. You'll meet some of them soon."

"Here on Ith," said Patrick.

"Yes," said Skwurl. "The Deacons call them abominations. Like in the video games. Or in the hunts you hear about on news programs. But they're not monsters. They're beings like us, only not *human* ones, obviously."

"You mean, so—"

"No time," she said, putting her hand to her lips. "Somebody will explain more to you later."

She cleared her throat and continued her prepared statement. " 'You, Patrick of Earth,' " she continued, " 'are here to help restore balance. It is too late to have prevented Ith's great decimation, but there's still a chance for Earth. It's not too late for sanity.' "

"I don't understand—you want me to do something?" said Patrick.

"Don't listen to her!" shrieked Kempton, finding his voice. "She's full of lies! She wants anarchy! Chaos! Evil!" He kicked his bound legs at the broken glass. "Do you need more proof—look what she's just done· to official property!"

"Will you *please* shut *up*? *Please?*" said Skwurl.

"Never! You disgust me and I want you arrested immediately! HE-EEELP!!! HE—"

The girl tore off a rectangle of tape and placed it over

173

Kempton's mouth. He writhed and rolled his eyes like a terrified animal.

"For now, it is merely hoped that you will keep your mind open, Patrick Griffin, and not fall in with the hypocritical manners of this world."

"You mean, like, wearing makeup?" asked Patrick.

"Sure." The girl smiled. "Or also, for instance, why everybody seems to be dismissive about the fact that you have no memory of your world's Hearer."

"That's what I told them—I don't know anything about a Hearer," said Patrick.

"And they don't quite listen, do they? Perhaps they implied that you have memory issues resulting from your transubstantiation?"

"Yeah, that's what they said," said Patrick.

"Interesting, don't you think? I mean you're the one who's from Earth—our first visitor since Rex himself—and yet they're so quick to discount what you have to say."

Patrick had indeed thought some along the same lines already.

The girl lifted her camouflage sleeve and glanced at an old-fashioned wristwatch. "Now, sorry, just one more thing—"

She broke off, sucking breath through her teeth.

Kempton had somehow spun himself around on the floor and kicked her in the shin.

"Actually, maybe I can make time for *two* things." She removed a black marker from her pocket, bent over Kempton, locked his head between her knees, and wrote **I brōk tenet 10** across his forehead.

"*That's* what you get for kicking somebody smaller than you," she said as she got up. "Now—before I go—" She gave another deft flick to her metal whip, dislodging the camera's glass lens with a *pok!*

"Check it out," she said.

"Is that what I think it is?" Patrick asked, cautiously stepping forward. But she didn't reply—she was gone.

"Mmmmf," said Kempton.

Patrick pulled the tape off the boy's mouth and helped undo the bonds on his hands and feet. Without a word, he helped Kempton to his feet and the two of them approached the busted-open camera. A large, vein-streaked, slime-covered orb dangled from a foot-long glistening pink cord. To Patrick's mind, the thing was either a prop worthy of a grade-A horror movie, or an actual *eyeball*.

CHAPTER 26
Roadside Assistance

CARLY GRIFFIN, PATRICK'S TEN-YEAR-OLD SISTER, looked out the BMW SUV's tinted window at the flashing lights and spotted her unharmed father and brother even as Mrs. Fettridge asked, "Is that your *father*'s truck, Carly?!"

Carly—busy wishing she was someplace very far away—didn't answer at first. In addition to being the most popular, Polly Fettridge was the prettiest and possibly the wealthiest girl in the fifth grade, and had a mean streak that made even Carly's older sister Eva seem like an amateur.

Mrs. Fettridge drove Polly and Carly home from their travel soccer clinic every Saturday. Carly had long since learned that the safest course was to only speak when spoken to and, even then, to do so only with the very shortest statements possible.

"What?" said Carly, intentionally looking out the wrong window. "Where?"

Polly peered at Carly, her nearly lipless mouth perched at the brink of a laugh.

"Oh, *dear*," said Mrs. Fettridge. "Let's stop and see if we can help."

"Uh, I—" began Carly, but cut herself off. There was nothing she could say that would make this any better. And a lot of things she could say that would make it worse.

"Your *dad* had an accident?!" said Polly. "And, look, your *brother*'s there, too."

"I hope everybody's okay," said Mrs. Fettridge. "My goodness, will you *look* at that car they're towing!"

The Prius that had rear-ended her father's pickup truck was entirely missing its windshield, and both its hood and grille were pushed back- and downward as if a giant had rolled his foot upon it.

"Your dad's, umm, truck doesn't look too bad, though," said Mrs. Fettridge, touching her hair with one hand and glancing in her visor mirror as she pulled to the curb and put the BMW in park. Mrs. Fettridge, like her daughter, was quite pretty, and amply pleased with the condition. "Well, and aren't we *all* lucky it's stopped raining?" she said, scooping up her iPhone and checking her side mirror as she exited the SUV.

Carly trailed out of the vehicle after Polly.

Neil was over by the curb berating himself for having done the honest thing and—on finding it under the passenger seat—given his dad's phone back to him. If he'd only thought things through and pretended to keep looking for it, he could right now be looking up information about the squid and also whatever that weird new insult was that his father had used. *Entack?*

"Rick! Is everybody all right?"

"Oh, hi, Andrea," said Mr. Griffin, spotting Mrs. Fettridge as he finished up a conversation with the police officer. "Yes, Neil and I are both fine. And the other driver, too. They took him to the emergency room to be safe—just cuts and bruises, though."

"Oh that's so *wonderful*," said Mrs. Fettridge. "Ambulance is *never* good, though. People are *so* litigious these days."

"Well, *he* rear-ended *me*," said Mr. Griffin. He'd thoroughly reassured himself on this score. "So, there won't be any judgments going his way. Anyhow, he seemed like a nice man. Just a bit of a tailgater, obviously."

"Well, what happened?" said Mrs. Fettridge.

"Somebody's dog got out of their yard and ran out in the road," said Mr. Griffin. "I hit the brakes, and then . . ."

"That's terrible," said Mrs. Fettridge, her hand fluttering to her chest. "And you didn't hit the dog?"

"No, it ran off."

"What kind was it?" asked Mrs. Fettridge.

"The dog?" asked Mr. Griffin.

"A big one," said Neil.

"Yeah, it must have been a Saint Bernard or something," said Mr. Griffin.

"Though it was gray," said Neil. "Which means it wasn't a Saint Bernard. That's for sure." He stifled an impulse to also note that Saint Bernards don't have antlers and carry crosses.

"Maybe it was a great Dane," suggested Mrs. Fettridge.

"Heya, Superstar!" said Mr. Griffin to the slowly approaching Carly. "How was soccer?"

"Fine," said Carly, trying to guess just how many minutes into school tomorrow Polly would be calling her "Superstar!" in front of all her friends.

"Well," continued her father, "the Fettridges have gotten you this far. You want to ride home with me the rest of the way?"

Carly gave her dad a shrug and gazed off at the horizon, still wishing she was someplace far beyond it.

"She was embarrassed about your truck even when it *had* a back bumper, Dad," said Neil.

"What?" he said, in mock shock, placing his hand over his heart.

"*I* like your truck, Rick," said Mrs. Fettridge. "It's very *you*."

"Uh, thanks, Andrea," said Mr. Griffin, looking over at her gleaming oversized luxury SUV and deciding it was best not to return a similarly veiled statement.

"Well," said Mrs. Fettridge. "Are you sure it's okay to drive—I mean, I guess it looks all right, all things considered—"

"Yeah, it's just going to need a new bumper and to have its airbags reset."

"What a *day* you Griffins are having," said Mrs. Fettridge.

"What?" said Mr. Griffin.

"I read on Facebook that Patrick's gone missing. Have you found him yet?"

"What?" said Carly. "Patrick?" She felt a sinking feeling suddenly. She'd been thinking about Patrick in the car just a little while ago, remembering his birthday was on Thursday. She and Mom were going to make him a pineapple upside-down cake, his favorite.

"You read that on *Facebook*?" asked Mr. Griffin.

"Yes, Laura Tondorf-Schnittman is watching the twins,

and Jenna Michaels said that Lucie's home and that your mother was picking up Eva from swim practice so—"

"Wow," said Mr. Griffin. "The Internet now knows more about my family than I do."

Mrs. Fettridge decided she'd detected a note of judgment and grimaced. "Well," she said, "let us know if there's anything we can do to help. I know it must be a scary time."

"I'm not too worried," said Mr. Griffin. "Patrick's a twelve-year-old boy and twelve-year-old boys sometimes go off and do things on their own. Or, at least, they used to."

Mrs. Fettridge raised a neatly plucked eyebrow and didn't say anything back.

"You know, it's this old-fashioned thing called independence that used to happen before everybody got personal tracking devices and began posting their status updates to major media companies every ten minutes."

"Ah, of course," said Mrs. Fettridge, grabbing her daughter's hand and turning to Carly. "You looked great at soccer today, Carly. You should come over and play with Polly sometime. We have a great big yard and she *never* goes out and practices on her own."

Polly gave Carly a withering look as her mother steered her back to their car.

Carly looked to her father. "Is Patrick all right, Dad?"

"I'm sure he's fine," he replied as he watched the

high-heeled Mrs. Fettridge slide back into her luxury auto-mobile. "He just went off someplace without telling anybody is all."

"Oh," said Carly, not entirely reassured.

Mr. Griffin ignored his cell phone as it buzzed. Whatever it was, it could surely wait till he got home in two minutes.

How could he have guessed it was his wife calling to say their children Paul and Cassie—the Twins—had also gone missing?

CHAPTER 27

What Meets the Eye

AFTER ALLOWING KEMPTON AND PATRICK TO
scrub the ink off the former's forehead, Gymnasiarch Frayne and two black-mustached men in dark blue
uniforms led them from the locker room, down two hall-
ways, and up an escalator to the plush reception area outside Provost Bostrel's private office.

Patrick had never seen such a fancy setup in his whole
life, much less in a school. From the silk-cushioned bench
with its lion's claw feet and fluted armrests to the large
and expensive-looking landscape paintings and portraits
on the walls to the crystal chandelier, it was the sort of

waiting room he would have expected to see maybe for the president of a very old bank.

To Patrick's eye, the only less-than-classy aspect of the room was the scrolling text upon the digitally enabled wallpaper. Textured messages circled, wobbled, and swayed around the room: **if ü sᴇ <u>sumð</u>ing, in<u>form</u>! <u>an</u>arkᴇ = <u>ɛ</u>vᴅʟ! <u>vij</u>ᴅʟᴅns ᴅ<u>buv</u> oʟ!**

"What the heck is *that*?" asked Patrick, for the first time noticing the gleaming, gold-leafed Egyptian-style pyramid set in the obsidian-walled tub in the middle of the floor.

"An award fountain," said Kempton. "Want to see it run?"

"Uh, sure," said Patrick.

"Fountain on!" Kempton commanded. There was a humming noise as the capstone lifted into the air on a jet of water. Jade-green eyes—one on each of its four sides—opened and seemed to track the two boys as the piece slowly rotated.

"What the heck is it for?" said Patrick, fascinated.

"It's our YSS award for best test scores in the prefecture."

"YSS?"

"Unified Society of Science," said Kempton. "Don't tell me you don't have YSS on Earth?"

"Well," said Patrick testily, "at least we don't have spy-cams in our locker rooms."

"We don't have spy-cams in *our* locker rooms," sputtered Kempton, "or in *any* private areas! In fact, we aren't even allowed to use our binkies in such places!"

"Well, la-di-da," muttered Patrick; it was one of Eva's favorite retorts.

Kempton gave him a hateful look and crossed his arms.

Patrick closed his eyes, leaned his head against the wall, and concentrated on the throbbing in his bruised nose. A door creaked and he opened an eye to see Kempton leaping to his feet for another impassioned salute.

"Please come on in and sit," said Provost Bostrel with all the exuberance of a telephone menu. Patrick followed Kempton into an office appointed in mahogany, velvet, and brass, illuminated by a single massive floor-to-ceiling window that looked out upon a vast field of amber grain in which, maybe a hundred yards distant, a green flag—the spider-and-stop-sign logo he'd seen on people's uniforms—fluttered atop a slender white pole.

From what Patrick had seen so far of the school and its surroundings—the trees, hills, winding streets, bleachers, and ball fields—this flat, sunny sea of wheat seemed out of place. He had an impulse to ask about it but stopped himself. It was his dream, after all, and, if things didn't make sense, there was nobody to blame but himself.

Following Kempton's lead, he sat in one of the wing-back chairs across from the provost's stately, richly grained desk.

"Care to try my nuts?" asked the man, pushing an **inRi**-logoed snack bowl across the desk.

"Oooh!" said Kempton. "They're at the *height* of ripeness!"

Patrick's stomach did a little flip-flop. He'd never much cared for nuts but there was something especially creepy about these ones. They were big as Brazils but paler, and fleshy-looking. He shook his head.

"Are they from the new hydroponic facility in Farmington?" asked Kempton.

"Umm, yes," replied the big-nosed man, preoccupied with his binky.

Kempton grabbed a handful and—before stuffing them into his mouth—explained, "Farmington has one of the most advanced agricultural laboratories in the world—this new strain of water chestnuts is one of the very latest cultivars. Our gen techs are amazing!"

"Jentex?" asked Patrick.

"The *gen*etic *tech*nicians in the Bureau of Comestibles," said Kempton.

"Oh," said Patrick. "I thought you told me one of your rules was you aren't supposed to do genetic stuff?"

"Ha!" snorted Kempton. "At least here on Ith, water chestnuts come from *plants*, which are *not* creatures. So, no, we have absolutely no prohibitions about genetically altering plants. Nor, for that matter, are there any issues with harvesting or *eating* them."

"Just no meat or fish?" asked Patrick.

186

"Nor other vertebrates, invertebrates, protists, or motile bacteria."

"What about mushrooms?"

"Mushrooms—fungi—are not considered creatures, either. Do you consider them so on Earth?"

Patrick shook his head. "So, like, you're all basically vegetarians."

Provost Bostrel looked up from his binky and raised an eyebrow.

"I mean, you don't eat any meat," explained Patrick.

Bostrel returned his eyebrow and turned his attention back to his screen.

"Most of us," said Kempton, "consume—in various forms—all manner of unfertilized eggs, dairy products, fungi, vegetables, fruits, saps, cotyledons, and endosperm."

"Okay," said Patrick, and then, though he instantly regretted having done so, asked, "And what's endo—umm—sperm?"

"Um, the nutritive part of a *seed*," said Kempton.

"And what was the thing you said before that?" asked Patrick.

"Cotyledons are the 'seed-leaves' of a nut or seed. Sometimes, as in walnuts, they are even the dominant caloric feature."

"And you don't eat meat because it's against the law to harm animals?"

"Yes—what, are you *obsessed* with Tenet Ten? Also, eating meat is highly inefficient. To say nothing of the cruelty involved, the energy and resource requirements to develop a kilogram of meat are tens or even hundreds of times what is required to generate a kilogram of equally nutritive plant-based product."

"Oh," said Patrick. He wondered what kind of reaction he might get for admitting he'd eaten beef, lamb, ham, chicken, turkey, and—once, memorably on account of how his face had swelled up like a balloon and he'd been taken to the emergency room—a fried clam (that vacation day on Cape Cod having been the day his shellfish allergy had been discovered).

On the whole, he was just glad this was a dream because he'd surely miss his two favorite foods—bacon and cheeseburgers—very, very much if he had to live forever in a world in which they were forbidden.

Another thought struck him: "What about the eyeball in the camera?"

"What do you mean?" asked Kempton.

"I mean that was a real eyeball—don't you kind of have to hurt something in order to take its eye and stick it in a camera?"

Kempton started to laugh but the provost once again looked up from his binky.

"Vitrogenics," said the provost.

"Sorry?"

"Laboratory-based tissue generation. What do you call it on Earth?"

"You grow eyeballs in labs?" asked Patrick, his stomach flip-flopping some more.

"Well, we can't break the Twelve Tenets," said the provost. "So of course we have to generate our own utility organs. Are you saying you don't have vitrogenic technology on Earth?"

Patrick was pretty sure he would have heard of people growing eyeballs in labs if that was a thing, and shook his head.

The provost's binky beeped for his attention and Kempton was already looking at his, so Patrick looked down at his own. He decided to look up the Twelve Tenets that people kept talking about.

Now that it was displaying in regular English, it was much easier to use.

The Twelve Tenets of Rex Abraham

   1. Promote order.

   2. Combat entropy.

   3. Shun the sickness of uncertainty.

   4. Resist the contagion of complacency.

   5. Conserve resources.

6. Respect directives.

7. Achieve measurable productivity in all tasks.

8. Seek all actionable knowledge.

9. Provide all actionable knowledge to your admins.

10. Do not harm the flesh of any living creature.

11. Do not alter the flesh of any living creature.

12. Disobey the Minder's emissaries in nothing.

"Patrick," said the Provost abruptly, "I don't suppose you've had any recollection about your Hearer yet?"

Patrick shook his head.

"No," said the man, squinting his eyes and looking back down at his screen.

"So, was that a *human* eye?" asked Patrick.

"What, in the camera?" asked Kempton, raising his binky in front of his face. "It's a modified *squid* eye. Probably *Onykia ingens*. Here, I'll do a rezref." He read aloud from his binky, " 'Deep-water squid possess some of the most supreme light-gathering organs in the animal kingdom and, with appropriate modifications to the lens and the introduction of avian cone cells for red-spectrum and high-definition viewing, they make ideal—' "

"Thank you, Kempton," sighed Provost Bostrel.

" 'The most impressive model currently in production,' " continued Kempton, " 'is the civic broadcast camera SBK43. It employs an *Architeuthis* vitroplant.' "

Patrick didn't know many scientific names but he at least recognized the single one his brother knew—*Architeuthis*, the giant squid. Patrick had been forced to watch more *Search for the Giant Squid* documentaries on TV than he could count. He didn't quite get the fascination—and it had always seemed pretty odd to him how there could be so many nature specials about an animal that had only once or twice been seen alive (and then by a robotic camera)—but he had to admit he preferred watching them to ESPN, which otherwise was Neil's top choice.

"You don't recall this technology from Earth, either?" asked the provost. "What about organ or limb replacement?"

"Limb replacement? You mean, if you lose an arm here, you can get a new one?"

"Yes," said the provost. "Provided it was purely accidental and that the replacement is generated from your own Minder-decreed genetic map—and is in no way augmented or altered—a *replacement* is not an *alteration* of the flesh."

"So the new arm couldn't be stronger or longer than the one you lost?" asked Patrick.

"Precisely right."

"That's amazing," said Patrick. "So people aren't in wheelchairs or anything?"

"Wheelchairs?"

"You don't have people who can't walk on Ith?"

"Can't walk?" asked Bostrel, as if he hadn't heard correctly.

"People they can't fix after an accident or that maybe were born without legs or something . . ."

"What's a wheelchair?" asked Kempton. "A chair with casters that you can roll around?"

"Never mind," said Patrick. "What about blind people? And deaf people?"

"Accidental blindness or deafness," explained the provost, "can be redressed. *Any* deficiency that comes about due to external influence can most always be reversed."

"So you're saying that only if you are born with it—"

"Yes, and then only if it came about from *non-external* factors."

"That's amazing," said Patrick, thinking of all the people on Earth whose lives could be helped if this weren't all a dream and they could come here.

"Well," said Provost Bostrel, looking up from a message he'd received on his binky. "It has been suggested we show you Rex's wikimentary."

"What's a wikimentary?"

"*This* is a wikimentary," said Bostrel, standing and moving to one side so that he wouldn't block the window, which Patrick now realized was rather part of the highest-resolution, most realistic-looking 3D display he'd ever seen in his whole life.

"Begin Rex Abraham: Edit twelve point seventeen," said the Provost.

The flag and field disappeared, as did the entire office wall—and much of the ceiling and floor. Speakers pumped the room full of studio silence and the remains of the room descended into inky darkness.

CHAPTER 28
Sunshower

THE GRIFFIN AND TONDORF-SCHNITTMAN TWINS stood at the mouth of the garage, staring into the damp gray woods past the driveway. A tiny slate-colored junco hopped among the leaves.

"Bird!" yelled Paul Griffin.

He took off in a purposeful if somewhat unsteady sprint. His three comrades laughingly followed. The sun was breaking through from the east and—had they not been so transfixed by Paul's chase—they might have noticed a rainbow arcing across the sky behind them.

The Griffin parents joked that their oldest son, Neil, was part Labrador for the way he chewed up his lacrosse mouth-guards. Lately, they had also begun to joke that their youngest son, Paul, was part bird dog. The boy had chased birds since he'd been old enough to run. It was cute on most levels—and it certainly seemed to have helped him become a very fast little boy. But especially when a seagull was loitering across a parking lot, a crow was perched on the other side of a stream, a sparrow was hopping down the middle of the bike path, or a pigeon was strutting along the curb of a busy street, it could create stressful situations for his parents.

He'd never quite caught one—much less thought through what he'd do if he did—but his dedication to the sport never wavered.

He chased the junco up and over the small wooded rise and then quickly forgot all about it because he was now able to see down to the golf course pond. A seven-foot-tall timber crucifix covered in vines had been stuck in the middle of its perfectly round island. In front of the cross, a large animal he had never seen in any museum, zoo, TV show, website, app, or picture book was bent over a cell phone.

"Guinea pig?" asked Cassie Griffin as the sun escaped a passing cloud and added ultravivid flecks of green to the prevalent early spring grays.

"Gi-ant ham-ster!" yelled Chloe Tondorf-Schnittman.

Across the shallow water, the creature looked up at the children and shook its antlered head with no small degree of mortification.

CHAPTER 29

The History of Ith, V. 12.17

WIKIMENTARIES, PATRICK CAME TO DISCOVER, were basically like Wikipedia entries, only they were videos. Very fancy videos.

The latest release on Rex Abraham—"Emissary from Earth and Savior of Ith, v. 12.17"—was a sweeping recreation of the historical record including dramatized scenes with skilled actors and the latest cutting-edge graphics, camerawork, and 3D effects.

Set to a majestic orchestral score that Patrick recognized as the basic tune of "Row, Row, Row Your Boat," the movie began with scenes of modern Ith life—sky-cars, satellites, public markets, pristine mountains, burbling brooks, sprawling sport stadiums, glass buildings that truly seemed to scrape the sky, gossamer communication satellites, massive robotic container ships, and taper-nosed trains that traveled too fast for the eye to resolve.

The scenes were incredibly realistic, and fully three-dimensional. A sky-car big as a baseball diamond seemed to take off through the ceiling; a speeding courier drone caused Patrick to duck as it swooped through the room and back out again on its way to deposit a package in the hands of a smiling businessman.

The immersive montage went on for a few minutes and then another spider-carrying-a-stop-sign logo filled the screen. Animated beams of light radiated from its hexagonal head:

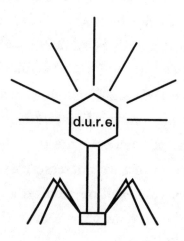

As the design shimmered, a narrator—a man with all the vocal charms of a middle school basketball coach—began:

THE TWO PRIMARY SENSES ARE THE MINDER'S GREATEST GIFTS TO HUMANITY. BUT AN ORDERLY BALANCE BETWEEN THE TWO MUST BE STRUCK! IF THE INTERRELATION BETWEEN SIGHT AND SOUND IS NOT PROPERLY MODERATED, CHAOS QUICKLY TAKES ROOT!

What followed was unlike anything Patrick had seen before. It basically told him the story of Rex Abraham, emissary from Earth and savior of the human race.

When Rex arrived, Ith was still in the Stone Age. He, on the other hand, had arrived in black ankle-high boots, jeans, black turtleneck, and was carrying a knapsack filled with high-tech gadgets, including a binky. Patrick immediately wondered about this—how could a man have arrived fifty years ago from Earth and yet be just as, if not more, modern than Earth was now?

Rex wasted no time introducing the wonders of technology to the primitive world and quickly unified Ith's people under the banner of progress and science. He introduced to them everything from the periodic table of elements to the quadratic formula to Newton's laws,

Avogadro's theorem, Planck's constant, Mendel's squares, Griffiths' inequality, and even Einstein's theory of relativity.

And so machines were invented, chemistry was advanced, diseases were cured, agriculture was revolutionized, communications were systematized, self-correcting bureaucracies established, knowledge compiled, language homogenized, and a new era of progress and harmony began.

And then it was explained that the whole reason Ith was lagging behind Earth in the first place was because the world had long been infested with *Anarchists*. These were some very bad, bad men—in the film, they wore long beards, brown robes, and pointy hats. For millennia they had been living in secret, emerging from their subterranean chambers only to stir up trouble, cause wars, engineer plagues, and set loose genetically engineered monsters, all with the single goal of causing chaos and generally keeping the human race from achieving its potential.

Now, Rex knew all about the Anarchists and it was his goal to advance technology far and fast enough that he could free Ith of their influence.

Battle scenes followed, in which they watched Rex driving a sky-car chasing a bat-winged serpent, Rex leading a troop of heavily armed soldiers as they gunned down a bigfoot-like creature, Rex standing on the bridge of a battleship as it shelled a tentacled sea monster almost as big as the ship itself, Rex flanked by a dozen broad-chested commandos breaking into an underground conference room filled with pointy-hatted men and making them all get on their knees . . .

But just as it looked like Rex and the people of Ith might triumph, might finally and completely rid the world of the Anarchist menace, the bad guys struck back. They unleashed the most deadly virus ever known—something called Solipsis Variant 4.

The plague had what was called a *two-pronged vector*: it traveled both through the air and via some very creepy little skin mites—tiny spidery things that actively stalked people and could lie dormant for weeks. This meant that even people wearing respirators were not immune.

Once inside the body the virus attacked nerve cells, and was lethal to people whose brains were past a certain stage of development. There were a lot of fancy terms including *myelination*, but the basic deal was that it killed everybody over the age of three. Everybody. Patrick kept closing his eyes to the enormous piles of dead people.

And yet there was a glimmer of hope. In the final days— as the plague raced around the globe (a single carrier of the disease could infect an entire community within a matter of hours)—Rex gathered the world's best young scientists to develop a vaccine. But before they could begin an assembly line to mass-produce the stuff, before they could even make enough to save themselves, a horrible monster—a revolting, filthy creature that was some sort of cross between a vulture and an overgrown pit bull (and not at all unlike the creature that Kempton had killed in his video game)—came onto the scene. It flew high over the laboratory where Rex and the scientists were working and dropped a single, very powerful bomb.

Rex crawled from the smoldering ruin. Bleeding and burned, he held a single glass ampule. The narrator explained:

WOUNDED BUT ALIVE, REX SURVIVED THE TERRIBLE BLAST. HE EMERGED FROM THE CONFLAGRATION WITH JUST ONE DOSE OF VACCINE AND, NOW, NO WAY TO MANUFACTURE ANY MORE. BUT HE WAS NOT THE ONLY SURVIVOR.

A soot-stained girl—maybe ten or eleven years of age—also clambered out of the debris. She was apparently the child of one of the scientists and, understandably, was crying her head off.

Rex went to her and gave her a hug. And then, for the first time in the film, he spoke.

"You must help all the little children you can find," he

instructed the girl, handing her his phone and then taking her face in his hands. "Although it will be tempting and their cries will break your heart, do not spend time with infants. They are too fragile, and hard to care for. But any child who can walk and talk—you must be their shepherd. They are still too young to be harmed by the coming disease. But they must be protected from wildlife, from cold, and they must be fed. This binky of mine will tell you all you need to know about finding food, shelter, and medicine. You may ask it *any* question and it will answer. Do you understand?"

The girl, clearly terrified, nodded bravely.

"Good girl. In this device is all the wisdom of the Minder, and all the achievements humankind has garnered from across the three worlds. You must be brave. You must be strong. And you must work to keep hope alive and well. Now, go live in the Minder's wisdom and adhere to the Twelve Tenets. And, most important of all, *fear no evil.*"

The little girl was crying her eyes out again and—though he'd seen better acting before—Patrick felt pretty bad for her.

"Take comfort. For even beyond this binky, the Minder will speak to you in dreams, and he will look after you. You are now his special one, you are the protector and savior of Ith. You are this world's *Seer.*"

And with that he grabbed her arm, rolled up her sleeve, and injected the world's only dose of vaccine into her arm.

AND SO REX SACRIFICED HIMSELF THAT A CHILD MIGHT LIVE, AND GROW TO LEAD US INTO THE BRIGHTNESS OF THE MODERN WORLD!

The next scene had Rex collapsing to the ground while the vaccinated girl looked on in terror. A terror which was not unlike Kempton's as the movie stopped, a siren began to wail, and a brilliant red strobe began to pulse.

"CRIMSON ALERT, CRIMSON ALERT!"

CHAPTER 30

Field Operations

ALTHOUGH HE'D BEEN BORN ONE OF THEM, Novitiate Frank Kyle didn't harbor a grain of sentimentality for the people of Earth. All one had to do was look at what they'd done to themselves for the past several millennia (plagues, wars, famines, economic collapse, and . . . repeat) and the only rational assessment was the very one that Rex himself had made: the world was in need of a forceful reset.

It was almost time. Now that the novitiates had delivered 4G informational technology into the hands of the leading corporations, now that Earth's billions of mistakes could be recorded, rebroadcast, reexamined, and ultimately corrected . . .

Now that, finally, the leading governments' security organizations were investing heavily in mass communications and data technologies so that the infrastructure would be almost entirely in place for the 2.0 to come . . .

Now he and his fellow novitiates had just to stifle this last-ditch ploy by the rebels and it would be clear sailing: Next week, the Purge. The week after that, the survivors could be rounded up, and education could proceed—and thanks to all this advance groundwork, the reboot would proceed much faster than it had on Ith.

He pulled his silver Mercedes into one of the puddle-pocked guest spots behind the Hedgerow Heights Country Club. Turning off the engine, he swiped his BNK-E from its cradle, exited the vehicle, and—after first smoothing back his newscaster hair—removed his golf bag from the hands-free, self-opening trunk.

All novitiates had received bags just like it. They were props to help them blend in with their influential clientele, although a close examination of this particular bag's contents would have set him very far apart from the average golfer. For while the bag did hold a pretty standard assortment of expensive clubs, it also contained a sniper rifle with a full magazine of depleted uranium bullets, each capable of punching through a decimeter of hardened steel.

He heard a tinkling noise as he rested his bag on the pavement and looked to see a big-bellied, skinny-legged man tottering down the footpath, jangling the keys inside the pocket of his salmon-colored pants.

"Course closed with all this rain, you know," said the stranger.

Frank Kyle gave the red-nosed man a hard look and flexed his right hand, his knuckles crackling with a noise like hail on a metal roof.

The man coughed nervously. "But I'm sure they'll open it soon—maybe you can get in a few rounds!"

"Yes, I will get in a few rounds," said Novitiate Frank Kyle as his dark eyes watched the man's car speed away across the parking lot.

He slung the golf bag over his shoulder, slammed closed the trunk, glanced at the sensor app on his BNK-E, and headed toward the seventh green to put a fatal hole in one unwanted visitor.

CHAPTER 31

The Color Crimson

RIGHT THIS WAY, IF YOU PLEASE!" SAID THE weaselly little man in the road-cone-orange uniform.

The provost stopped screaming and cleared his throat self-consciously. Kempton, a degree more rattled, kept on screaming.

The orange man cleared his throat, too, and was starting to seem impatient until his eyes settled on Patrick, at which point he looked rather astonished.

"What's the sitrep, Safety Warden Schoen?!" asked the provost.

"Um," said the little man, wrenching his eyes from Patrick's ears, "sir, POP has declared a Code Crimson."

"Yes, I heard that," said the provost, reasserting a measure of his proper administrative stature. "What is the *causal* situation!?"

At this point Kempton broke off screaming to listen.

"Oh, uh, Anarchist incident. They've somehow blue-screened the prefectural grid and undertaken multiple propaganda attacks. I am supposed to—"

"So we're to return to our domiciles—"

"The superattendant is *on premises*, sir, and wants a debrief."

The provost visibly flinched at this news. "Of course," he said.

"So, again, if you'd please follow me."

"All of us?!" asked Kempton.

"Yes, all of you," confirmed the safety warden, gesturing to the doorway and stomping his foot like a soldier at attention.

"This is *unprecedented*," said Kempton, running his fingers along the part in his hair as he and Patrick got up from their seats. "A Code Crimson *and* we're going to see the superattendant—all in the same *day*!"

"Code Crimson?" asked Patrick.

"Everybody but admins and authorized personnel

confined to domiciles," said Kempton. "It's the highest level of emergency there is!"

They made their way down the main hallway, out the school's front doors, and onto a driveway loop crowded with vehicles covered with logos and retina-staining strobes. Though the aircraft were similar in size and shape to the sky-ambulance that had come to the field earlier, these were mostly gray and bristling with knobs and struts.

Brown-booted, olive-uniformed soldiers were standing around the aircraft. A crew in white jumpsuits was working power-brushes and sprayers along one side of the school. Somebody had spray-painted a message on the smooth concrete wall—

TRUST NOBODY WITH 2 FIRST NAMES

"Is that graffiti in *Earth* writing?" asked Kempton. "What's it say?"

Patrick read it aloud.

"Interesting they wrote it in Earthish," said Kempton. "It must have been for your specific benefit."

"You are to report to the command tent," said Safety Warden Schoen, stopping suddenly and gesturing.

The provost squared his shoulders and led the boys in the direction the safety warden had indicated. As they crossed the turnaround, the gathered soldiers began oohing, ahing, and taking videos of Patrick on their binkies.

Patrick didn't much enjoy the experience but Kempton was lapping it up. He kept bumping into Patrick as he tried not to drift outside the frame of anybody's video.

"Go right on in," said the provost, stopping at the side of the tent. A formerly invisible slit in the white fabric peeled open, and Kempton, with a smiling turn to the cameras, ushered Patrick into the dim, buzzing interior of the tent. The place was pulsing and flickered with the light of dozens of electronic displays and holographs. But, more than all the gadgetry, what drew Patrick's eye was an imposing, broad-shouldered, short-haired woman dressed in khaki like a general and standing over a holographic map of what looked to be the northeastern part of the United States.

Her voice—a degree lower than Bostrel's baritone—was imposing as her appearance. "Ah, there you are!"

Provost Bostrel gave a quick bow. "Superattendant Stifel—*what* an honor!"

Patrick looked over to Kempton to see if he was going to bow, too, but he was just standing there, jaw hanging open.

"Good to see you again, Provost Bostrel," said the woman, her large flint-colored eyes turning to Patrick. "And you must be *Patrick Griffin*."

He felt as if he were being x-rayed. "Nice to meet you," he said.

"Yes," said the woman. Patrick guessed she must be his mother's age but she was a whole lot harder looking: her chin was square as a cleaver and the skin of her face rigid as uncured leather.

She smiled now, revealing an expanse of surprisingly big gums and small teeth. Patrick decided there was a whole lot more pink than white in there at any rate.

"Now, can you please tell us about that unpleasant young Anarchist who accosted you in the locker room?"

A brown-uniformed man stepped forward with a two-handed apparatus consisting of a long-shafted, fabric-covered microphone together with camera barrel inside which, Patrick surmised, there might possibly be a not-quite-giant-squid eyeball. The device was plugged into the technician's belt-holstered binky via slender silver cords.

"Your Eminence," blurted Kempton, "she was a female aged approximately fourteen to sixteen yies, weight close to thirty-five kilos, shaved brown hair, gray costume, and she was *armed* with a telescoping metal whip!"

"And, Patrick Griffin, *your* impressions of the perpetrator?" said the deep-voiced superattendant as Bostrel put a corrective hand on Kempton's shoulder and whispered something in his ear.

"Umm," said Patrick, "you mean, like—"

"What pops into your head when you think of her? Did she seem nice? Pretty? Smart? Short? Physically fit? Articulate? Talented?"

"Well, she was good with her whip thingy."

The woman cocked her square head at him.

"I mean her aim was pretty good."

"She was adept at interpersonal combat?"

"Sure, well, she was kind of dressed like a ninja and she definitely took down Kempton pretty fast, so, yeah, I guess."

Kempton shifted uncomfortably but didn't say anything. The woman meantime pursed her narrow lips and looked at her binky. "Thank you. And, please, to the best of your ability to recall, tell us what she said to you."

"Well, I guess she was talking about how cameras were everywhere and that's when she busted the mirror," he replied, trying to make room for the encroaching brown-shirted cameraman and his microphone boom. "I think she was sort of making a point," he continued, "that there are too many cameras here on Ith."

"Well," said the woman. "Of course, you know there *are* cameras in lots of places. But does it strike *you* that there are actually *too* many, Patrick Griffin?"

"What do you mean?" asked Patrick.

"That there are more cameras here than you would like to see? Surely you have them on Earth?"

"Yeah," said Patrick. "Like at school and in malls and stuff, you know . . ."

"Yes," said the superattendant. "And presumably there, as here, they are installed for the public good—a means to help people make the very best decisions, and to keep public services functioning at maximum efficiency?"

Patrick gave a confused look and she went on. "For instance, if there's a signaling issue at such-and-such an intersection, it allows the Department of Thoroughfares and Byways to reroute traffic to ameliorate the situation. But the notion that the government hides cameras in bathrooms—*or* in private homes, *or* in designated privacy zones—is completely ludicrous. You may in fact be gratified to see," she said, waving at the table map and causing it to transform into an array of hovering locker-room architectural plans, camera schematics, evidence labels, and text reports, "a *wealth* of evidence has surfaced proving that the camera you saw was indeed a malicious plant."

"Oh," said Patrick. She was obviously trying to convince him it was the way things were but it still just didn't make sense to him. What would happen, he wondered, if he pushed back on her the way he had pushed back on Kempton in the locker room about not wearing makeup?

"Well," he said, resolving again that it was his dream, after all. "It still seems like it must have been a lot of trouble to put a camera behind the mirror like that."

"What do you mean?" she said.

"I mean," explained Patrick, voicing what seemed pretty obvious to him, "they had to figure out there was a hollow space in there and then they had to replace a whole mirror with a big giant sheet of one-way glass without anybody noticing and whatnot."

"Ah," she said, smiling like an indulgent parent, "you will come to find their perniciously clever efforts can result in feats of ingenuity far greater than *that*."

The cameraman bobbed his head in rueful support.

"But why a camera in a bathroom? I mean, if they wanted to cause trouble, wouldn't there be easier and better ways?"

"Easier, perhaps, but *better*?"

"Yeah, you know, like more destructive. Like, you know, a bomb or something."

"Physical destruction is one thing, but the sort of destruction they seek is more potent. They seek to create *doubt*."

"Doubt?"

"Yes, and bombs don't create doubt. *Questions* create doubt. Consider: Did seeing that planted camera not lead you to *ask questions*? Did you yourself not just *ask* why they'd put a camera in the bathroom?"

Patrick thought this through.

"Fortunately, science and common sense will triumph

as they always have, and they will fail to infect your mind, Patrick Griffin."

"*My* mind?"

"Your mind—your *opinions*—Patrick Griffin, are of tremendous interest to us all. You being a person of such significance, these selfish, short-sighted criminals will continue to do everything they can to poison you against us."

"But why am *I* so important?"

"Because the *eyes* of the world are upon you. Because you are the first emissary the Minder has sent us since Rex fifty yies ago."

"Okay," said Patrick, thinking of the way the kids at school and the soldiers just now had reacted to him. Still, what she was saying sounded more like a smart thing to say than it did an actual explanation.

"But," he continued, "how about this: to plant a camera there, they must have known I was going to be in that bathroom, right? But even *I* didn't know I was going to be there until I had to change my clothes, and I didn't know I'd have to use a sink till—"

"It's not immediately obvious but the explanation is quite simple: they operate in *sleeper cells*. In a case like this they merely need to keep their local agents on alert and give them the authority to self-activate. Clearly, this young woman—or a nearby co-conspirator—was watching and realized you would be at that particular place, a place where she and her fellow deviants had prepared a 'trap,' if you will. We have deactivated such installations all over the world. It fits to a tee their standard modus operandi."

"Their what-erandy?" asked Patrick.

"Their MO, their method of operation. That said, rest assured—now that we've gauged their keen interest in your arrival—POP and the YSS subministries are scanning *all* locations you might possibly visit in the coming days, and necessary protocols are being put in place to ensure minimum disruption. Take comfort that we have long had these Anarchists on the run, and it's only a matter of time before we entirely extirpate their movement."

"Minder be praised!" exclaimed Bostrel, and Kempton looked up brightly.

"Well, now, let's give you some tests and get you on your way."

"Tests?" asked Patrick.

"Tests, yes—a physical examination so we can benchmark your physical condition and ensure you enjoy the greatest possible wellness.

"And, after the exam is complete," she continued, "you and your host family are to visit with the Seer in Silicon City."

"Are you *kidding* me!?" screamed Kempton, clapping his hands to his cheeks like a game show contestant.

"What a *wonderful* honor," said Bostrel, shaking his head in admiration as he exchanged an elbow-bump with Kempton.

The brown-uniformed cameraman put a protective cap on his camera lens and faded back into the shadows. Meantime a fabric panel on the other side of the tent zippered open to reveal a person wearing a white jumpsuit and reflective faceplate.

"Ah," said the superattendant. "Here's the Physiological Assessment Technician now. It's been rewarding to speak with you, Patrick Griffin. And I trust I have helped free you from those spurious questions with which our enemies have tried to impede your mind, and judgment."

CHAPTER 32

Ixnay on the Odentrays

MR. BUNBUN WOULD HAVE BEEN LYING TO SAY HIS feelings weren't a little hurt at being called a hamster. But how to explain to a bunch of four-year-olds that he was perhaps part rabbit and part deer—and zero parts *rodent*?

And, really, what would be the point?

He pushed a whiskered smile across his furry snout and loudly said, "Oh, hello!"

The children's jaws fell open.

"Oh, dear, am I using the correct language? *¡Hola! Bonjour!*"

The children—all four—laughed with delight.

"You can tawk!" said Cassie Griffin.

"Yes, oh good, it *is* English, isn't it? Why, yes, I *can* talk! And I *quite* enjoy doing so."

"What is that?" demanded Paul Griffin, pointing.

"Oh," said Mr. BunBun. "This crucifix? Ah, well, I am performing a funeral."

"Somebody died!" squeaked Phoebe Tondorf-Schnittman.

"A squirrel," said Mr. BunBun.

The children nodded somberly as if this made all the sense in the world.

"Would you like to come watch?" he asked. The children nodded again—not exactly somberly this time—and trooped across the plastic-planked footbridge.

"What's your name?" asked Chloe Tondorf-Schnittman. She had the very agreeable sensation she had somehow stepped inside the world of a children's TV program.

"Well, I have different names in different places. Some call me Sentient Jackalope, some call me John Pertolope, and mostly, these days anyhow, people call me Mr. Bun-Bun."

"Where's your home?" asked Paul.

"Well, I come from very far away—a place called Mindth."

"Is that in Russia?" asked Cassie.

"Not entirely," said Mr. BunBun.

"What happened to the squirrel?" asked Paul, pointing at the little gray body in the hole.

"A domesticated *cat* happened to it," said Mr. BunBun.

"Aw," said Chloe Tondorf-Schnittman, bending down.

"Would you like to help bury him?" asked Mr. BunBun.

"Yes, please," said Paul.

"Here, we can do it like this, don't you think?" said Mr. BunBun, tossing a pawful of excavated earth into the hole.

Paul reached down and did the same and the three girls followed suit. BunBun then turned and quickly shoveled the remaining soil into the hole with his rabbit-like hind feet.

"And now," he said, turning back to the enraptured children, "how about a prayer?" And here he sang a little Commonplace song that reminded the Griffin children (the Tondorf-Schnittmans didn't attend church) of a certain Easter hymn:

We all fear an ending
For an ending is change
And we like what we know
And we abhor the strange
Though we say we like fresh
Versus what has grown stale
Let's sometimes hold breath

And not always inhale
Be-cause—
Expiring can be inspiring
And there is no ascending
Without a real ending!

"Again?" said Cassie.

"You like it?" beamed Mr. BunBun. "It's one of my fa-vorites." He repeated the song three more times, pausing after each line till the children were mostly able to sing along.

"What are you?" asked Paul afterward.

"Ah, well—scientifically speaking—I'm a cervidic lago-morph. What you might call a rabbit-deer chimera. In com-mon parlance, as I think I mentioned, I'm a jackalope."

"Rabbits have big ears," said Paul.

"I didn't say I *was* a rabbit; I'm just sort of related to them. Much in the way a mule is related to a horse. Or a liger to a lion. Or a griffin to an eagle—"

"Our last name is Griffin," said Cassie.

"*Is* it?" remarked BunBun. Before the children had ar-rived his binky had shared with him some local police news report about a missing boy with the same last name.

"And do you have a brother named Patrick?"

Paul and Cassie nodded.

"He's a good boy?" asked BunBun.

"Patrick likes dinosaurs," said Paul.

"What a small world," said BunBun, thinking through the odds of running into the siblings of the boy he'd just caused to be transubstantiated to Eyeth.

"My hands are dirty," observed Chloe Tondorf-Schnittman, displaying her muddy palms.

"Hmm," said Mr. BunBun, turning out his own paws. "Mine, too. Shall we wash them in the pond?"

Cassie Griffin began to laugh.

"There's no soap!!" exclaimed Paul.

"There's soap in the bathroom," suggested Phoebe.

"Let's go to the bathroom!" laughed Cassie.

Paul nearly collapsed to the wet turf in a fit of high-pitched laughter.

"Bathroom?" asked Mr. BunBun.

"Yes," said Phoebe bossily. "Let's go, Deer Rabbit."

"It would be a pleasure," said Mr. BunBun, clearing his throat. "But I'd really best be on my way—"

"And we can have a snack!" announced Cassie.

"Do you like carrots, Deer Rabbit?" asked Paul. "There's carrots."

"Yes, I very much enjoy carrots, young man, but I've got a long way to go today. Speaking of which—do you know of a place called New York City?"

"There are dinosaurs there!" said Cassie. The American Museum of Natural History was the Griffin twins' favorite place in their so-far discovered world.

"And mammoths!" said Paul.

"Dinosaurs and *mammoths*?" said Mr. BunBun.

"And a giant sloth," said Cassie.

"And a giant squid," said Paul.

"And a blue whale," said Cassie.

"Ah," said Mr. BunBun, furrowing his brow ever so slightly. "And there are people, too, right? In the city? A lot of people?"

The children gave him a blank look.

"It's crowded?"

Cassie nodded emphatically. "The lines get *very* long."

"My dad got mad one time," said Paul.

"Oh, good," said Mr. BunBun. "Not about getting mad— I just mean it's good that there are a lot of people there. I need to see a lot of people."

"Why?" asked Cassie.

"Well, I've got to put on a, umm, show of sorts," said Mr. BunBun.

"You do magic tricks?" asked Chloe.

"Well, in a manner of speaking, yes."

"Will you be on TV?" asked Phoebe.

"TV? Television, is it? Well, yes, I do hope so."

"When?" asked Phoebe.

"In a few days, I expect."

The children seemed awfully impressed.

"Well, it's been a pleasure meeting all of you, but I really must get going."

"Aw," said Chloe, looking like she might cry.

"Thank you for helping me with the funeral," he said. "And are those *pens*?"

Chloe nodded emphatically and proffered three capless markers she had taken from the playroom.

"May I, really?" asked Mr. BunBun, touched.

Chloe handed them to him.

"Thank you very much—they may prove to be quite useful," he said as he delicately touched one of their felt tips. "I don't suppose they have some sort of covers?"

Chloe shook her head.

"Don't stain yourself," said Cassie.

Mr. BunBun nodded somberly, accepting the markers with good care.

"Bye bye, Deer Rabbit," said Paul.

"Goodbye, my friends," said Mr. BunBun, bowing nearly to the ground. Then he turned and hopped across the five yards to the mainland and onto the early spring golf course.

CHAPTER 33
Baseline Conditions

THE PHYSIOLOGICAL ASSESSOR LOOKED UP FROM the screen of her red-and-white-skinned binky.

"Well"—her voice tinny and distant through her mirrored faceplate—"you have good LDLs, excellent nerve conductivity, top-level immune indicators, blood pressure within normal limits, adequate dentition, no evidence of scoliosis, dermatitis, gingivitis, halitosis, psoriasis, or any viral or bacterial infection."

"That was it?" asked Patrick, impressed. "That was the test? You were able to tell all that just now?" He'd just emerged from a glass-walled cylinder that basically resembled the cleaning machine that had destroyed Neil's T-shirt. The procedure had taken less than thirty seconds and had been entirely painless.

"Yes, the holiscan is complete. You're cleared for normal travel and physical activity. The only significant suboptimal condition itemized"—the woman paused to lift her faceplate. She had a thin face and a long nose that hooked sideways at the tip—"is that you would appear to be at risk, due to an enzymatic conformational issue expressed in some of your lymphocytes, to an immunological hyperresponse to certain glycoproteins."

"What?"

"It's a fairly narrow range of molecular structure. I don't think it will pose an issue as such conformations naturally occur only in mollusks."

"Oh, yeah, I'm allergic to seafood."

"Seafood?"

"Well, fish are okay, but I'm not supposed to eat clams and things."

"No," said the medical technician, raising her cosmetically enhanced eyebrows. "Now, do you have any subjective complaints?"

"What kind of complaints?"

"The objective portion of your examination is complete. Now we check for any subjective issues that may have been missed by our instruments. Do you experience any pain or discomfort on a recurring basis? Headaches? Stomachaches? Tiredness? Soreness of throat? Excessive itching of the skin or mucous membranes? Stiffness of limbs? Frequent diarrhea? Difficulty with micturition?"

"What-er-ition?"

"Micturition."

"What's that?"

"Do you have any difficulty passing urine?"

"Um, no," said Patrick. At least not since he'd figured out how to work their waterless, high-tech toilets.

"Good," said the woman, scanning her binky. "Then the examination is complete."

"That was it?"

"Unless you have any questions."

"Actually," said Patrick, "you're like a doctor, right? Like you know about health and exercise and how much sleep to get and things?"

"That is my subject matter expertise, yes."

"Good," said Patrick. "Because I think I've been getting too much sleep and was wondering if there are any techniques for waking yourself up? You know, so you don't sleep too much?"

"You don't have alarm apps on Earth?" asked the woman.

"Well, I was thinking more like are there any ways to do it yourself—like, say you're in a dream and you decide to wake up from it, how would you do that?"

"Dreams are the Minder's province," the woman quipped. "You are not supposed to have any control over them."

She glanced at her binky again and said, "I've just summoned your escort."

"Thanks," said Patrick.

"Now you'll just need to swallow this," she said, handing him a silver pill.

"What is it?" asked Patrick, glancing at the little shiny capsule.

"It's your PB."

"My what?"

"You don't have personal beacons on Earth?"

Patrick shook his head.

"The beacon contains a transponder that inertly knits to the wall of your small intestine, monitors your vital signs, and, in the event of a medical emergency, allows you to be located by an MHY, especially in the event you lose your binky or are incapacitated."

"So is it, like, permanent?"

"The beacon? This latest model has a hundred-yie lifespan. Should you live longer than that, you will be issued a replacement."

"Everybody has one," said a voice behind him. He turned to see Oma had entered the curtain-partitioned exam chamber.

"That's precisely right," said the woman. "Now would

you like to wash it down with wheat grass, tomatillo, kale, celeriac, yucca, or grapefruit juice?"

"Uh, grapefruit, I guess," said Patrick.

"We have a sweet tooth, I see," said the woman, smiling woodenly. As she turned to retrieve the proper beverage from a small refrigerator behind her, Oma quickly grabbed the pill from Patrick's hand, passed it through the loop on the ankh pendant she was wearing, and handed it back.

"It's okay now," she whispered. "I'll explain later."

Patrick looked down at the pill in the palm of his hand as the woman rummaged in the fridge for his drink. "Where's Kempton?" he asked.

"My brother wanted his oat snacks and smoothie—and I guess he felt he'd weaseled his way into enough vidfeeds with you already today—so he agreed to let me take over for a bit. Why? Would you rather we switch back?"

Patrick started to blush. "I just meant—"

"Well, *he's* not happy with the situation; I can tell you that much. But that's what happens when you don't think things through. I mean, I suppose it was slightly unkind to suggest his Lasters treats *might* have been sent home for him, but I certainly didn't say for sure that they had."

"You mean he thought he was going to get his dessert from the school and it wasn't actually there?"

"What's worse, the Code Crimson means he's confined

to our house with my parents and without any Interverse access. He's probably having a nervous breakdown as we speak."

"Here's your juice, Patrick Griffin," said the assessor, handing him a plastic specimen cup filled with a dingy yellow liquid.

Oma winked and whispered, "Time to become one with the Deacons!"

Patrick didn't much like the idea of swallowing something that would stay in him for the rest of his life but it was just a dream, after all, and whether it was Oma or the assessor who was on the level, he guessed it wouldn't kill him either way. He put the pill on his tongue and swallowed.

The assessor looked up from her binky and nodded approvingly.

"It's transmitting just fine," she said. "Now, no solid food for one dunt."

Patrick nodded and decided against asking her to remind him how long a dunt was. Provided it was shorter than a week, it didn't really matter—he was far too queasy and tired to even think about food.

"And don't forget your garment," she said, indicating the ruined T-shirt.

"Oh, yeah," said Patrick. He picked up the singed piece of clothing and, in something of a daze, followed Oma out of the examination chamber.

CHAPTER 34

Loco Parentis

RICK GRIFFIN HAD BEEN PREPARED FOR HIS WIFE, Patrick's mother Mary, to be worked up, and even devastated about Patrick's situation. But, finding her sitting on the damp front steps, staring at the sky, he hadn't quite imagined her to be so quiet.

"Where are my children?" she whispered, more statement than question.

"He'll turn up."

"You didn't listen to my message, did you?"

"Oh," he said, folding his hands, "sorry, no, Neil and I had a bit of trouble getting home and, well—"

"You can always listen to it later," she said with a weird little laugh.

"I'm sorry, honey. What was the message?" His heart seemed to fall into a lower chamber as it occurred to him that something bad actually had happened to Patrick. Could he have *really* gone missing?

"Cassie and Paul are gone, too."

"What!?" said Rick, startling to his feet.

"I expect," she said, "that they're probably just fine. Laura Tondorf-Schnittman apparently left the back door unlocked and they wandered off."

"What?"

"With her kids, too. You may want to go over and help them look. She thinks they're probably just out on the golf course."

"What?" he said, not knowing what to do beyond sitting back down and giving her a hug.

"What's wrong with your truck?" she said, noticing its missing rear bumper.

"Somebody ran into us on Benedict. That's why I was late. Everybody's okay."

"Three missing children and a car accident in a single morning," she said.

"What a day," he said.

"Yes," she said, the flatness in her voice cracking. "I've been sitting here, Rick, trying to figure out what to do—should I go help with the Twins, should I stay here for Patrick, should I worry about the other kids—but, really, more than that I'm just wondering if it's even really happening."

She buried her head against Rick's chest and began to cry. "Maybe we just never woke up this morning," she choked out between sobs. "Maybe it's all just a nightmare. And, honestly, I don't know why, but *Patrick*'s the only one I'm worried about."

CHAPTER 35

Talking to Girls

UNLIKE MOST GIRLS PATRICK KNEW, OMA WAS NOT a big talker. And the strange thing was, he wouldn't have minded if she had been.

It wasn't just that she was pretty—she certainly was, at least in a weird, big-eyed way. The thing that got to him was that she seemed to have more expressions, and combinations of expressions, than anybody he'd ever met. He kept finding himself staring at her as if she were saying something really interesting—telling a great story, perhaps—only she wasn't saying anything unusual, or even necessarily speaking at all. But the movements of her dark eyebrows, the flickering tension on her cheeks, the different ways she could shape her mouth . . . he found himself constantly wondering and guessing what was going on inside her head, like she was a book he'd been reading but whose final pages were glued shut.

And so, as they walked back toward her house across the school grounds, he kept trying to think of things he could say to get her talking.

He'd already asked her if it was normal—since there was kind of a state of emergency going on—that they were being allowed to walk home by themselves. She'd explained that they only had a few blocks to walk and that the entire area was in lockdown. So, really, nothing bad could happen to them.

But she'd said it all very flatly, clearly not interested in the topic. He wondered if he should talk about something more personal. Maybe he could ask why she wore less makeup than most people. Or, maybe he could inquire how had her own game of kill the carrier been? But that just seemed stupid. He toyed with the idea of finding out whether she liked any music—she'd seemed interested in Neil's They Might Be Giants shirt—but that was the cheesy sort of thing teenage boys were always asking teenage girls.

"So what was the deal with the silver pill?" he finally

managed. That, at least, seemed a reasonable question. After all, he'd swallowed the thing.

"It's a PB, like the technician said," replied Oma, offering a bemused sideways glance.

"Right, okay."

"Why do you ask? Didn't you trust her? Or, is it *me* you don't trust?"

"Oh, I didn't mean it like that."

She laughed. "I'm just messing with you. You absolutely should be curious about the fact that a machine was put inside your body."

"A machine?"

"Yes, one that broadcasts your vital metrics to the government."

"I guess, when you put it that way . . ."

"And that mechanically adheres to the wall of your small intestine for the *rest of your natural life.*"

"Well, she was a medical expert—and you yourself said it was okay to swallow it, right?"

"But think about it. It really does make you want to ask a whole bunch of *questions*, doesn't it?"

Patrick recognized the same line the superattendant had used and gave her a quizzical look.

"Hey! What's that on your arm?" She grabbed his wrist and examined the burn.

"Oh, yeah, I bumped it against this hot pipe at home. The letters kind of transferred, only backward—"

"Does it hurt?"

"That's the weirdest thing—it doesn't really at all unless I pinch it or something. I keep forgetting it's even there."

"What's it say?"

"Now? I mean it reads backward from the pipe like I was saying, but I guess it spells 'Ya Way.' "

Oma let go of his arm. Her eyes, he noticed, were glistening.

"Do you want to know why I put the pill through my ankh before you swallowed it?"

He had noticed her doing this and thought it strange, but hadn't exactly been dwelling on it—in terms of weird things that deserved some thought, his mind had lately become a crowded place.

"Okay, why?" he asked.

"Well, *if* I tell you, you have to swear not to say anything to *any*body, and especially not to Kempton."

Patrick nodded. And promptly had his mind blown.

PART III: IMPRESARIOS

Keep smiling is what I say, it's better
to laugh than to do the other thing.

—Anthony Burgess, *The Wanting Seed*,
bcp §3¶356

CHAPTER 36

Situational Assessment

REX ABRAHAM WAS PROUD OF MANY OF THE THINGS he had achieved, but the implantation of a computer into his brain—knitting the neurons of his mind directly to a synaptic chip—had been one of the very smartest things he'd ever done. It had, after all, made him *even more* of a genius.

He waited a few moments as the feed petered out, then—via a few very simple mental commands—reactivated his ears and eyes. He was sitting in his expensive Otto Williams chair in the viewing room of his cliffside home, looking out at the purple-tinged Pacific Ocean. He allowed himself a moment to observe a propeller-driven plane putt-putting across the morning horizon before closing his eyes and turning his augmented mind inward to consider the download he'd just received about the boy who had just gone to Ith or—as more than a billion English-speaking morons here might spell it—Eyeth.

Identification had been achieved in a matter of high-bandwidth moments, from the first hysterical 911 call to the spate of emergency responder transmissions that followed, to the hundreds of cross-referenced social media posts, private messages, and voice communications from the family, friends, and relations: the child was Patrick Griffin of 96 Morningside Drive, Hedgerow Heights, New York.

He was in what his local regional educational system called the "seventh grade," where he was a slightly above-average student in a fairly competitive, affluent, well-educated community. He had mostly received threes (the second highest mark on their scale of four), although he had achieved some low fours in math and science classes. His worst subject appeared to be French—just a 2.4—for which Rex couldn't quite blame him. Even if the world's French-speaking percentage wasn't already plummeting, the Purge was coming and would soon render the study of *any* foreign language moot.

Soon all the French anybody would need to know would be *Renaissance*, which is what Earth's own Division of

Recorded Events would publicly call the Reboot, just as had been done on Ith.

The boy's parents were not especially significant—the father was a modestly successful sales representative for a book-publishing corporation, the mother a midlevel human resources consultant. His blood type was O-positive, he lacked any common genetic disorders, and he was in the 65th percentile for height, and the 55th for weight, at 41.1 kilograms.

A pretty unexceptional specimen in all regards. Still, the facts that his native language was that of his new hosts—and wasn't French or any of the other soon-to-be-obsolete languages of Earth—and that he had decades of natural life expectancy ahead of him were troubling. The same two conditions had been true of certain prophets, cult leaders, kings, saints, martyrs . . .

Still, the boy's journey to Ith was just the playing out of the necessary physics. He was nothing but a randomly determined counterweight to whatever creature those idiot Ith Anarchists had sent here. If 41.1 kilograms of sentience moves one way, then 41.1 kilograms of replacement sentience must go the other way.

And all Rex's organization had to do now was ensure that the entire 82.2 kilograms was terminated in case it in any way slowed his plans to bring Earth into compliance, to unify the three worlds in his vision.

CHAPTER 37

A Spy in the House of Puber

THE OAK-SHADED, SHRUBBERY-PENNED PLAYGROUND somehow reminded Patrick of the one on Sunset Drive near his family's house, although they were hardly interchangeable. For one thing, rather than swing sets, climbing castles, overhead bars, seesaws, and slides, this one featured foam-coated stairs, low-to-the-ground balance bars, and variously sized elliptical trainers, stationary bikes, rowing machines, treadmills, and gymnastics pads.

Patrick tucked his ruined shirt under his left arm and followed Oma over a series of foam-coated exercise bars.

"What is this place? An outdoor gym?"

"It's a KFP—a Community Fitness Park."

"Weird," said Patrick, dragging his foot and inadvertently kicking wood chips onto an exercise mat.

There was a scrabbling sound as a blue-collared squirrel darted out from some nearby bushes, stuffed its mouth with the chips, carried them back onto the border, and then vanished into the bushes on the far side of the playground. The entire performance kind of reminded Patrick of a ball boy at a professional tennis match.

"Is that squirrel like the park janitor or something?"

"We'll get to that soon," said Oma, climbing onto a stationary bicycle.

"So what's the deal?" asked Patrick, getting onto the one next to her. "People come out here and exercise?"

"Yep."

It suddenly occurred to him that nobody in this dream had seemed at all fat.

"So are we going to—"

"You're free to pedal if you like; I just figured this would be a good place for us to talk privately—nobody will be out here with the Code Crimson on," she said. "And I'm supposed to ask you a kind of important question."

"What is it?"

"Do you want to run away with me?"

"What?" said Patrick, blushing outright.

"I'm leaving tonight. The storm should give us some cover from the Peepers and their sky-eyes."

"You want me to *run away from home* with you?"

She looked down at her toe-shoes and nodded. Her big eyes seemed to be glistening.

"Wait, *who* wanted you to ask me this?"

"The Anarchists, as the Deacons call them—the Commonplacers, as we call ourselves," she said. "Look, it's either coincidence or the opposite of coincidence that you ended up arriving in my front yard. But either way, it's kind of not an opportunity to be missed. My-Chale—the leader of the entire movement, the *Book of Commonplace*'s editor-in-chief—himself has asked me to help you disappear."

"What?" asked Patrick, feeling a little dizzy. He had suspected Oma had some secrets, but being a member of the group that the entire government seemed dedicated to exterminating was not as far as his mind had been ready to go.

"Wait. You mean, like . . . you're really working with them, these Anarchists?"

"Yes."

"So, wait, you want me to *disappear*?"

"Yes, we need to get you away from the Deacons. And I'm to go with you."

"What about Kempton? What about your parents?"

"Look, I love them, and part of the reason I joined the Commonplacers is I want their lives to be better. I—we—want everybody's lives to be better."

"So you're, like, a *criminal*?"

"The worst kind of criminal there is, according to them," she said, gesturing up at the green spider flag flying above the playground.

"Oh," said Patrick. "But . . . are you sure about all this? I mean your family seems pretty normal and happy, don't they?"

"Have you *seen* how stressed my father is? How he's constantly struggling not to overeat? Or my mother's addiction to terrible video entertainments? Or Kempton's cultish belief in the Deacons' patriotism program? They're all classic symptoms of unfilled human potential."

Patrick considered what she said about her family. It was true Kempton didn't exactly seem to be the happiest, most well-adjusted kid. But he'd seen bigger head cases in Hedgerow Heights.

"But on Earth," he said to her, "I don't think there's a government conspiracy or anything, and there are still a lot of unhappy people."

"Does your government torture and *enslave* its people?"

"They used to allow it but—no, slavery's illegal these days. Wait, you just mean they enslave people with, like, video games and propaganda and—"

"No. I actually mean physical *slavery*. You asked what would happen if I got caught—if they found out I sympathized with the Commonplacers and was planning to take you away from them?"

He nodded again.

" 'The nail that sticks up gets hammered down,' " she said.

"What would they do?"

"They'd make me a belty."

"A belty?"

"Somebody in a MoK collar."

"A mock collar?"

"You saw that cleaner squirrel before? And you see that llama over there pruning the hedges?"

Patrick looked over at the creature. It was wearing a blue collar much like the sheep that had greeted him upon his arrival on Ith, or the animals Kempton had pointed out to him behind the grandstand at the school.

"*That* is a Mok collar. I'm going to guess you don't have them on Earth, either. It stands for Motor Operative Control. They use them to control your body from the neck down."

"So, you mean—"

"You see how neatly trimmed the grass is? Or, thanks to our belty squirrel friends, how there's not a leaf or a speck of dirt on the mats? Or what a neat job that llama's doing on the bushes? You think if that llama weren't wearing a collar it would be all neat like that? Or do you think it would be choppy and it'd skip certain bushes altogether and wander over and poop in the sandbox sometimes, too?"

"Umm, choppy and the sandbox thing?" said Patrick.

"So, what happens if you get caught doing anything subversive is you end up in a work camp with one of those collars on your neck *for the rest of your life*. Belties. That's what they're called."

"Wait, they do this to people—to human—"

"If I got caught even talking to you like this, they'd ship me off to a collar camp."

Patrick shook his head not because he disagreed but because it felt as if his head were filling with a dark cloud and he was hoping to shake it out.

"Yeah. So, well, that's why we're here taking risks. We need to wake everybody up to this stuff."

He found himself staring at the llama. He didn't have a lot of experience with llamas but it didn't look like a very happy one. There was something glassy and almost dead about its eyes.

"Seriously?" said Patrick. "They'd really put a collar on you and then they'd, like—"

"Control everything I do from the neck on down."

"Not your head?"

"Apparently the mouth and tongue are extremely complicated to program. Which isn't to say the Deacons probably aren't working at it. Their technology just keeps getting better and better."

Patrick felt a little panicky as he thought of a person—as he thought of Oma, actually—walking around unable to control her own body.

"So," she continued. "Are you going to come along? I can't promise it's going to be easy. Or even safe. But there's so little time left."

Her big eyes locked on Patrick's and he heard his heartbeat in his ears as he gazed back. There was an honesty and seriousness about her, a degree of—he didn't quite know what to call it, *realness*, maybe—that was unlike what he'd seen in anybody else he'd met in this dream. Except maybe also for that Skwurl girl from the locker room.

Kempton was clearly a confused kid. What Bostrel did and said seemed a little shifty. And that superattendant lady had definitely been a weird character.

And, besides—what was he going to do here? Go tattle on her and spend the rest of this dream hanging out with Kempton?

"Sure," he said. "I'll go with you."

Oma smiled with relief and her eyes—though dark as polished onyx—somehow brightened as she heard this.

Patrick felt as if a marching band was warming up behind his ears.

"Looks like they're getting the grid back online. Quick," she said, climbing off the bicycle and coming toward him, "let's fix your makeup."

"What?"

"Your makeup is a mess and while personally I don't care how you want to look, it'll make for a good cover story for why it took us so long to get home: we stopped here so I could fix you up."

"Oh, *did* we?" said Patrick.

She laughed and blushed a little herself as she came up to him.

Somehow seeing her like this, and the feeling of her standing close as she looked inside her makeup kit, made him for the first time really wish this weren't just a dream.

"So what time are we running away?"

"That's a funny way to talk about it," she laughed. "This is serious business, Patrick!"

"Okay then, *seriously*," he said. "What's the plan? You said we had to wait for this big storm Kempton's been talking about?"

"Exactly," she said. "Yes, we're supposed to be picked up sometime before seven. So just go along like everything's normal, and don't be surprised by *any*thing, okay? Could be some weird stuff happening."

"Like what?"

"Like you wouldn't believe me if I told you," she said. "Now, sit still."

"But," said Patrick, not minding her giving him attention like this but still really not liking the idea of having makeup on his face. "Umm, maybe we can come up with another reason for us to be here, like—"

"Like *what—this*?" asked Oma, leaning forward and kissing him on the mouth. Her lips were very soft. And smooth. And, beyond his ability to tell that much, they seemed to have the power to stop his mind from working.

Fortunately, the awkwardness of the moment was diffused as a sky-car thundered overhead, hovering a moment as Oma rubbed some cool red gloss across his recently kissed lips. Then it rocketed back the way it had come.

CHAPTER 38

Youthful Followings

BUNBUN LOOKED BACK AND FORTH FROM HIS BINKY to the words he'd just written on the halfway hut's big white message board,

> *If civilization were acne, the other*
> *planets would tease Earth.*
> *—Rex A. [BCP§421ᚳ43]*

He supposed it was one of the more cryptic Commonplace sayings, but cryptic was good, at least if it provoked any degree of curiosity, and questions, in whoever found it.

He was just lowering the marker when laughter burst out behind him and he turned to see that the four youngsters—rather than returning home—had apparently decided to follow him.

"Deer rabbit!!!"

BunBun was torn. He had plenty of time for another chat, but it would be highly unsafe for them to be seen with him. Still, it would be rude to just run off. He smiled gamely and began to wave back but his binky-watch chirped.

"Oh no, oh no, oh no!" he said, looking down at the screen.

The device was informing him of a Deacon-protocol transmission—and from only a kilometer away! His rabbity eyes nearly bugged out of his head as he considered what to do. The innocent children's safety was paramount.

"Deer rabbit—are you still going to New York City?" asked Paul Griffin.

"Deer rabbit—what did you write on that board?" asked Phoebe Tondorf-Schnittman.

"Deer rabbit—did you use *my* markers?" asked Chloe Tondorf-Schnittman.

"Children," said BunBun, thinking quickly. If Rex and

his killer Deacons were on their way, there was no time to spare. "I'll answer all your questions later. But only after we have a sand castle competition. Do you know how to build sand castles?"

The answer was a very enthusiastic yes.

CHAPTER 39

Attitudes on Gratitude

NANTUCKET BEACH SCENE, HALF A DUNT BEFORE sunset!" announced Mrs. Puber as she bustled into the dining room. The room's walls and ceiling changed to an open, airy view of a sandy beach and grass-stubbled dunes. Overhead, gulls wheeled and cried in the slanting sunlight.

"Let's eat while everything's still warm," she continued. "Tell me, Patrick—on Earth, does your family give thanks before dinner?"

"Um, yes," said Patrick. "We do."

"Would you like to do so for us now?"

"Well—" Patrick said, as a blessing from Bible camp popped into his head:

Fruit us
Bread us
Rice us
Cheese us
Let us thank thee
Loving Jesus

But he couldn't see himself saying it out loud. He wondered was this a test of some kind? Did they really want him to say grace? Hadn't Kempton said they didn't have religion here? Did Mrs. Puber just want to see for herself if he really believed in God and Jesus?

"Um, actually, I'd rather not," he said. "I mean, not without my family here."

"You poor dear," said Mrs. Puber, her face scrunching up with pity. "*Without your family*—how you must miss them!"

"Of course, of course—we didn't mean to put you on the spot like that, son," said Mr. Puber. "We just wanted to give you the opportunity—"

"Oma," interrupted Mrs. Puber, "why don't *you* give the appreciation tonight."

"Aw, Mother!" said Kempton.

"Quiet, Kempton," said Mr. Puber. "You say it every night, Oma needs to say it sometimes, too."

"It's okay by me if Kempton—" Oma began.

Her mother cut her off. "Oma. The gratitude. Now."

Oma took a deep breath and inclined her head.

"With profoundest appreciation, we bow our heads and offer thanks for the Minder's will, which has enabled this bountiful moment. Illuminated by the vision of the Seer and informed by the ingenuity of the Deacons, the implementational expertise of the departmental superattendants, and the executional adeptness of all our smees, deputies, admins, and subalterns, we affirm our supreme gratitude to the nurturing, life-sustaining, and joy-bringing order that has been set before us."

"Affirmed," said the family.

Patrick was about to ask what a smee was but caught an eye roll and brief smile from Oma and lost track of the thought.

"Nicely articulated, Oma," said Mr. Puber.

"Yes, it certainly is nice to see *some* evidence of your top-decile scores," said Mrs. Puber, sighing as she took a dollop of sanitizing gel.

"Oma," said Mr. Puber, "had top scores in her communications class this yie."

"Yeah, I'm sure Patrick knows all about that since he

had to spend a whole bunch of the afternoon with her braggy self," said Kempton.

"Um, that would be you, Kempton, who talks about himself all day long," replied Oma.

"Okay, so what *did* you guys talk about all afternoon?" said Kempton.

"Mostly how proud we all are about how you get by despite your chronic *mustela nervosa.*"

"What's *mustela nervosa* . . . wait. *Mother!*—she's calling me a *weasel* again!"

"Never mind them, Patrick," said Mrs. Puber, blotting her lips with her red napkin, "they're just going through a tough socio-developmental phase right now. The counselor tells us it will pass. Do I understand you have a sister, too, Patrick?"

"Yeah, four," said Patrick.

"She's four yies old? What a wonderful age."

"Actually, Cassie is four. She's twins with Paul. But I was meaning to say I have four sisters."

"Bu-u—what?!" exclaimed Mr. Puber.

"Did you say *four* sisters, dear?" asked Mrs. Puber.

"FOUR SISTERS!?" exclaimed Kempton, nearly dropping his sanitizer pump. "And who's *Paul?*"

Oma shook her head sympathetically and perhaps, it seemed to Patrick, to indicate that he shouldn't be so quick to answer their questions.

"And—and—you have *brothers*, too?" said Mrs. Puber.

"Just two. Neil and Paul, Cassie's twin."

"THERE ARE SEVEN CHILDREN IN YOUR HOUSE-HOLD!?" asked Kempton.

"Nice arithmetic, Kempton," said Oma, clapping.

"Are you a conjoined family?" asked Mr. Puber.

"Sorry?" asked Patrick.

"Do you have more than one set of parents living in the same, um, domicile? Or are any of the children adopted from families whose parents were unsuited for child rearing or are deceased or—"

"No, we're all my two parents' kids," said Patrick, wondering if that was the best way to say it. It seemed an odd thing to have to explain in the first place.

The kitchen door slid open and a wire basket on four rubber-tipped legs stalked up alongside Mrs. Puber. She placed her red predinner napkin inside and it moved to Kempton.

"Families here on Ith only have two children," said Oma. "It's the *law*."

"Ahem," said Mr. Puber, "yes, the human population on Ith has been at its optimal level for nearly two decades, so parents, except in rare cases of municipal-level shortfall . . . Occasionally a family will have three if there's been a nearby case of infertility, accident, or—"

"Oh," said Patrick, still having some trouble adjusting

to using scissors and tongs. Kempton had laughed at the notion of forks and knives. Apparently scissors and tongs are far more efficient and, as Mrs. Puber pointed out, less likely to scratch the plates. "I think China's like that back on Earth."

"China, ah," said Mr. Puber dubiously. "So, umm, your family is so large because Earth has become underpopulated?"

"No," said Patrick, looking down as the automated basket strode up next to him. "I mean, maybe in some places, but I think actually it's the other way around. Like, we were just learning in social studies that 350,000 people are born every day, and only 150,000 die every day, so that means we're—"

"TWO HUNDRED THOUSAND NET GAIN IN POPULATION A DAY!" exclaimed Kempton.

"Excellent math skills again, Kempton. Gold star," said Oma.

"But that must mean," said Mr. Puber, "with a birth rate that high, your overall population is at—"

"I think we're about to hit eight billion."

Mr. Puber put his sanitizer pump back on the table without having given himself any.

"Are you making a joke?"

Patrick shook his head. "No, sir."

"But, Rex told us," he spluttered, "I mean, according to

261

the Minder's plan—there are supposed to be *101 million* Earthlings . . . this would be almost an 8,000 percent discrepancy!"

"Why don't you have something to eat, dear?" said Mrs. Puber to Mr. Puber.

"But I should immediately text the—"

"Stay right there in your chair and let's have dinner as is proper—*without accessing the Interverse.*"

"But, Mother," said Kempton, "this is huge!"

"Kempton, we were told to feed Patrick Griffin dinner, and we do not *ever* break etiquette in this family, much less *at mealtime.* The house is not on fire, abominations are not at the door. And, as the Commission on Family Values has long recommended, there will be *no binkies at the table.*"

"Nicely put, Mother," said Oma.

"And I want no more speaking of population mandates or politics or any kind of scientific theories. We are a *normal* family and, even if we have an *extraordinary* guest, we are going to have *normal* conversation."

Mr. Puber and Kempton both fidgeted like schoolboys but nodded their acquiescence.

"Did we get rutabaga compote?" asked Mr. Puber, waving his tongs excitedly.

"Yes, dear," said Mrs. Puber. "It's coming."

Patrick recalled that Oma had said they were getting

"picked up" at seven and figured it had to be close to that late already.

"So," Mrs. Puber continued, looking brightly around the table. "Tell us about your days, children. Was the weather okay at Lasters? I was so concerned it was going to rain, what with this horrible storm coming. Did you see those awful clouds this morning?"

"Mother, the forecast *said* it wasn't going to get here till this evening," said Kempton. "You *know* the Meteorology Bureau is *99.8 percent* accurate on precipitation predictions out to sixty-three dunts."

"Kempton's got a thing for meteorology," said Oma. "It's his backup if he doesn't make it as an Arso. Which he won't."

"At least I'm not going to have a niche entirely forced on me, loser!" yelled Kempton.

"Both of you, stop!" said Mrs. Puber. "Patrick's siblings—none of them, I am certain, ever indulges in such petty bickering."

Patrick folded up his napkin as neatly as he could and placed it inside the collection cart.

"All ready, everybody? Let's eat!" said Mrs. Puber. The bin almost impatiently collected Mr. Puber's napkin and sprinted from the room. A heavier-duty six-legged model entered the room in its place. It bore a wide silver disc divided into six pie-piece-shaped trays, each heaped with what Patrick presumed must be dinner, though it was, if possible, even less appetizing than last night's. The main dish looked like some sort of seed-filled pudding, surrounded by chickpeas and drizzled with pink mucus.

Mr. Puber moaned rapturously as he set his tongs to work, but the gloppy stuff had the exact opposite effect on Patrick. He blanched and wondered again when his and Oma's escape was going to happen.

"What time do you figure it is, Kempton?" he whispered.

The boy, though he was sitting right next to him, didn't seem to hear the question, so he repeated it a bit more loudly.

"The serve-bots always come in at four-point-five dunts," said Kempton. "Why? Got an appointment?"

"Just curious," said Patrick, and gave himself a mental kick in the butt. Seven *dunts*, not seven o'clock, was what Oma had meant, of course. He sighed and resigned himself to eating the most disgusting-looking meal of his entire life.

CHAPTER 40

Children and Fools

DESPITE HAVING SPENT SEEMINGLY HALF HIS LIFE training in the field, Novitiate Frank Kyle was no fan of the outdoors. It was simply impossible to discount the distractions and discomforts that came with having no climate control or furniture. To say nothing of the bugs.

The devastating agricultural damage insects had caused throughout human history, together with their role in human disease—the brain-cooking fevers, the skin-bursting plagues, the lung-drowning infections—unleashed more chaos than flood, fire, and earthquake combined. The day when all nonessential insects, arachnids, and other subsentients were eradicated from populated areas (as Rex said had already happened on Ith) could not come soon enough.

But that day, of course, was contingent on the Purge.

Till then, the only thing to do about the midges aimlessly dancing in the early-spring sunlight was to keep squinting and not to inhale any of them. The thought of one of their swamp-birthed fleshy little bodies entering his eyes or mouth or nose or—

A voice spoke just then. It emanated from the wireless receiver knit to his auditory neurons. Nobody else—not even a gnat that had flown all the way inside his ear—could have heard it. But Novitiate Frank Kyle surely did.

He stopped walking and activated his retinal display: "Pawprint: lagomorphic, subject approximately 41.1 kilograms, moving at 4.8 kilometers per hour. Recency: 129.8 quats."

He shut off the data and looked down at the soft, rain-soaked grass. A pair of long, thin prints, half a meter in length, were there as plain as day.

"A lagomorph!" he exclaimed aloud. "Well, *that*'s interesting; if not terribly *scary*."

It was almost encouraging, really, that the enemy had taken their last big shot and hadn't chosen anything more formidable than a rabbit. Had they sent a half lion, flying horse, or a venom-spitting giant lizard, or something else fairly radical—*that* could have been somewhat challenging to address.

But a large rabbit—even if it turned out to be somewhat chimeric (perhaps it had the head of a chicken or the arms of a monkey)—was

A) going to be relatively easy to kill and

B) something that could be explained away.

The educated population here was now coming to terms with genetically altered crops, cloned sheep, and miniature horses. A giant rabbit could simply and easily be construed as an escaped laboratory experiment.

"Oh, those horrible, horrible scientists!" he said aloud in a mocking falsetto voice.

But Novitiate Frank Kyle wasn't here at this podunk suburban golf course to allow such a scenario in the first place. Because if *nobody* ever saw a giant rabbity monster—if nobody knew it had ever been here—then *nothing* would ever need to be explained.

The voice traveled into his auditory cortex once again: "Second print set: human, approximately 19 kilograms, moving at 4.8 kilometers per hour. Recency: 132 quats."

And indeed, close to the first ones, Novitiate Frank Kyle now discerned another imprint, that of a human child's shoe.

"Third subject," continued the voice. "Human, approximately 21 kilograms, moving at 4.8 kilometers per hour. Recency: 132.1 quats."

And then, in rapid succession, the voice announced two more pairs of indentations, each of which had been made within moments of the others.

Novitiate Frank Kyle scrolled through some hyper-linked pages on his retinal display and determined—based on the size, spacing, and depth of the footprints—that the enemy combatant's companions were approximately four years old.

He continued to walk as he read reports, examined charts, and reviewed his decision-making protocols.

Witnesses younger than five years were considered highly unreliable. But, still, above two there was risk. And risk had to be minimized.

He pulled out an ammunition clip just as the automated voice made another announcement: "Voices, 442 meters, east northeast. Acoustic analysis suggests three to five English-speaking entities."

Novitiate Frank Kyle sighed as he slid his gun from the bag, removing the knit sock from the end of its barrel. Then—just to be certain—he removed one more ammunition clip from the golf bag.

Disengaging the gun's safety as he went, he walked up the crest of a wooded hill, lay down in the filthy, muddy (and doubtless insect-infested) leaf litter, popped the protective caps off his rifle's scope, and examined the figures he could see gathered in a sand trap near the seventh green.

The four young children were there—playing in the sand—but that was all. Nothing else, much less anything rabbitlike, was with them.

Well, he'd find it soon enough. Doubtless after making contact with the children, the creature had moved off to pursue whatever futile objective it had been sent here to achieve.

His BNK-E suddenly buzzed in its belt loop. The device's screen was asking if it was okay to disengage silent mode on his neural implants, and to replay three recent alerts.

The color drained from Novitiate Frank Kyle's short-bearded face. He hadn't engaged silent mode. *How could it have been in silent mode?!* The interface was located inside his own head and he'd surely have remembered if he'd done anything so stupid! He hastily selected the unmute icon and gasped in horror as his motion detector exploded onto his retinal screen. A large red dot was racing toward the center of his range-finder.

He turned just in time to see a very large furry foot closing in on his face.

All became very bright for Novitiate Frank Kyle right then. And then black. And quiet.

CHAPTER 41

To Sleep, Perchance to Dream

CAN YOU TURN DOWN THE MOON A LITTLE?"
Patrick asked. Kempton had them sleeping under a
tree-framed country sky bright enough to read by. Either
Kempton hadn't had the moon on last night or Patrick
had been so tired that he hadn't noticed. But—between
his nervousness about his and Oma's coming escape and
the way that vegetarian glop from dinner was sitting in
his stomach—there was no missing it tonight.

"Turn it down?"

"It's so bright," said Patrick.

"That's my prescription."

"Prescription?"

"My counselor prescribed elevated ambient light levels because of my stress dreams. It's this or the aurora borealis routine. But that can be annoying. All those colors moving around, you know. The moon's good, though. Nice and calming, don't you think?"

"I guess I'll get used to it," said Patrick. "And what's the deal with the bed?"

"What do you mean?"

"Can I turn off the massage? It's kind of annoying."

Wherever Patrick rolled or however he lay, the mattress came up to meet him. It was a strange sensation—like hands pressing upward.

"Massage? No, it's just the active response," Kempton explained. "The Commission of Public Health says there's been a 43 percent reduction in spinal complaints since it became standardized."

"So, like, you can't turn it off?"

"Did you not hear me? It's good for your back. You'll get used to it."

Patrick sighed and tried to stay still so that the mattress would leave him alone.

"Say," said Kempton. "I was thinking, is the reason you have so many siblings because you are in a *celebrity* family on Earth?"

"Celebrity? Us? No, definitely not," said Patrick.

"Oh," said Kempton. He looked over to Patrick in the not-so-dim light.

"Patrick?"

"Yes, Kempton?"

"What would you say is the chief difference between Earth and Ith? I mean other than for your eyes being small and your ears being big. And the population issue. And not being as technologically advanced."

"Between Ith and Earth?" said Patrick, and thought about it a moment. "I guess things are more organized here."

"Organized? How do you mean?"

"Well, it's like you guys seem to have all these rules and things—and all the machines—this bed, and the robots, and how your toilets are all automated and stuff."

"Okay, but what else? You said your written language is different, right? And, really, there are *no* abominations?"

"Kempton," said Patrick. "I am not going to talk to you anymore because I'm feeling very tired right now and—no offense—I think this is all a dream and I don't need to answer your questions."

"You *what*?!" said Kempton, sitting bolt upright. "That's just like Rex! He went *three days* before he stopped suspecting it was all a dream! Do you want to see a psych counselor?"

"No," said Patrick, his heart sinking. "I want to sleep."

"Okay, but if you need help—they told us to watch for adjustment issues and, if you're feeling disoriented—"

"Good night, Kempton," said Patrick, turning his pillow and pushing his face into its dark, soothing coolness.

"Good night, Patrick," said Kempton, lying back down.

Patrick closed his eyes and began to count in his head. He remembered how Kempton had counted *One Missouri, two Missouri* rather than *One Mississippi, two Mississippi*. It occurred to him this was because a tert—or was it a quint?—was a little shorter than a second, and Missouri is a little shorter to say than Mississippi.

"Patrick."

"Yes, Kempton?" said Patrick, raising his face from the pillow.

"Our trip to Silicon City is going to be *awesome*."

"Sure," said Patrick. "Good night."

"Good night, Patrick."

Patrick reburied his face in the pillow. A moment later there was a weird raspy, whiny sound and Patrick rolled over to see Kempton asleep and snoring like a sick little lamb.

Frustrated, he lay awhile watching the boy and found himself thinking about school, his real school. The year was almost over—just another couple months to go. He couldn't wait for the summer. He hoped they'd go to Washington, DC, again and see Uncle Andrew. Everybody had complained about the trip last year—how hot it had been, how small the hotel rooms had been—but they complained everywhere they went. And he knew he and his parents, at least, had really enjoyed all the museums and the tours and the . . .

And here Patrick's mind wandered from the llamas at the National Zoo and the toothpaste tube Neil had left in Patrick's sneaker with the cap off while they were in the hotel room and how he got toothpaste all through his sneaker and then Uncle Andrew taking them to that picnic at the cemetery and the Smithsonian and the Library of Congress and . . . the images flowed and changed without his control yet it was perfectly natural—this was what happened when you fell asleep. But then something made him start. It was a noise or maybe, rather, it was that there was no longer any noise at all. The buzzing of the room's displays had completely stopped. He sat up in the pitch-dark and noticed the mattress was no longer matching his movements. Kempton was still snoring softly, but other than that, everything was silent. It was like the power had been cut.

He felt around for his binky to check the time—was it seven dunts already?—but, just as he located the holster on the bedside table, there was a house-shaking tremor and what sounded like a distant clap of thunder.

Kempton whimpered and left off snoring.

There was a clunking noise then, and the door slid open, the word **egzit** glowing red from its lintel.

Patrick picked up his binky. It didn't seem to be working—the screen was entirely blue like it had been during the locker-room incident. There was another tremor and rumble, this one bigger than the last.

"Wha!?" said Kempton, and Patrick heard his sheets whipping around. "Why's it so *dark*!?" he pleaded. "What's happening!?"

"I don't know," said Patrick. "There's a thunderstorm or something. Maybe the power's out?"

"What?!" said Kempton. "That's not even *possible*!"

"Well, it's pretty dark. And my binky's offline. And the bed's stopped doing its thing when I move."

"Deacons' eyes!" blurted Kempton. "You're right! Look—the evac lights are illuminated! Maybe the derecho—"

He was cut short by a tremor that knocked the boys flat onto their backs. The emergency lights went out and there was a blast of windblown rain. A little bit of light returned, too, though not much—just enough for Patrick to detect that the wall and ceiling of Kempton's room had been torn away and that the blue-black sky was being blotted out by the smudgy but distinct shape of a very, very large woman.

CHAPTER 42

Backup Driver

EVA SCOWLED INTO HER IPHONE. SHE WAS ALREADY in a bad mood from having had such a terrible night's sleep. She'd kept waking up from the strangest dream about her family going on vacation in this weird place where there were friendly monsters, like a super-realistic theme park for *The Lord of the Rings* or Narnia or something. And then her brother Patrick had climbed over a fence and disappeared into one of the exhibits and then she and her brothers and sisters and parents began running around and fighting the park guards, who were like these blind robot-zombie dudes who were really strong.

Anyhow, it hadn't exactly been a nightmare—most of it had actually been more fun than scary—but it sure hadn't made for a restful night.

But what was specifically pissing her off now was that Nana was coming to get them from practice. She loved her grandmother, but this was not good. Nana was a *ridiculously* slow driver and Eva was meeting Lindsay and Madison at Starbucks at three—Ashton Lane and his friends had lately been spotted hanging out there after Saturday lacrosse practice—and she absolutely had to shower before Carly got back from soccer and hogged the bathroom herself.

Also, Nana *always* struck up inappropriate conversations with Eva's friends.

"Nana's picking us up," she said to Sabrina. "Do *not* give her anything but yes-or-no answers, okay?"

Sabrina looked up from her own iPhone and blinked at Eva through her too-small Kate Spade glasses. Sabrina was Eva's swim-team training partner and, at least during the season, Eva spent more one-on-one time with her than with any other human being. But Eva made sure their bond ended there. Out of water, Sabrina was sensitive, gawky, and hesitant—Eva's antithesis.

It also didn't help that Sabrina was now starting to beat Eva at meets. Eva had always been the better natural athlete in terms of coordination and general athleticism, but

Sabrina's freakishly long arms and legs were clearly becoming a decisive factor in the pool.

"Um, okay," said Sabrina.

"Really," said Eva, slamming closed her locker. "Just shut her down. She needs to concentrate on the driving. Trust me."

Sabrina nodded and tried to smile, not that Eva was even looking her way.

"Come on," Eva said, shouldering her bright yellow Speedo bag and starting for the door. Sabrina struggled with her sweatshirt and hurried to follow.

Nana drove an ancient Renault Fuego. Renault hadn't been selling cars in the United States for decades, but Nana had a mechanic in Mt. Kisco she'd been going to forever and he and she somehow kept the thing going. Eva had to admit it was a little cool driving around in an '80s French automobile—it did turn some heads—but the interior was appalling.

Thirty years of incessant cigarette smoke had basically turned the vehicle into an ashtray on wheels.

"There she is," said Eva. "And, who'd've thunk it—she's parked illegally."

The silver hatchback had pulled in from the wrong side of the drive and stopped smack in the middle of the yellow hash marks of the fire lane. Through a partially opened window, Nana's bony, jewel-encrusted hand beckoned frantically. The two girls pulled up their hoods and hurried down the still-rain-dampened steps.

"Remember, *no spreken zie* English, okay?"

Sabrina nodded.

"And you better sit up front. There's no way you'll fit in that backseat. Nana says it was designed to hold a baguette, a bouquet, a bottle of wine, and nothing more."

"Hurry up, girls!" shouted the old woman as they crossed the drive. "Emergency, emergency!"

Eva crinkled her brow as she opened the passenger door. "What's going on, Nana?"

"You've lost a brother!" said the old woman.

"What!?" said Eva, climbing into the tar-stained back.

"Your silly brother ran off someplace and didn't tell anybody."

"Why is this a surprise? Somebody just discovered Neil's selfish and inconsiderate?"

"Not Neil, Patrick," said Nana. Eva arranged her legs sideways and snapped the passenger seat back into its forward position.

"Patrick? I guess *that's* a little weird, then." She paused a moment, remembering her dream last night. "But, on the other hand, it's not like he's not a little weird himself. You remember Sabrina?" she asked as her friend got into the front seat.

"Of course I do! My how you've grown into a lean green bean—you're a veritable fashion model!"

Unobserved, Eva rolled her eyes as her friend stammered a protest.

"Well," continued Eva, "so what's the big deal? I think we can rule out that he's gone and joined a gang."

"I expect you're right," said Nana, popping the Renault into gear and continuing the wrong way down the driveway. "But your mother's making quite a fuss—the fire department and the police have both been to the house."

"Really?" asked Eva.

"She's quite convinced something bad's happened."

"Well, Mom does sometimes overreact, you know."

"I suppose I *do* know that. But she's claiming maternal intuition in this case, and I happen to know something about that, too."

"Intuition? You mean like ESP, Nana?"

"I guess that's right. Sure. But I'm not talking woo-woo stuff. When you're a mother, sometimes you just know things about your kids that other people can't grok."

"Grok?"

"It's a '60s word, dear," said Nana, tapping her cigarette at her window as she turned left on Riverside. At least half the ash blew back inside and swirled like snow around Eva. "Came from a science fiction novel. It kind of means *comprehend*."

"Well, what's the plan, then? I have to shower and then I've got a thing in town—"

"Huh. You going to this *thing in town* too, Sabrina?"

"Uh, no, I have to study," said Sabrina.

"You hear that, Eva—Sabrina has to study."

"We take different classes, Nana."

"Ah," said Nana, bringing the Renault almost all the way up to the thirty-mile-per-hour town speed limit that nobody but she observed. "Well, I guess you'll have to see what your mother wants done when you get home. It might be a good idea for you to stay home till they locate Patrick."

"Great," muttered Eva, her mind already turning to what she was going to do to her little brother if he screwed up her afternoon. "Just great."

CHAPTER 43
Biggy Packing

A FLICKER OF LIGHTNING ILLUMINATED THE RAIN-lashed space where Kempton's bedroom wall and ceiling had been. The enormous figure occupying it was a woman—maybe thirty feet tall—very hairy, very wet, and generally very giant-like except that she wore running sneakers, a backpack, and an ugly flannel shirt tucked into army pants that were pulled up too high—way over her belly.

Patrick decided the big woman basically resembled a giant version of one of the vegetable-stand workers at the

Hedgerow Heights Farmers' Market. Her face was big chinned and twinkly eyed, and she was clasping her hands in apologetic fashion like she'd sort of ripped open the house by accident and was expecting to be scolded.

Kempton was more than a little freaked out: the scream he let loose was maybe only a half note lower than a coach's whistle.

The giant spoke up, her voice conveying a distinct lack of threat. "My apologies for the rudeness of this introduction," she said above the howling wind. "My name is Purse-Phone, and I'm here to pick up Patrick Griffin and take him on a behind-the-scenes tour of the Deaconry!"

"Run, Patrick, RUN!" yelled Kempton.

The giant seemed annoyed for a moment. "You needn't be a-pointing out to me that you're not Patrick, Kempton Puber!" said the giant. "I know which a you is which, and no harm'll come to you, so whyn't you just simmer down and butt'n your lip, ay?!"

There was a peal of thunder just then and Kempton recommenced shrieking.

Lightning flashed twice in quick succession. Patrick wondered if she had really said her name was Purse-Phone.

"Eeeee—iiiiiii!!!!" said Kempton

"Aye-yi-yi, you're a nervous critter, ain'tcha? Okay, here's what you say, Kempty: you tell those blind bastards that I said I'd mish ya up like a mosquito if ya didn't let Patrick go with me and so you had to go along and so you *did* go along. Ka-peesh?"

Kempton went quiet for a moment. The blue light of his binky showed his face to be frozen in consideration of what the giant had said. "Wh-what?" he finally asked.

"You're givin' up your heretofore valiant defense of Patrick Griffin and your home so that I don't kill ya, right?"

Kempton began keening again.

"Right," said the giant, turning to Patrick. "I heard he was high-strung but mercy, he's a ravin' half-plucked chicken!

"Here," she continued. A strobe of electric light showed her to be turning around and squatting. Her backpack, partially hidden by a massive braided ponytail, was actually not a pack so much as an open wooden frame with straps and handles all over it.

"Come on over, Patrick Griffin, and we'll piggyback," she said over her shoulder.

"What?" asked Patrick.

"There's a ledge for yer feet, and handholds a'top. It'll be much faster if it's me that does the walking. And feel free to use my ponytail for climbing purposes, if it's a help."

Patrick looked at the big gray rope-like braid hanging down her back and gave a why-not shrug as he got up from the bed. It was all too crazy to take seriously.

284

"Unless you'd rather have me squish-squash Kempty here," the big woman added. Kempton broke off from his latest scream to plead for his life.

"Take it easy, Kempton," said Patrick. "You can tell she's kidding. And, anyhow, I *am* going to go with her."

Kempton stopped blubbering and, leaping from his bed, fled into the hallway, arms pinwheeling as he ran.

"Yah, that's one nervous lad," said the giant. "Think it's too many video games, and not getting out enoof?"

"Where's Oma?" asked Patrick as he approached the giant.

"We'll be picking her up shortly," she replied. "Didn't want her family to see her going willingly—leave them the chance to think she was abducted."

"Oh," replied Patrick as he grabbed hold of her big wet ponytail and clambered up onto the back-platform.

"Say," said the giant, peeking over her shoulder, "that's some shirt you're wearing—what color is that, dark zebra?"

Patrick looked down at his new shirt and shook his head. In the monochrome flashes of lightning he supposed it was hard to see that the stripes of Bing Steenslay's shirt were yellow, not white.

"Um, I guess it would be dark bee."

"Ah," said the giant, squatting slightly. "Dark bee. Well, just don't sting me, ay?"

Patrick smiled and wondered if she might be Canadian.

"All comfy?"

"Sure," said Patrick, twining the handhold straps around his arms.

"Good. Now hold tight!"

And with that, the giant carried Patrick out into the stormy night, quickly crossing several streets and at least twice as many backyards.

"Got elbow room back there?" asked the giant over her shoulder, her booming words loud enough to be understood through the storm.

"Yeah, sure," yelled Patrick. The only trouble was that the giant's wet gray ponytail kept swishing back and forth and sometimes hitting him in the face.

"Good, 'cause here's our friend!"

The big woman squatted and Oma stepped forward from behind a tree, quickly clambering aboard the platform next to Patrick. She was wearing a ninja suit, just like the girl from the locker room.

"Hello, Patrick Griffin!" she said, and gave his shoulder a squeeze.

"So what's the plan?" asked Patrick as the giant stood. "Where are we going?"

"We're going to go learn a thing or two."

"Grip tight, we've reached the woods!" announced the giant.

A welter of torn leaves and small sticks drove home the point. She forged forward maybe a half mile into what seemed to be a proper forest, and then the big woman stopped and tensed.

Patrick craned his neck to see what was going on. The giant was looking intently at a nearby pine tree and, after a moment, her hand darted down through its boughs. A horrible screeching noise ensued as the giant brought the same hand down and over her shoulder to Oma. Extending from the top of her massive fist was the head of a very unhappy raccoon.

Oma smiled and quickly secured a band around the panicked animal's neck.

"What the!?" said Patrick.

Oma fist-bumped the giant's finger and turned her attention to her binky. She pulled her ankh necklace up, swiped the pendant against the back of the device, and pressed it into Patrick's belly.

"What are you doing!?" asked Patrick.

"What?!"

Patrick yelled the question more loudly. The storm's roar was not easy to overcome even at a standstill.

"Had to disable—tracking—personal beacon!" she replied. "—raccoon—false signal—me, both. Red herring—better chance—"

"Okay!?" said the giant.

"Okay!" said Oma. The big woman opened her hand and the terrified raccoon scooted off into the storm.

"Come back soon, raccoon," said Oma.

"Now," said the giant, holding up a pair of earbuds the size of strawberries, "I hope you don't think me unmannerly, but I make mooch better progress when I keep a beat."

"Enjoy!" said Oma.

The giant smiled affably, popped the buds into her ears, quickly did something to her oversized binky, replaced the device in the pocket of her flannel shirt, and took off running.

"—what—you think of Purse-Phone?!" asked Oma, leaning in close.

"Who is she?!" asked Patrick, trying to stop his head from banging against the pack.

"A Commonplacer!" she replied.

"Okay, and *what* is she?!" asked Patrick, looking up at the back of the woman's hairy—woolly, actually—neck.

She gave an answer but a thunderclap shook the very ground just then. It sounded to Patrick like maybe she'd said "sock scratch."

Patrick shook his head.

"—talk more when—get there," she yelled. "It's kind—hard—hear!"

"Okay!" agreed Patrick.

Oma leaned up against him again and he in turn against Purse-Phone's back. The volume on the giant's buds was up very loud and the beat—with which she was keeping pace—reminded Patrick of a Green Day song he'd always quite liked, "Warning Sign." Despite the strangeness of it all, despite the noise, and despite the pelting rain, Patrick felt pretty warm and happy.

And, before very much longer, he fell sound asleep.

CHAPTER 44

Course Correction

NOVITIATE FRANK KYLE HAD HEARD OF "SEEING stars" but it wasn't till this moment, trying to stand, that he had experienced the condition firsthand.

Whatever had hit him had hit him very hard. Hard enough to have given him a concussion, hard enough to have made him lose consciousness. He explored his face with his fingers. The socket of his left eye was puffy, the bridge of his nose tender. Now, as long as his—

A horrible realization dawned as he tried to focus his eyes through the swirling spots in his vision: his golf bag was right there on the grass next to him—but the gun was gone!

He kicked the bag over in case somehow the weapon had ended up underneath. It wasn't there.

He reached into his fanny pack for his BNK-E so he could initiate the weapon's homing signal, but now an equally if not even more horrible feeling overcame him— the spare ammunition was still there, but his BNK-E was missing, too!

Only decades of training kept him from outright panic. He judged the sun's position hadn't radically shifted— probably he hadn't been unconscious for more than half a deuce—then he reached down to his ankle to make sure his ceramic combat knife was still there. His assailant hadn't known about that, at least. He removed it from its sheath and, as he did so, noticed something wrong with his knuckles. In blue permanent ink, *N-I-C-E* was spelled out on his left knuckles, and *F-A-C-E* on the right.

He tamped down his anger. He had to stay rational. Clearly the enemy combatant was employing psychological warfare, was trying to discomfit him, was trying to throw him off his game.

He tucked the blade up inside the sleeve of his Tommy Hilfiger jacket and inspected the putting green beneath his feet. Head down, he walked four, five, six meters and finally spied the telltale impressions—long, thin footprints that could only belong to the enemy combatant. He followed them a few meters and confirmed that there was only the one set—the creature was alone.

Lips closed and without a sign of worry or strain upon his bruised face, he hurried along his enemy's path.

Novitiate Frank Kyle followed the trail down the gently curving green. His target was sticking to the winding but easy-to-navigate fairway. His surgical augments allowed him to sprint at over fifty kilometers per hour, and he took full advantage of them as he turned off the course and sprinted up the wooded hill to the south. Hurdling the old stone wall at its crest, he half hoped to see his targets on the next green, but instead, standing next to a golf cart in the middle of a gravel path were a middle-aged man and woman. Each was wearing a Tommy Hilfiger golfing outfit identical to his own.

His stomach surged upward as if he were standing in an elevator whose cables had been cut. He considered running back the way he had come—running with abandon, running till he dropped from exhaustion. But there would be no point. They would overtake him as surely as the night. He dropped his shoulders and went to meet his fellow novitiates from—and competitors for—Prefecture One.

"Nice face," said the broad-shouldered woman, Novitiate Sara Michel.

"Yes, I expect the contusion will last a good while," admitted Frank Kyle.

"Is that all just contusion?" said Novitiate Greg Andrew, his voice dripping with unkind amusement.

"There's *writing* on your face, brother," said Sara Michel, pursing her perfectly glossed lips as she held out her BNK-E.

Frank Kyle put his hand to his face.

The screen of Sara Michel's BNK-E pushed upward, quickly adopting the shape of a man's head. Frank Kyle recognized the subject of the communications holograph and quickly lowered his hand, which had begun to tremble.

"Are we correct in observing that you have lost your BNK-E?" said the deep-voiced, dark-eyed head. This was none other than Victor Pierre, Rex's very first novitiate here on Earth. Rumor had it that it was he who had personally oversaw the last winnowing—the elimination of unfit novitiates after the annual review. The fact that he was personally involved in this, was directly communicating from his European post, was a terrifying sign.

"Mirror app, horizontal inversion," said Greg Andrew to his own BNK-E, and passed it to Frank Kyle, who now saw on his forehead the words *BAD MAN*.

"Oh," said Frank Kyle.

"Let's get moving, shall we?" said Sara Michel.

Frank Kyle briefly stared into Victor Pierre's depthless, data-dilated eyes.

"I have another call. We'll debrief later," said the head, and promptly melted back into Sara Michel's screen.

"Did you at least get a good look at the enemy combatant?" asked Greg Andrew as he gestured for Frank Kyle to get into the golf cart.

"Umm," said Frank Kyle, marshaling his thoughts, "lagomorphic, maybe forty-one, forty-two kilograms."

"So you got beat up by . . . a *bunny*," said Sara Michel.

Frank Kyle ignored the taunt. He'd still beaten them to the target. And he had known they weren't going to be supportive. Until and unless they made the final twelve, they would remain his competitors, not his friends.

"It's not a flier, at least—it *can't* have gotten too far," he said as he sat. "It was heading southeast—"

"Rex has cut short the mission," said Sara Michel.

"We," said Greg Andrew, "have a vid conference in less than a deuce."

Though his mouth had gone entirely dry, Frank Kyle found himself swallowing. He wondered if he'd have a chance to wash his face before then. Not that it probably mattered.

CHAPTER 45

To Dream, Perchance to Sleep

THE NEXT THING PATRICK KNEW IT WAS DAYTIME.
He was awake and lying upon the narrow strip of grass behind the garage.

He was glad to be back home, back in the real world. But he couldn't help feeling a little wistful. He'd been proud of himself for deciding to join Oma, and that adventure with her and the giant had been genuinely exciting.

But there was no question about falling back asleep here, about getting back to the dream. The grass was wet and he was stiff and sore and thirsty and he absolutely had to get back inside and clean up the kitchen before his parents came back and he found himself grounded for the rest of his life.

His being outside behind the garage like this wasn't any big mystery. He must have staggered out when the kitchen had filled with fumes, and then, obviously, passed out.

He hurried around the garage and crossed the yard to the side door—the same door through which he'd let out the cat.

There were voices down the hall. His father's—and Neil's, and Carly's, and maybe Eva's.

And while he knew he should be worried about being in trouble, he realized suddenly, acutely, that he had missed them all—really actually missed them. He burst through to the kitchen door, knocking right into Neil.

"Hey, buddy. What's that on your face!?" his older brother yelled, grabbing him by the shoulders.

"What!?" asked Patrick, anger and embarrassment clutching at his chest.

"No way," said Neil. "Hey, everybody—PATRICK'S WEARING MAKEUP!"

CHAPTER 46

Executional Assessment

REX TURNED DOWN THE CREED ALBUM, PUT HIS hands behind his black-turtlenecked back, cleared his throat, and began the meeting. The ocean view faded and the windows went entirely black. One hundred twenty tiles illuminated around him, each containing a middle-aged face—men and women of all racial and ethnic descriptions, though wearing nearly the same humorless expression.

These were the remaining candidates, the novitiates, for Earth's first Deaconry.

Rex gave a cool smile and addressed his virtual audience.

"I apologize for the interruption but Novitiate Kyle from Prefecture One is here to recount highlights from his recent mission, and I wanted us all to witness the debrief in real time. Novitiate Kyle—if you please?"

"Oh, uh, yes, Your Awarenence. I tracked the subject from the insertion point to a golf course at latitude 41.14534, longitude minus 73.83089, approximately two kilometers to the east. Somewhere between insertion and my intercept, the visitor made contact with four humans—juveniles, all approximately age four and therefore on the lower spectrum of witness reliability."

Rex raised his dark, well-tended eyebrows. "Please remind us how this might impact your mission objectives, if at all?"

"Well, of course I had to address that situation, too. 'Failure to manage risk is mission failure,' " he said, reciting a line from the training manual.

"Indeed," said Rex, smiling. "And how did you proceed once past this decision juncture?"

"I picked up their trail and, by approximately one point four-two dunts, I achieved contact."

"And then?"

Novitiate Frank Kyle wondered if the pounding in his head was visible to the camera as he proceeded to recount everything that followed—from his discovery that his neural alarms had been muted to his getting knocked unconscious (presumably by the enemy combatant) to his discovery that his equipment had been stolen—right up to the point where he encountered his fellow novitiates and was taken back to regional headquarters.

"And, so," said Rex, his words staccato with impatience, "how would you characterize the overall success of your mission?"

"Umm, 42 percent, Your Awarenence."

"Really? Tell us, how did you arrive at this figure?"

Novitiate Frank Kyle tried to assume a confident smile but it looked more like he was trying to crimp an invisible piece of foil with his lips.

"Well," he said, coughing softly, "successful assessment is half of mission success, but I of course lost my equipment and had to give myself a deduction there."

"But you give yourself *some* credit?"

"Yes, Your Awarenence. I tracked and located the enemy combatant, plus I personally discovered it had the ability to access my neural network, which certainly would be unprecedented, so it seems to me that—"

"And did you visually register the enemy combatant— did you actually *see* it?"

"Well, umm, not entirely."

"And the lost equipment? You are referring to your field-issue rifle and BNK-E?"

"Yes, Your Awarenence."

Rex's eyes wandered upward thoughtfully. "Anything else go missing?"

Victor Pierre gave a little bark of a laugh. He was the only novitiate who could have gotten away with such a piece of spontaneity in front of Rex, and everybody—himself included—knew it.

"No, I did a thorough inventory and—"

"You also lost an *opportunity*, did you not?"

"Well—"

"And you lost us *time*, didn't you? You lost valuable *time* for our team, for this world, and for the Minder himself?"

"Well, in a manner of speaking, I—"

"A manner of speaking?! Are you accusing me of communicating information in a roundabout or colloquial fashion?"

"Of course not—I—"

"Quiet. I actually am inclined to concur with your self-assessment."

Novitiate Frank Kyle breathed a sigh of relief.

"But let's put a *minus* symbol in front of it."

"Uh," said Novitiate Frank Kyle, more than just his hands shaking now.

Rex, too, seemed to be shaking—with rage. "You are *personally* responsible for setting our mission back dunts if not entire *days*. Your assignment was simple and you managed to let yourself be overtaken by an enemy combatant that had only moments to prepare itself. Tell me: How strong is an organizational chain?"

"As strong as—as—its *weakest link*."

"And, for the good of mankind and the three worlds, are we to be a pillar of strength, or a puddle of weakness?"

"Please, Your Awarenence—"

"Are you not answering a very clear, direct question?"

"A pillar of strength, my master!" shouted Novitiate Frank Kyle.

"To my mind the only positive thing to come out of your utter failure is, perhaps, some confirmation of the theory that our enemies possess the ability to compromise our neural implants! Unless you disrupted them yourself?"

"Sir, I would never—"

"Which is actually not all that surprising since this agent came from Ith, where they may have had a chance to learn the technology. You agree with me that it's not that surprising, don't you?"

"Y-yes," stammered Frank Kyle.

"So, it's actually quite fair to have expected us to be prepared for such a thing, is it not?"

"Well, I—I—"

"Shh," said Rex, raising an index finger to his lips as 238 other judgmental eyes joined his upon the quavering novitiate.

"How do you feel about beta-testing human subjects, Novitiate Kyle?"

"Beta testing?" said Frank Kyle, closing his eyes. "It's necessary to advance technology."

"Your informational implants, your strength, your speed—they all are the fruits of human testing, are they not?"

"Of—of course."

"And MoK collars—they, too, come from such testing, do they not?"

Frank Kyle blotted at his sweat-beaded forehead and nodded enthusiastically.

"So, *are* you in favor of testing beta-rated technologies on humans?"

"Yes, Your Awarenence!"

"Good. Because we wouldn't want you to arrive at—which facility is it, Novitiate Pierre?"

"KF-1, sir," smiled Victor Pierre.

"We wouldn't," continued Rex, "wish for you to arrive at KF-1 harboring any hypocrisy or cynicism."

"*KF-1? The collar* facility?" asked Frank Kyle.

"Yes, in fact yours is all ready."

"*Mine?*"

"Shh," said Rex, putting a slender finger to his lips. "It's a brand-new prototype. We may have finally cracked a key component of the verbalization issue. We may finally be able to control the subject's speech."

"But you can't do this! I am inn—" said Novitiate Frank Kyle, leaping toward the camera in desperation.

Whatever else he said didn't get picked up. His microphone had been shut off and two large men in black suits came up behind and pulled him out of frame. Then the feed went entirely blank and his tile disappeared.

"And so," said Rex to the remaining 119. "Let's use this as a cautionary tale, shall we?"

Every head nodded; a few, following Victor Pierre's lead, even smiled.

"Any fresh progress to report on the enemy combatant, John Michael?"

The visage of a muscular man with wire-framed glasses and a dimpled chin moved to the center spot on Rex's screen.

"No," replied the man, "we still haven't relocated the creature, Your Awarenence."

"Well, if there are no results to report by EOD, then I trust you, too, will be prepared to let me know how you feel about human beta testing?"

John Michael blanched but smiled gamely. "There will be no further failure, Your Awarenence."

"Good," said Rex. "Because I'm sure I could find another

who would be willing to prove him- or herself at this juncture."

John Michael bowed his head and his tile receded back to its place.

"And," continued Rex, "will somebody remind me who's now on point for the Ministry of Communications—Cathy Lauren, is it?"

"Yes, Your Awarenence," said a thin-lipped blond woman in a royal blue turtleneck as her face tile moved to the center of the screen.

"How's the cover-up story coming?"

"We're ready, Your Awarenence."

"All right, give me the elevator pitch."

"Your Awarenence?"

"Gah!" he exclaimed in frustration. "It's in the *white paper*! You know, if you only have an elevator ride in which to pitch somebody, what do you say that gets them leaning *over the plate*?"

"Apologies, Your Awarenence," she said, looking like she was blinking back tears. "My elevator pitch is, 'Ag-Gen, the company that created the recent sheep-goat hybrid, is behind the creature, and they must be punished.'"

"And we expect the scientific establishment, such as it is, to go along with this idea that this company could have really done such a thing? Made a giant rabbit-like creature?"

"Yes, we've identified all key opinion gatekeepers and will ensure that they play along."

"Good," Rex said, and then was silent a moment.

The woman's face tile shrank and resumed its former place among the many.

"And," he continued, "am I to understand the juvenile witnesses are still with their parents?"

"Yes."

"And no indication of them reporting the creature's existence?"

"If they told their parents, the parents have chosen not to disseminate."

"Who in their right mind," snorted Rex, "would believe a bunch of four-year-olds saying they saw a giant bunny?"

The 119 remaining heads nodded gravely.

"Still," he said. "We should consider apprehending them once we have the enemy-combatant situation buttoned down." Which, he reflected, would require a good deal of his personal attention. He scowled and dismissed the tiles with a wave of his hand. The Pacific Ocean reappeared, and the neatly produced, inspiring strains of Creed came back up.

CHAPTER 47

Underground Movements

AM I WHAT—WAIT!—WHAT!?"

Patrick opened his eyes.

In the flickering lightning he saw that Oma was looking at him and that they were still plunging through the forest.

"Are you okay?" she repeated. "You yelled out in your sleep."

"I did? What did I say?"

"Um, *dillhole* I think is the word you used."

"Huh," said Patrick, wiping his mouth in case he'd been drooling, not that anybody would have been able to tell in the rain and dark.

"Nightmare?"

"Kind of," said Patrick. "How long was I asleep?"

"A good dunt or so."

The storm had quieted somewhat and the music thumping from the giant's earpieces was a bit more down-tempo than the former Green Day–sounding song.

"We should be almost there," Oma continued. "I hope I'm doing the right thing."

"What do you mean?"

Even in the dark, the look Oma gave Patrick made him realize he'd just asked a pretty stupid question. "You mean running away—all this," he corrected himself.

"Don't you miss *your* family? And don't you worry about them?"

"I guess," he said, thinking on it. "I mean, yes, mostly." It was pretty different situations for him and Oma. Other than for deciding to join her on this trip tonight—he actually hadn't made any choices. He wasn't really responsible for being away from his family. He'd just sort of ended up here and gone along for the ride. She, on the other hand, was apart from her family because she had *decided* to be apart from them.

"But your family will be okay, right?" he said. "I mean, they'll miss you and worry and stuff I'm sure."

"I *hope* they'll be all right. But things might get hard on them—they'll be investigated at least."

Patrick thought of Oma's parents discovering she was gone. They must be freaking out right now, much, he guessed, as his own parents would be if he went missing. Which he supposed they might be doing right now, were this not a dream. A dream in which the person he was talking to was stressed out and obviously needing some reassurance.

"But," he said to Oma, "it's all worth it, right?"

"What's all worth it?" replied Oma, her voice tight.

"You know, saving the world, or—you know—helping to anyhow."

"It's worlds, not world."

"Oh, you mean Earth and Ith both, right?"

"Yes, and Mindth."

"What?"

"The world of dreams, the realm of the Minder. Purse-Phone is from there."

"And the Minder is who exactly?"

"The soul behind the three worlds. Some old traditions would call him or her or it a God or Holy Spirit."

"So, wait. This Commonplace stuff—it's like a religion?"

"I guess so," said Oma. "But probably not in the sense you think. You see, it's not about a God in charge of everything and the little people obeying him. It's a God who is built of everything. The Minder relies on Earth, on Ith, and on Mindth to keep sane. The Minder depends on the lives and doings of every single one of us.

308

"That," she continued, now seeming to Patrick a degree less impatient than she had been, "is why the book, the collection of everything wise, our guide, is called *The Book of Commonplace*. It all comes from the *common place*. From real life."

"So it's a book. That's what you were talking about with editors and stuff?"

"Exactly," she said. "And it's being updated all the time."

"And the government doesn't like this book."

"Ha!" she shouted more than laughed. "No, the government does *not* like this book. It's kind of exactly against everything the Deacons stand for."

"And the Deacons, they're like a group of priests or something . . ."

"No," she said, scowling, "they're not priests. They're a bunch of augmented freaks."

"What do you mean?"

"You know how the Tenth Tenet is 'You shall not harm or alter flesh of any living creature'?"

Patrick shrugged.

"Well the Deacons don't obey that one. That one's just on the books so that we peons don't try to augment our bodies or brains like they have. They're not real keen for any rivals."

"So they're, like, supervillains or something? Part super-robot?"

"Part human, part machine, total control-freak creeps," she said.

"So how are you guys going to fight them?"

"I don't really know. All I know is they called me up, and they asked that I help bring you over." She aimed her—glistening, Patrick noticed—eyes up into the sky.

"I can't believe I just left my family."

Patrick very much wanted to reassure her. He just didn't have any idea how to do it.

"Well, enough of that," she said, looking back down, her eyes purposeful and even slightly hard now. "As it says in the *Commonplace*, 'Rolling in the muck is not the best way to clean.' Sorry, I'm over it. The die's been cast and all that."

"Here we go!" boomed the giant, and sat down upon the ground so that Patrick and Oma could clamber down.

They were at the edge of a clearing and in the next pulse of lightning Patrick saw that it extended in a straight line right and left—a swath cut through the forest like for a highway, only there wasn't any pavement—just overgrown grass.

Purse-Phone wandered out in the middle of the narrow field. She appeared to be looking for something.

"Here we are!" she shouted, and bent down.

There was a scraping metallic sound.

"A manhole?" asked Patrick.

"What?" said Purse-Phone.

"Did you say *man-hole*?" asked Oma.

"Well, yeah," said Patrick.

"That's awe-some!" laughed the giant.

"Why, what do you call it?" asked Patrick.

"Umm, a maintenance access lid?" said Oma.

"Well," said Patrick, racking his brain, "I guess, you know, it's like a mouse hole or a snake hole or something: it's a hole that a man goes into."

"Well, you better get down that hole, little man," chuckled the giant. "The Peepers'll be back on their game soon enough."

"Thanks for the lift, Purse-Phone," said Oma. "And it's a thrill to have finally met you."

The giant bowed and daintily shook Oma's hand—no elbow-bumping, Patrick noticed. "Likewise, my friend. Now, just make sure you get the soothboond or you'll end up in Canada, ay?"

"The southbound what?" asked Patrick as a roaring noise erupted from the darkness below them.

"We're catching a train," said Oma.

The giant patted him gently on the back. "Be safe, little man," she said.

"Thanks," said Patrick, leaping backward as a mottled gray face peeped out of the dark hole.

"Boo!" said the face.

"Holy—*what the*—?!" shouted Patrick.

"It's just Skwurl," said Oma, laughing at Patrick's reaction.

"Aye! It's me, Skwurl the *tunnel monster*!" said Skwurl.

Patrick, the sudden picture of sheepishness, dropped his arms and hung his head as Oma and Skwurl exchanged bemused looks.

"Sorry," said Purse-Phone. "Forgot to mention I was passing you off to a new guide. I can't fit down that tiny little hole. Now, be safe down there."

"Thanks," said Patrick.

"See you later, Pursey!" said Skwurl, and then turned to Oma and Patrick. "Now come on, you two. We've got a train to catch."

CHAPTER 48
Stay Close

OMA, PATRICK, AND SKWURL WERE STANDING ON
an empty flatbed car somewhere in the middle of a
miles-long robotic train that was part of the Underground
Rail Line—URL—system. Skwurl had explained that it
was the primary method of moving freight on Ith—the
extensive tunnel system crisscrossed the entire globe, keeping the surface pristine and the surface environment un-
affected. It also offered the Commonplacers a relatively
safe method of getting themselves from place to place
without being seen.

"You're both rather narrow-shouldered," said Skwurl,

appraising Patrick and Oma's new skin-suits in the dim light of the train tunnel. "But they fit just fine. And now Patrick doesn't look so much like a bumblebee. Now go ahead and put on the headpieces, like this."

She pulled the fabric at the back of her neck forward over her head and face, joining the forward seam right to the suit's collar. It was basically like one of those Halloween Morphsuits, although there were two patches of lighter gray fabric where her eyes were, kind of like a SpiderMan costume. She struck a pose with one hand low and the other high in the air like she was holding an invisible platter.

"Really?" said Oma.

"Really," said Skwurl.

Patrick pulled his on. Amazingly, the fabric didn't seem to hinder his vision or hearing in the slightest, although it did kind of scrunch up his ears and nose.

He looked over at Oma, standing arms akimbo and apparently looking right back at him because as he turned to her she nodded her head, pivoted on one leg, and did a karate-style kick in his direction.

"Now, any questions?"

"Umm," said Patrick, "how did I get here?" He was meaning to be funny but Oma had turned and was wandering away across the open train car. And Skwurl clearly entirely missed the humor.

"Ith?" she replied. "You were transubstantiated."

"What?"

"When somebody has enough transcense and they burn it in an enclosed area, the person or persons who are in that space, they get sent to the other world."

"So, wait, does that mean I made transcense—that's how I got here?"

"I don't think so," continued Skwurl. "You see, there are two parties to a transubstantiation—the intentional one heading one way, and the unintentional one that replaces the intentional one.

"It works like a counterbalance, and since you are roughly the same mass as the agent we *intentionally* sent to Earth, you were the *unintentional* result."

"Oh," said Patrick, on some level disappointed that his kitchen sink chemistry experiment hadn't been responsible for this whole thing. "So what is transcense?"

"Transcense?" asked Skwurl. "I frankly don't know what it *is*. I just know what it does. You get enough of it, and know how to use it properly, and it can send you from Ith to Earth, or Earth to Ith. Though, like I said, always in exchange for somebody on the other world."

"Like lucky you," said Oma as she strode up next to Skwurl, apparently finished with her martial-arts moves.

"Lucky," said Patrick, trying out the word as if he'd never pronounced it before.

"So, Skwurl," asked Oma, "who was the person they sent to Earth that caused Patrick to come here?"

"Actually, Mr. BunBun's a sentient jackalope," said Skwurl.

"Wait. What?" asked Patrick.

"Part antelope, part rabbit. Only he's more antelope-sized than rabbit-sized. Same mass as you, of course."

"Oh," said Patrick. "So this, umm, Mr. BunBun landed in my house in my place?"

"Well, not exactly," said Skwurl. "There's a three-hundred-cubit displacement due to the time it takes for the process to occur, and the fact that the worlds are always in motion. So he probably didn't quite arrive *in* your house—unless your house is pretty huge."

Patrick looked at her and at Oma. It was hard to tell with their hoods on, but neither appeared to be cracking a smile. "And the reason you sent him to Earth was what?"

"To save it."

"Save *Earth*?" asked Patrick.

"Yes," said Oma.

"Huh," said Patrick.

"You don't sound all that blown away," said Skwurl. "Are you thinking that sending a jackalope to save an entire world is maybe not the greatest-sounding plan?"

316

"Let me ask you, Patrick," said Oma. "In your experience, are there a lot of giant talking jackalopes on Earth?"

"Umm, no."

"So if one showed up," she continued, "might it cause people to *ask questions*?"

"Oh," said Patrick, remembering what the superattendant had said about causing doubts. "I think I gotcha. It's kind of an attention-getter. Like, you know, a publicity stunt."

"And hopefully a massively effective one," Skwurl said. "The plan is simply to draw attention to what's about to happen on Earth so your people start asking questions and do something before it's too late."

"What's about to happen on Earth?"

"I'm right now taking you guys someplace where you can see for yourself. For now I'll only suggest that you maybe don't believe every single thing in that wikimentary you were shown. Now," Skwurl said, glancing at her binky, "let's get ready to jump."

"Jump?" said Oma, looking apprehensively over the side of the speeding train.

"What? Shouldn't we wait for the train to stop again?" asked Patrick. It was very dark down there on the rail bed but he could make out plenty of passing metal ductwork and buttresses that seemed like they might be fairly suicidal to land upon.

"It's not going to stop till after our destination," said Skwurl. "Come on, it's not going that fast. Trust me."

"Do we have a choice?" asked Oma.

"Wait—hold still—I almost forgot!" said Skwurl.

"Forgot what?" asked Patrick.

She reached up, pulled off their hoods, and stuck something in each of their left ear holes.

"Hey, what the—" said Patrick, jerking his head away and reflexively trying to pull the thing out.

"Leave it—it's an audio plug in case we get separated and I need to talk to you."

"Okay," said Patrick. "And what if I need to talk back?"

"Just talk—your hood has mic fibers. Wait—you feel that?—the train's starting to slow. Pull your head cover back on and hand me your old clothes there. We're getting close."

She threw Patrick's and Oma's former clothes out into the roaring darkness.

"That shirt wasn't very comfortable anyhow," said Patrick.

"They might spot them eventually," she explained, "but if we left them here on the train, they'd find them as soon as they offloaded. We can't be giving them clues quite *that* obvious.

"Okay," she said. "Now, join hands. And then be ready to let go after we jump."

"Wait, how fast are we going?" asked Oma.

"About a hundred kilometers a dunt," Skwurl said and leaned out over the side of the flatbed. "Just tuck and roll when you hit the ground."

Patrick did some quick math. He'd figured out last night that a dunt was about two and a half hours, and he knew a 5K run was like three miles, so converting the units, you'd get about twenty-four miles per hour.

He looked down into the pulsing darkness and considered what would happen if a person jumped out of a car going twenty-four miles per hour. He figured it probably wouldn't be fatal unless they hit something stationary, like a tree, or a rock, or a metal train-tunnel buttress.

"Are you sure—" he started to say, but just then Oma tugged on his hand, startling him. He lost his balance and fell after her into the roaring black maelstrom.

There was a sensation of weightlessness, and then Oma's hand jerked from his own, and then his left foot kicked into the ground (or, rather, the gravel bed seemed to kick into his foot), and he realized—as he tumbled like a rudely thrown rag doll—that he'd forgotten to tuck and roll.

Elbow, hip, right knee, left elbow, left side of his face all felt the full fury of the sloping gravel rail bed, and then he was lying on his back and all was still and he listened as the train continued to trundle past, and then away.

"You both okay?" said Skwurl's voice from somewhere close by in the darkness.

"I can't believe we just *did* that," said Oma, panting slightly. It was too dark to see but Patrick sensed a smile in her voice.

"I think I'm okay," said Patrick. His tailbone was killing him, and his elbow. And the side of his face. But he was pretty sure he hadn't broken anything.

"Good," said Skwurl. "Now let's go show you what the Deacons are all about."

There were some low lights along the magnetic tracks and he barely could make out the girls' receding forms. He scrambled to his feet and followed them up a series of metal rungs in the wall, through another manhole, and up into a forest clearing.

"Shouldn't be too bad a walk from here," said Skwurl. "But let's get cracking—we don't want to be strolling around in broad daylight. Quick, put the access lid back and let's get to the trees."

A noise like a foghorn boomed through the darkness and off to the east the sky glowed orange.

"Was that an alarm?! Were we spotted?!" asked Patrick.

"No, *that's* what we're going to see," said Skwurl. "Now, come on." She took off toward the woods.

"Oh," said Patrick, and dropped his eyes as the glow

turned pink and drained out of the sky. It was pretty dark now—he could just make out where the light-colored grass stopped and could see the gray, spidery silhouettes of trees against the star-pricked sky—but Skwurl's camouflage was already as hard to discern as a drop of ink in a pot of coffee.

"Hey, where'd she go?!" said Patrick to Oma. "I can't see jack."

"You can't?" asked Oma.

"No, seriously, it's *dark* out here."

"It's not so bad. Maybe it's your little Earthish eyes? Come this way," she said.

"What way?" he replied.

"Here," she said, actually taking his hand.

"Shh!" Skwurl scolded through their earpieces. "They do use microphones sometimes, too. So, if you make *enough* noise . . . wait—you're having trouble seeing? I forgot to have you engage your night vision!"

"Night vision?" asked Patrick.

"Well *that* might help," said Oma.

"Behind your head you'll feel a little bump on your suit hood, just at the base of your skull. Press it."

Patrick did as he was told and his vision exploded with green light. Now he could see all kinds of detail— the texture of the seamless asphalt, the spiky roadside grass, the young scraggly clumps of bushes toward the tree line and, just a few paces in front of him, Oma shaking her fabric-covered head in wonder. She turned and waved at him.

"See better now?" asked Skwurl.

Patrick and Oma both nodded. They could both now see her standing at the tree line.

"Sorry about that," said Skwurl. "How on Ith did you manage to stay with me coming out of the tunnel?! Let's all try to stay close, okay? Much easier to coordinate if I don't have to keep stopping to wait for you to catch up, okay?"

"Coordinate what?" asked Patrick.

"Umm, coordinate not getting caught," said Skwurl.

"And sent to a collar camp," added Oma.

"Or simply killed," said Skwurl.

"What?" said Patrick.

"You heard me—the Deacons won't be asking to play checkers if they catch us at this point."

"But what about the Tenets—they aren't supposed to harm anybody, right?"

"What, you don't have any two-faced liars on Earth?" asked Oma.

Patrick found himself wondering if Oma would get along with Lucie. Lucie was always saying presidents and everybody else in government were a bunch of lying murderers for letting wars happen and stuff like that.

"Now," said Skwurl, "let's go—it's not far from here but we want to get there before the sun comes up."

She turned and—despite her talk on staying close—sprinted into the trees. Oma obediently ran to catch up but Patrick undertook a more leisurely jog. He was enjoying his new super-vision. It was kind of like what Neil had in his high-tech FPS soldier games although the virtual-reality aspect of it was about ten times better.

He especially couldn't help marveling at the brilliant green sky. Some of the stars were brighter than streetlights, and the Milky Way was like a solid ribbon of radioactive waste in the sky.

"Patrick, get to the tree line, quick!" said Skwurl's voice in his ear.

"Huh?" he said, looking back down just in time to see Oma disappear into the forest.

"Hurry!"

Patrick heard a distant rumbling and picked up his pace. The roar grew louder and light began to lick at the tops of the leafless trees ahead of him—and rapidly began to drain downward.

He broke into a sprint and—deciding it was more important to be able to breathe than to see his surroundings in high definition—pulled down the smothering hood of his Morphsuit. It was like running through surf the way the grass and weeds slowed his steps and tugged at his feet—only it was worse than that because beaches were at least sandy and generally not littered with ankle-twisting rocks. And the closer he got to the trees, the longer the grass became, and soon he was stumbling into bushes that had to be gone around or—as they became more and more dense—plowed through.

But there was no slowing down now. The light on the trees ahead was already at the lowest branches—and growing brighter—and the roar had become so deafening he barely could hear Skwurl's shrill voice. "Lie down on the ground when you get to the trees, and stay still!"

"Patrick!" came Oma's terrified voice. "Do what she says!"

He burst through another thorny tangle of shrubs. His skin-suit might be wonderful at many things, but protecting his skin from prickers was not one of them. He would have cried out in pain if he'd had the breath to do so.

He tripped over a root and fell, brush flaying his face, hands splaying out across the mud, a fist-sized rock punching painfully into his chest.

"Unnh," he managed as he let go of what air remained in his lungs.

"Patrick!?" came Oma's hushed voice.

"I—"

"Line-of-sight in nine quints!" said Skwurl. "Stay where you are, stay absolutely still!"

Patrick flattened his cheek to the cool moist ground and watched as the world grew brighter than if there had been a dozen suns in the sky.

CHAPTER 49

Hanging on the Line

HAVING LONG SINCE FINISHED THE SAKI BOOK (which was wonderful but far too short) he'd taken from the old man's house, BunBun entered some of its lines into *The Book of Commonplace*'s "suggested entry" queue, and then proceeded to do his reading. Every day he read from *The Commonplace*—the central document of their movement, the so-far assembled total of the three worlds' wit and wisdom—and just because he was on this crazy mission didn't mean he was going to break the habit.

He snorted as he came across a quote by somebody named Martha Washington:

I'VE LEARNED FROM EXPERIENCE THAT THE GREATER PART OF OUR HAPPINESS OR MISERY DEPENDS ON OUR DISPOSITIONS AND NOT ON OUR CIRCUMSTANCES.

"Clearly," he muttered to himself, "Martha Washington was never sent on a crazy mission to an entire other sense-world and made to hide all by herself for almost two straight days without a shred of entertainment."

After making sure the little children had been safely returned (he observed the tearful reunion with Mrs. Tondorf-Schnittman from the clandestine safety of the woods), he'd had absolutely nothing to do but sit. He'd now made it through two entire nights without losing his sanity but he still had probably another half day of doing absolutely nothing before he was supposed to proceed on his mission to ring Earth's alarm bells. My-Chale had been very explicit about this. He'd told BunBun there was a good chance he would receive a message on his binky, and needed him to stay near his arrival point. After that, *then* he was clear to go play Paul Revere and put his life in *real* jeopardy.

For now, he supposed, at least he was safe. He'd deployed a decoy program (a digital ghost of his binky that leapt from cell phone tower to cell phone tower making Ith-protocol transmissions) to throw Rex's killers off his trail.

So far, it seemed, so good. Perhaps they really believed

he'd headed east into the region the "Google Map" called "Connecticut." By now his transcense trail had entirely decomposed so they'd be relying on standard electronic surveillance only. And doubtless they wouldn't assume he'd have stayed put, spending the night behind the steering wheel of a golf cart parked inside a country-club storage shed, less than a quarter mile from where he'd first arrived, just . . . sitting.

It was a good thing the Minder had given him a fluffy tail.

CHAPTER 50
Proving Ground

PATRICK STAYED MOTIONLESS—EXCEPT FOR HIS furiously beating heart—for a couple minutes as the aircraft's roar faded.

"You can get up," said Skwurl. "They've moved on."

Patrick rolled over and pulled his night-vision hood back over his face. Oma had run out of the woods and was now reaching down to help him up.

"And this evening's lesson," she said, "is . . ."

"Stay close?" said Patrick as he took her hand.

"Think you two can remember that?" asked Skwurl's voice.

Patrick brushed at the leaves and mud all over his skin-suit. "Were they looking for us?"

"Probably not for *us* in particular," said Skwurl. "They would have been a bit more persistent in that case. No, I don't think they expect we could have gotten so far so quickly—hopefully our decoys will have them looking in other directions. But that was definitely an *active* patrol. I'm guessing either we or some deer triggered a motion detector, or were spotted in a low-res sat scan.

"Anyhow," she continued, "we've lost at least a deuce now—we need to get going if we're going to get there by sunrise."

Still not having any idea where "there" was, Patrick and Oma followed Skwurl up a steep forested slope to a level patch of ground. The woods stretched out ahead of them and, beyond, through the leafless, mossy oaks and maples, there was a glow—maybe the first traces of morning light—bleeding up into the sky.

"What's that smell?" Patrick panted—there was something like burning rubber on the breeze. And then there was a low rumbling.

"And that noise?" asked Oma.

"You'll see soon enough," said Skwurl.

"What the—?" said Patrick.

They had entered a grassy clearing. A large, red-roofed, dilapidated, tan brick building stood to one side. It was unlike any of the sleek modern buildings he'd so far seen here on Ith. It was really much more Earth-like—blocky, old-fashioned, the patterned bricks around its vaulted windows generally looking like they had been laid by hand, not machine. It reminded Patrick of the convent above the reservoir where the Griffins sometimes ice-skated in the winter.

"What is this place? It looks pretty old," said Patrick.

"I think it was part of a college or something," said Skwurl.

"Wait," said Patrick. "Didn't they say it was fifty years ago that Rex arrived and this whole world was living in the Stone Age—"

Skwurl exchanged a look with Oma. "We'll talk about *that* later," she said cryptically. They jogged around a corner of the building and skirted a brick wall that had been painted with a small white spot inside a large black one.

"What's that?" said Patrick, stopping to get his breath back as much as because he was curious.

"Yin wins," said Oma.

"What?"

"You know Yin and Yang?"

"Like that Chinese symbol thing?"

"Buddhist," explained Oma.

"You know about Buddhism?" asked Patrick.

"Yeah, I've been doing some extracurricular reading

here and there," Oma replied. "Anyhow, so this is what it looks like when Yin beats Yang's butt."

"Huh?"

"It's from *The Book of Commonplace*. That's what that BCP thing is, and then the section and paragraph."

Patrick walked up close to the circle. The paint was fairly fresh. "Who made it?"

"An agent. Skwurl, do you know who painted it?"

"A pretty senior one," said Skwurl.

"Why do you say that?" Oma asked.

Skwurl ignored the questions and kept on walking.

"And what about the other graffiti I've seen?" asked Patrick. "What was the point of those messages?"

"What others have you seen?" asked Oma.

"He means the one I left on the bathroom mirror," said Skwurl.

"Something about how the Seer does well because she listens," said Patrick. "But the Hearer didn't listen, so he's dead, right?"

"Yeah, something like that," said Skwurl.

"So there was a Hearer?" asked Patrick. "And he was on Earth?"

"Well, an important thing with that one is to know where it came from. I didn't have time to write that part out."

"Where'd it come from?" asked Oma.

"One of Rex's communications experts," said Skwurl. "An otherwise anonymous stooge named Franklin Shone."

"Why would you quote one of Rex's people?" asked Patrick.

"*The Book of Commonplace* recognizes all useful contributions. It doesn't matter if you're an evil warlord, a carpenter, or a friendless clerk. If it helps a reader understand the world, it goes in."

"And what about the message on the side of the school?" asked Patrick. "The one about not trusting people with two first names."

"I know about that one!" said Oma. "You see, last names are often so abstract, right? But first names are generally familiar. So if you have a first name as a last name, it most always seems recognizable to people. So basically Rex *Abraham* and all his henchmen always have a second name that can be a first name because they've discovered it makes them even a tiny degree more popular and recognizable than they would be otherwise."

"Rex sounds like a weird dude," said Patrick.

"You don't know weird till you know Rex," said Skwurl.

"Wait," said Patrick. "You're talking about Rex like he's alive? But the story about the girl and the vaccine—"

"Didn't she tell you not to believe every wikimentary you see?" said Oma.

"So, but, where is he?" asked Patrick.

"Umm, on *Earth*," said Skwurl.

"Wait," said Patrick, stopping in his tracks. "He's there right now?"

"He's been there all your life."

"But—" said Patrick, trying to figure out if that was remotely possible.

"We'll get into it later," she said. "Here, we're almost to the overlook."

Skwurl led them across the field to an old stone bench in the middle of a patch of bare rock. It was still too dark to see but he had the impression they were up pretty high.

"Where are we—the top of a mountain?" asked Patrick, gesturing toward the darkness ahead of them. The brightening predawn sky began lower than where he'd have expected the horizon to be, and he had a sense of emptiness before, and below, them.

"Cliffs, actually," said Skwurl. "We're above the Palisades."

"Wait—like the ones along the Hudson River?" asked Patrick.

"That's what people *used* to call it," Oma replied.

"What's going on?" Patrick asked, not doing a very good job of disguising his uneasiness.

"Watch right there," said Skwurl.

"Oh my God," said Patrick as a cloud moved off the horizon and the predawn sky illuminated a broken, crooked, but instantly recognizable landscape. "But, they said—"

CHAPTER 51

Sibling Relations

MONDAY MORNING THE TWINS GOT UP AT THE crack of dawn.

Being just four years old of course they had been less impacted by the traumas and dramas of the past two days. They were aware that their brother Patrick was missing but it wasn't something keenly disturbing to them. The rest of their family had explained he was just on a trip and would be back.

And as for their own brief disappearance Saturday morning (they'd been found by Laura Tondorf-Schnittman shortly before one o'clock on the golf course, not far from the ninth hole), there were no lingering aftereffects other than an obsession with a character named Dear Rabbit.

Indeed, as Lucie—herself wakened early by a strange dream—came down from her room, she found them in the third floor hallway talking to Neil about the creature.

"No," Paul was correcting Neil, holding a plastic allosaurus in front of his older brother's face. "THIS ONE is DEAR RABBIT."

"Mom and Dad banish you to Jurassic Park?" Lucie asked.

"Nah," said Neil, clearly a little embarrassed to be seen playing dinosaurs-and-mammoths with his youngest siblings. "Just seemed like, you know—"

He broke off, entirely disconcerted that his big sister was smiling at him without a trace of sarcasm or irony. This was not the Lucie he was used to seeing first thing in the morning. He knew it was not right to think that Patrick's disappearance was a good thing, but it sure was interesting how it seemed to be changing all the members of his family.

Lucie sat down on the stair. Cassie backed up against her leg.

"You think he ran away?" Neil asked his older sister.

"He's being Dear Rabbit!" the little girl said, pointing at the plastic allosaurus.

"Ah," said Lucie.

"I don't think he's the sort of kid who would run away," said Neil, answering his own question. "Now *I* might run away. In fact I was thinking of doing it next weekend. So I could go see that squid since there's no way Mom and Dad would ever let me otherwise. But, Patrick?"

"I don't know," said Lucie. "Whatever happened, clearly he's capable of surprises. He's always been a still-waters-run-deep kinda kid, you know?"

"What am I, a puddle?"

"Of Mountain Dew," said Lucie.

"Well, *awl* right then," said Neil. "As long as we have that straight."

"Dear Rabbit buried a squirrel," interrupted Paul.

"A dinosaur buried a squirrel?" asked Lucie, smiling.

"No, *Dear Rabbit* buried a squirrel," said Cassie.

"Ah," said Lucie indulgently.

"How big was it—this rabbit?" asked Neil, strangely serious all of a sudden.

Lucie looked at her brother curiously. Maybe he just spent so little time with the kids that he didn't understand the line between whimsy and downright weird.

"Big!" said Cassie.

"Like a big dog?" asked Neil.

Both children nodded.

"Holy *crap*," said Neil. "It's not Dear Rabbit, is it? It's *Deer* Rabbit. Where'd you see it?!"

"At Phoebe and Chloe's pond," said Paul.

"The other morning when you guys went out on the golf course, right? And it had antlers like this?" he said, putting his fingers up on his forehead.

"Neil, what are you doing?" asked Lucie.

"I saw it, too," he said.

"Neil, you shouldn't mess with their minds like that—"

"I'm not messing. I *saw* it. It's why Dad and I had an accident on Saturday—it ran across the road—*hopped* across the road, actually—and we almost hit it! I knew I hadn't gone crazy!"

"Wait. Wait. What?"

"I kid you not. It was like this big rabbit with antlers— like one of them whatchamacallits—jackalopes. Only big. Dad said it was a dog but he didn't get a good look, he was too busy freaking out because I was trying to look up about the giant squid on his iPhone."

"And he smells like church," said Cassie.

Here Lucie sat up, remembering the smell of incense in the house the morning Patrick disappeared.

"Where'd the Deer Rabbit go?" asked Neil.

"To see the dinosaurs," said Paul.

"And mammoths," said Cassie.

"And you say he buried a squirrel at the golf course?"

The twins nodded.

"If we go there, can you show us where you saw him?" Neil stood.

"Umm, we are *not* taking the Twins over to the golf course," said Lucie.

"Why not? It's, like, not even seven yet. And Mom and Dad said yesterday we weren't going to school today with Patrick still missing. Just like we didn't have to go to church yesterday. Plus, Mom and Dad will appreciate it if we take the kids for a walk, get them out of their hair. Come on."

"Are you serious?"

"Patrick disappears and there's a weird animal wandering around town? Don't you think there might be a connection? Don't you think we should at least check it out?"

"But what will there be to see? If there is a big rabbit deer, it's probably not even there anymore."

"I don't know. Maybe it left footprints? Maybe we can track it. Let's bring your phone so we can take pictures, okay?"

Lucie looked down at the kids.

"You guys want to go look for the big rabbit?"

"And dinosaurs!" said Paul.

"And mammoths!" said Cassie.

"And griffins!" said Paul.

Lucie had been smiling at them but the corners of her mouth fell into a line at her littlest brother's saying this.

"Griffins like our last name you mean?" she asked.

Paul shook his head. "Griffins that fly!" he said.

"Sure, why not?" said Neil.

"Let's go," said Lucie. The dream that she'd just had this morning—she'd been running through turnstiles, like for a subway or the entrance to an amusement park. They seemed to go on forever, and she didn't know what they were for, but she just kept going through them. But then a voice had come to her, telling her to stop. A deep voice from overhead. Circling high above was a griffin. He'd told her to wake up and go help her family. And that Patrick was just fine.

CHAPTER 52
Site Seeing

PATRICK RECALLED THE SCENE AT THE END OF THE original *Planet of the Apes* movie—one of Neil's and his father's favorites—in which the astronaut hero sees the Statue of Liberty's torch sticking up above the sand and realizes that—rather than being a different world—the chimp-ruled planet he's landed on is actually a future Earth. (The astronaut had gone through a time rift up in space, Dad had explained, like it was perfectly normal.) "You maniacs!" the man yells, condemning his fellow humans for presumably destroying the world as it was.

There was no sign of the Statue of Liberty from here but the smoldering skyline on the other side of the river sure looked like New York City. His eyes locked on the Empire State Building. It was missing its antenna mast—and the light of the eastern horizon was shining through its left side like it had been gutted by fire—but he'd done a fifth-grade project on the construction of what had once been the world's tallest building, and he knew he wasn't mistaken. There was no sign of the Nordstrom Tower to the north, nor the Freedom Tower beyond to the south, and it seemed like a lot of other buildings had been knocked down—there were big gaps in the skyline like missing teeth in a giant's jawbone—but from the shape of the river to the nearby steel towers of the George Washington Bridge, there was no question that he was looking at New York City . . . a *ruined* New York City.

And now, even as he and Oma and Skwurl watched, one of the remaining skyscrapers wobbled and fell, a plume of dust rising into the sky in its place. A moment later, the tremendous boom of the collapse reached their ears.

"I *knew* it," said Oma.

"What the—?" said Patrick.

"A little hard to jibe with the stories they were telling you yesterday, right, Patrick?" asked Skwurl. "We were still living in the Stone Age fifty years ago here on Ith and all the technological wonders around us were brought to us by Rex? The world was a dark and primitive place till the light of the Minder lit up the world?"

"What *is* this place?" he asked.

"Here? New Jersey, you mean?" replied Skwurl.

"No, I mean this *whole* place."

"You starting to accept that maybe this isn't a dream?" she asked.

Or maybe, he considered, what they were seeing just made it even more certain to be one. "Why are they knocking down New York City?"

"It's one of the last few bits of evidence left. The bigger sites—because they're more work to erase—they've left for last. But Oma's town used to have other houses in it. And that building behind us, that'll be torn down pretty soon. Probably tomorrow. The Reclamation Squad is working its way up this side of the Atlantic Coast right now. Here," she said, standing and leading him to a patch of woods to their right.

She led them down a path and then out to a bulge farther down the cliff. There, through a gap in the trees, they could see the river's near shore. A large crane was docked directly below them. People in green work suits were driving machinery back and forth from what looked to be an old boatyard. Old white-hulled boats and a few outbuildings were being broken up and their wreckage taken over to a pile by the shore so that the crane could dump it out in the river.

"See anything interesting about those workers down there?" Skwurl asked.

"They're wearing green and they don't like boats?" said Patrick.

"Say '20-X' to your suits," she said.

"What? Okay, '20-X,'" he said, and nearly lost his balance. It was as if he'd been shot out of a cannon—the command had caused his view to telescope so that he felt like he was only twenty yards rather than a quarter mile from the scene.

"They're all wearing those collars," said Patrick as he got his bearings. The people in the green suits were wearing blue fabric collars like the animals he'd seen in the Pubers' hometown. He realized these must be some of the people Oma had told him about when they'd been in the exercise park.

"Belties!" said Oma.

"Criminals and enemies of the Deacons," said Skwurl. "Conscripted for manual labor, and especially for the sort they can't have regular citizens knowing about."

"What'd they do? Were they Commonplacers?" asked Patrick.

"Some were. But many were people who were just in

the wrong place at the wrong time, and also any survivors of the Purge."

Patrick's telescoped vision locked on a woman shoveling debris. Her face was tear-streaked and she seemed to be talking to herself like she was crazy. He hastily aimed his eyes at the horizon and told his suit to turn off the zoom.

"I've never seen one in real life before, only heard the stories," said Oma. "It's so *sick*, Skwurl."

"How can it happen? How can they enslave people and get away with it?" asked Patrick.

"Remember," said Skwurl, "how they told you that fifty years ago a virus killed every person over the age of three but the Seer? Well, when you have a population of a couple billion, even the craziest genetically engineered virus isn't going to get *every*body. So they captured and collared all the adult survivors and turned them into secret slaves."

"What?" said Patrick.

"Crazy, right?" said Skwurl. "But you know the first thing Rex had mass-produced after the virus particle, and its vectors? MoK collars. Kind of revealing, don't you think?"

"What's it like?" he asked.

"What, living in a world run by a bunch of evil freaks?" replied Skwurl.

"No," said Patrick. "I just meant wearing one of those collars."

"Well," said Skwurl, "you can still think your own thoughts and speak your own words, but basically from the neck down, you're just along for the ride. Depending where you are, certain motions are mandatory, allowed, or prohibited. They set up grids and algorithms so a single operator can oversee up to a hundred belties."

"Does it hurt like they say it does?" asked Oma.

"Imagine not just having no control of your body, but *somebody else* controlling it."

Patrick and Oma both nodded.

"Well," said Skwurl. "My replacement should be here any second and I've got to get back to the train."

"Where are you going?" asked Oma.

"Back to headquarters," said Skwurl. "We've got a lot going on."

"But—" Patrick started to say.

"Don't worry," she said, already hurrying back up the path. "You're in good hands . . . or something."

As they watched her disappear into the woods there was a soft whooshing noise in the sky behind them, and a sudden wind. They quickly turned and saw—coming in just over the treetops—a sight that fairly proved to Patrick that this indeed was all a dream.

CHAPTER 53
Twin Tailings

WHERE ARE *THEY* GOING?" ASKED CARLY. SHE'D been standing at the window halfheartedly looking for her cat—it seemed to have disappeared along with her brother. Or maybe a day before or after. She couldn't say for sure. It wasn't like she saw it every single day. But nobody could remember having seen it in at least a day, and they'd looked through the entire house yesterday. It was definitely gone.

Eva, who'd been sullenly eating a bowl of granola at the center counter, looked up from her iPhone and asked her younger sister what she was talking about.

"Lucie, Neil, and the Twins. They're going someplace."

"What?" asked Eva. Because of all the hubbub about Patrick's having gone missing, their parents had instructed them to stay home—no church or sports yesterday, no school today. She got up from her stool and joined Carly at the window, just catching a glimpse of the four figures turning off the driveway and down the sidewalk.

"Isn't that weird?" asked Carly.

"That's more than weird—it's seven in the morning. I don't think I've ever seen Lucie or Neil up at seven in the morning, umm, ever."

"What do you think they're doing? And why are they bringing the Twins?"

"Freaky. Let's follow them."

Carly looked at her older sister, wondering if she'd ever said "let's" do anything to her before. "Sure," she replied, trying not to seem too excited. "Why not? Should we go tell Mom and Dad?"

"I don't think so," said Eva. "Let's just leave a note."

MY-CHALE!" SAID OMA, AWESTRUCK.

"Hello, Oma Puber," said the griffin, his voice deep and slow as he tucked his enormous wings along his leonine flanks.

"And you are Patrick," it said with a kindly wink that somehow reminded Patrick of his school librarian, Mr. Kirschner.

"Yes, hi," said Patrick, unsuccessfully trying—along with Oma—not to stare too hard at the fantastic creature. Its feathers glinted like they were spun from metal fibers, its beak was massive and intimidating, and its eyes were large and somehow human despite the lack of eyebrows or even regular lids. He was also struck that while its body was definitely that of a lion's, it was that of a lion at least three times bigger than any he'd ever seen at a zoo—the creature was as tall at the shoulder as one of those big Budweiser horses, and doubtless a whole lot heavier.

And yet once again—as with Purse-Phone the giant—Patrick somehow didn't feel any fear of the apparent monster in front of him. Despite the wicked beak, the massive claws, the overall sense he had that it could have plucked a small car from the highway and flown off with it, there was something considerate, respectful, and even shy in its manner.

"Let's get inside the old building," it said, gesturing back up the path. "The sky-eyes will be back online momentarily."

Oma and Patrick mutely followed the enormous eagle-lion back to the sand-colored building, entering the debris-strewn lobby through its splayed, broken-hinged front doors.

"I hate to be brusque," began the griffin, sitting back on its haunches in front of what looked to have been a reception desk, "but we don't have much time. And we have a problem to address."

"What problem?" asked Patrick.

"The fact that you still think you're dreaming."

"What makes you say that?" said Patrick.

"Most people, the first time they see a griffin, they get a little worked up. In fact, they tend to *flip out*. But you seem pretty composed. Like you probably have decided that you're *imagining* me."

Patrick figured there was no point being less than honest about it and nodded.

"These past two days have been implausibly strange, have they not? So strange that you have decided that you can't be awake and that the reason you don't remember any other dream being like this—so detailed, so intricate, so real, so complete—is that the *details* of dreams are forgotten when people wake up from them."

"Well," said Patrick, "I mean all of this is pretty, umm"—the word *unrealistic* popped into his head, but he worried it might be unkind to say—"*different* from what I'm used to."

"But is it *so* different that you can't possibly believe it to be the same reality that you believed in the day before yesterday?

"Sometimes it helps to think of a problem the other way around," continued the griffin. "One might ask, how can a person who's awake ever prove that what's around them is *not* a dream?"

"Well, that's pretty easy," said Patrick. "Doesn't it kind of depend on what you know to be usual?"

"Usual?" asked Oma.

"Well, what you're used to. Real life goes on for longer than a dream, right? So you're more used to it. And it fits with what you know when you're awake. Like, until two days ago, I never heard about a place called Ith where everybody's eyes are big and their ears are small and there are giants and griffins and sky-cars and stuff."

"But why, then," asked the griffin, "does it seem like it's all part of the same experience? Is it *usual* that while you're in a dream you remember everything from your *waking life*?"

"Well, I mean," replied Patrick. "I thought about that but maybe it happens all the time, and—like other details— you just forget it when you wake up?"

"That," said My-Chale, "is called the Dreamer's Dodge: people will forgive their actions, or inactions, because they treat life itself as a dream. It's a practice especially common among people who believe in an afterlife that is more substantial and meaningful than this one."

"So—I'm sorry—what's your point?" asked Patrick.

"If you *suspect* something is a dream, then you'll care somewhat less about what happens to somebody in it, and how your actions affect them, than you would if you believed it was *real life*, right? You'll maybe give yourself an out. You'll maybe make excuses, you'll maybe feel okay dodging a responsibility you feel to them—and especially so if that responsibility is difficult."

This made sense to Patrick. If you thought something was just a passing dream, you wouldn't care quite as much than if you didn't.

"So you want to be sure I care about you?"

"I'm not talking about me, or even us," My-Chale said, gesturing at Oma. "I'm talking about how we are trying to save three entire worlds from a peril that has already ravaged one, is about to subsume another, and will not stop until it has destroyed the third. We are up against a man who has more power than any being in all of history. The chances of us prevailing are slim to begin with. And, if our greatest hope isn't quite sure that it's all even happening—"

"And you're saying *I'm* your greatest hope? You do know I'm twelve? And that I don't have any superpowers except, maybe, for having a better sense of hearing than most people here?"

The griffin allowed himself a quick laugh—far more lion- than bird-like—before continuing. "The people of Ith have been enslaved by Rex. Rex is the one and only person from Earth they've ever known. And they revere him like a deity. You are from Earth, too. It wouldn't take a very clever schemer to portray you as something of a second coming, a prophet even.

"The Deacons were entirely surprised by your arrival— if you sensed a little confusion about what to do with you, that's because they were fighting among themselves

354

about what to do with you. Some wanted to kill you immediately, and prevent news of your arrival from getting out there.

"But the faction that prevailed watched you and decided that you weren't a threat, and they had this realization. You, Patrick Griffin, could be made into a very powerful propaganda tool for them. That invitation to Silicon City was basically an excuse to get you out there so their media experts could get you 'on message' and train you to be a public relations figure, a celebrity to help maintain the order."

"And I would have agreed to it?"

"You might not have. Perhaps you would have seen through their lies, perhaps you would have resisted— perhaps taking courage in the thought that it was just a dream. And, in that case, probably they would have engineered a convenient way for you to disappear from public view."

"Disappear, like, kill me? How do you know all this?" asked Patrick.

"We Mindthlings have some abilities to see things in dreams. And since—for all the machinery in their heads— Deacons still dream, every so often we get some crumbs of useful information."

"So," said Oma, "the Deacons wanted Patrick to be a public relations tool for them. But isn't that what we're asking him to be for us now?"

"Yes, that's true," said My-Chale.

"Though they started it," said Oma.

"And," said My-Chale, "I think you'll also see we will not be lying, coercing, or giving him drugs as we *ask* him to do this great favor for us."

"And what am I supposed to do? You want me to tell them the Deacons are bad? That Rex was a fraud?"

"That might be useful," said Oma.

My-Chale turned to Oma. "Had you ever seen a ruin before today?"

Oma shook her head. "I'd heard of them—" Her voice quavered.

"Oma is a recruit to our cause," continued My-Chale, "and even she has barely an idea of the magnitude of what Rex did here. For the sake of power, for the sake of control, he destroyed an entire world. Nearly three billion souls died here that horrible year. And now Rex is on Earth preparing more than twice that for the same fate."

"He's really there," said Patrick, trying to wrap his head around the implications of this. If it were true, if it were real, didn't that mean his entire family—

"The people of this world will listen to you," said My-Chale. "They can push back on the Deacons. They can maybe even do enough to distract Rex, to help prevent him from going ahead with his plan. It will be a difficult path. But you see why we absolutely need you to *believe*?"

Maybe he was just tired, but Patrick was having more and more trouble resisting their logic. If nothing else he was going to have to admit that he must be pretty crazy himself to dream up something so mind-blowingly strange as all this.

"I need to stop believing this is a dream to do the job right is what you're saying?"

"Yes."

"Okay," said Patrick. He was starting to get frustrated, and maybe even angry. He felt like they were talking in complete circles. "So, prove it. *Prove* to me it's real already. You guys know all this stuff, and you still haven't gotten me to believe this crazy crap."

"And how can we do that?" asked My-Chale sadly. "What would *proof* be?"

"I don't know, maybe if I could be awake on Earth so I could remember all of this and realize it wasn't just a regular dream . . ."

"Yes," said My-Chale. "It still might not work, but that's what we were thinking, too. We will send you back to Earth."

"You're going to send me back to *Earth*?!"

"Skwurl told you about transubstantiation," said Oma.

"We have just enough transcence for a round trip," said My-Chale.

"A round trip?"

"So you can return, too," he replied. "*If* you wish to."

Patrick found himself staring at Oma's enormous eyes. She seemed as surprised at all this as he was.

"So the plan is you'll send me back to Earth and then *I* get to decide if this is all real and then, *if* I want to, I can come back? You'd let me go just like that?"

"It has to be this way," she said, the situation dawning on her. "It has to be *your* decision to come back, Patrick."

The griffin inclined his head and, without a trace of smile in his voice, said, "Patrick, we're sending you home."

CHAPTER 55

Point of Some Return

PATRICK WAS LYING ON THE FLOOR OF THE abandoned building's boiler room. The door was closed (the griffin said it was important that transcense be trapped in a nearly airtight area so that it could achieve suitable concentrations).

He reviewed the transubstantiation preparations Oma and the griffin, My-Chale, had made him memorize:

One: Lie down on your back.
Two: Hold close any items you wish to bring with you.
Three: Close your eyes and relax.

Four: Do not struggle—let your impulses run free.

Five: Hold fast to your mantra.

Well, he could check off the first one. Oma had found a somewhat clean rug, and he was definitely lying upon it, on his back. He looked over at the burbling censer, the metal cylinder that contained the transcense, a half dozen paces away on the floor. Scary, squid-like tendrils of inky vapor were already snaking their way across toward him.

He shut off the binky and clutched it, and his return ticket—a second censer My-Chale had given him—to his chest. It contained nearly all of the Commonplacers' remaining stockpile of transcense. In other words, there would be nobody coming after him to help and, if he didn't use it come back to Ith, he'd never see My-Chale or Oma or anybody from Ith again.

He closed his eyes and concentrated on his relaxation exercises. My-Chale had told him to flex and loosen his toes, then his feet, then his ankles, and so on up to his forehead.

It seemed to be working pretty well and, having managed to get through the full course twice, he was nearly at the edge of sleep when he was racked by the world's most massive sneeze, a blast so forceful his ears rang and his muscles went all crampy and sore.

"My mantra!" he whispered to himself. Oma had

explained it as a combination of familiar words or sounds that would help him focus; something nostalgic was good, she said, but it absolutely had to be something he knew by heart. He ended up deciding to go with a nonsense rhyme that his father used to read to him and Neil before they went to bed when they were little.

It was called "Song of the Stuntman" (even though it was a poem, not a song) and it went,

All right
All set
All fright
No net

He whispered it to himself, once, twice, then partway through a third time before a familiar keening tone filled his ears.

CHAPTER 56

Fosse aux Lions

YOU'RE GETTING CLOSE," SAID REX. HE WAS teleconferencing with Victor Pierre, the highest-ranked of all his novitiates. A rainy suburban scene was visible through the car's rear window behind the man's angular face.

"Yes, Your Awareness. Estimate three terts to the insertion point." Victor's voice betrayed nothing but cold-blooded mastery.

"Good, very good," said Rex. "Now, don't let me distract you. Report back as soon as—what's that?! What's going on?"

Victor was checking his mirrors and appeared to be slowing his car. Red and blue pulses of light stained the teleconference projection.

"Nothing significant, Your Awarenence," replied Victor. "Just a local law enforcement vehicle."

The sound of sirens rose and faded.

"They're dealing with a missing-person report," the aspiring Deacon continued. "Still no reports they've discovered the enemy combatant's arrival."

Rex knew this already. He hadn't been fomenting a telecommunications revolution on this planet so that he would *not* be able to tell what was going on in any corner of it at any moment in time.

And especially so if it had anything to do with a transubstantiation event. He'd been studying the transubstantiation process for close to a hundred years and he knew everything that there was to be known about it—how to initiate it, how to control it (at least to the extent it could be), and certainly how to detect it.

This was how—two days ago—he had almost immediately known about the arrival of the first Commonplace agent in and the simultaneous disappearance of the Griffin boy from a small town in suburban New York. And this is why he now knew of the arrival of yet another Commonplace agent—this time in rural France—and, from the ensuing police broadcasts there, the sudden, inexplicable (at least to the locals) disappearance of one Lilian Carruth, a retired secondary school language teacher.

"Well then, I'm going to leave you to it, Victor," continued Rex. "You know the desired outcome."

"I do, Your Awarenence."

"Report back as soon as your objective is achieved."

"Of course," replied the stone-faced man.

Rex shut off the teleconference application. He was distinctly annoyed, but not very worried. Of all the places for an enemy to have arrived—for it to have landed within a thirty-tert drive of Victor Pierre's residence—it was, if not quite in the den, at least just about at the lion's doorstep.

Now Victor's colleagues on the east coast of North America had just to finish taking care of the other visitor, the rabbit creature, and Rex could fully turn his attentions back to the final preparations for Earth's cleansing and rebirth.

CHAPTER 57

Surreptitious Returns

COLD RAIN JOLTED PATRICK AWAKE—*REALLY, really* awake. His eyelids fluttered open and left him staring up into the gray, drenching sky.

He rolled over and sat up. He was in a muddy, weed-filled lot surrounded by low stucco walls and a rusted chain-link fence.

He was light-headed and disoriented but was struck that this place just felt, well, *real* somehow. He was in the rain and he wanted to go inside and get dried off and warmed up. This was not the sort of thing you dreamed about—it was too boring, too normal, too usual, wasn't it? This was not an experience filled with big-eyed people, giants, sky-cars, or griffins. This was being outside on a rainy day. Which was weird in itself but . . . He let the thought trail off and started to sit up. But as he went to place his hands on the wet ground he realized that each was clutching something: his right held his binky, his left the transcense censer.

And the fact of these two things he could see in his own hands meant that the dream, or nondream, was still going on.

And that meant Rex Abraham was quite possibly a real person in this dream or nondream. And that meant, as My-Chale the griffin had warned him—whether dream or not—he didn't have much time.

There was a road nearby and he decided it was probably best that he get out of sight. He staggered across the lot, reached a low row of just-budding fruit trees, and dashed to the overhang of a doorless one-car garage. A rust-spotted white van was parked inside.

Patrick breathed deeply, taking in the loamy smell of the rain-damp air. After pocketing the return-trip censer, he reached down to grab a handful of wet brown dirt. He supposed at least it *seemed* like Earth. What exactly had *not* seemed Earth-like about the dirt or the rain or the plants of Ith he couldn't quite say.

He also couldn't say quite where he was, although he

was pretty sure—judging from the skinny, white, black-lettered license plate on the van, and from the small stucco houses with the flower-pot-tiled roofs—he had not landed in Hedgerow Heights. My-Chale had warned him that there was no controlling a transubstantiation in terms of where one would arrive.

He looked down at his binky.

"Location and time," he whispered.

The rain-beaded screen promptly displayed:

Mauléon-Licharre, France, EU local time 2:46 p.m.
Monday, March 14, 2016

So he was in France. Sure, why not? He could call his Uncle Andrew from there as well as from anywhere on Earth—his binky just needed to be able to find a cell tower or satellite. It was just, of course, between the worlds that calls were physically impossible. An electromagnetic signal doesn't have any more ability to travel through the fabric of reality than a thrown rock does, My-Chale had explained.

And then he would call his parents, too. Afterward.

The reason for calling Uncle Andrew first was that—probably even in a dream and definitely in real life—his parents would be freaked out and would only confuse things. Uncle Andrew, on the other hand, was a scientist; he'd care about Patrick's situation, but he was more likely to keep his head. He'd help Patrick actually figure things out and decide what to do, rather than—as he was sure his parents would do—insisting he call the police and get home. He'd talked all this through with My-Chale (who nevertheless felt he needed to call his parents and tell them he was okay—they'd have been missing him for almost two days now), and they'd agreed that talking to Uncle Andrew first made the most sense. Unless something else happened first to convince Patrick this wasn't—or was—all a dream.

"Current time Washington, DC," he whispered next.

8:47 a.m. Monday, March 14, 2016

"All telephone listings for Andrew Lancaster Meyer, Washington, DC."

Uncle Andrew's telephone numbers and address appeared on the screen. Patrick took a deep breath and placed the call to his cell number. It rang once, twice, three times, four times, and then went to voice mail. He tried Uncle Andrew's work and home numbers next but, again, no answer.

They'd talked this possibility through, he and My-Chale, but disappointment and worry still gnawed at his stomach. It was always possible Uncle Andrew would be away from his phone—in the shower, out for a jog, commuting to work, asleep with the ringer turned off, whatever. Patrick jabbed his sneaker toe into the ground, dislodging a divot of muddy earth in frustration.

The seesaw sound of sirens came to him through the rain. He popped his head out from around the side of the garage and saw four little police cars coming off the main road and zooming down the lane that bordered the far end of the scrubby lot. They stopped in front of the multi-level gray house at the far corner of the field.

Probably, he guessed, they were investigating a report of a missing person, and a mysterious cloud of transcense smoke. My-Chale had reminded him about how his transubstantiation was going to cause somebody from Earth to go back to Ith in his place. Whenever somebody goes to one world, a replacement comes back for him or her. Again, this was why when My-Chale had sent the agent BunBun to Earth, Patrick had been swapped out to Ith.

He tried Uncle Andrew one more time, but still there was no answer. He was starting to feel some real panic now. What if this whole thing was true about Rex unleashing a plague on Earth? And about his Deacons on Ith meaning to finally kill all the Commonplacers including My-Chale and Skwurl and Oma? And about him, Patrick, actually being able to make a difference about any of it?

But now a new dark thought entered his head. My-Chale had said Rex—who for years would have been plugged into everything happening on Earth—would know Patrick's name. Would know that *he* had been the person who had counterbalanced. He'd have intercepted the police reports. And he'd have detected the transubstantiation itself— both the Commonplace agent BunBun's arrival and Patrick's disappearance.

And My-Chale and Skwurl had also said he would not have much time. When Rex—if there really was a Rex— detected Patrick's current transubstantiation, he'd doubt- less think the Commonplacers had sent another trained agent. And he'd send his own agents to try to kill it.

But what occurred to Patrick now was something he and My-Chale and Skwurl *hadn't* discussed—what would happen if Rex somehow had figured out that it was Pat- rick who had come back? And suspected he was working with Rex's enemies, the Commonplacers of Ith? What if the reason Uncle Andrew hadn't answered the phone just now was that Rex had gotten to him? What if Rex had got- ten to his entire family? If he was as bad as everybody said he was, might he not hold Patrick's entire family hostage? Or even kill them?

He tried calling Uncle Andrew a third time and still there was no answer. This time he left a message, "Hi, Uncle Andrew, it's Patrick, your nephew. Um. I'm calling from, uh, well, I guess you can't call me back because I don't think I have a number on this phone but anyhow, and I'm not sure how long I'm going to be around, but I'm okay. I'm going to call my parents now but in case I don't get through, please tell them I'm okay, all right? Okay, love you. Hope I see you soon."

He lowered the binky. Had that been a mistake? My-Chale and Oma had said his phone was secure but might Rex be able to hear Uncle Andrew's voice mails?

He was starting to feel really sick to his stomach. Dream or not, this was all too crazy and complicated to figure out.

One thing he knew, though, was he had to call his parents and make sure they were okay, and knew he was okay.

Not doing that—even if it was just a risk that all this was happening and wasn't a dream—would be inexcusable.

He'd dial the house first. Somebody should be home. It would be about nine in the morning there. But before he could say the phone number his binky vibrated. There was a message on his screen, written in regular English:

Dear Patrick,

I had your binky programmed to send a message to the agent we sent to Earth. Again, his name is BunBun. I just wanted to let him know that you were

371

here. I hope you don't think I've taken advantage,
but it was complicated to explain and we have so
little time. I've asked him to get in touch with you.
If he doesn't, we will assume that Rex got to him.
I wish you great wisdom and strength in this
moment. We all trust that whatever you decide, it
will be the right thing, and for the best.

Gratefully yours,
Michael

"Michael," said Patrick aloud even as he realized it
was another stupid pronunciation issue. One said *Ith*, not
Eye-th. *Irth*, not *Ear-th*. And, at least on Eyeth/Ith, one
said *My-Chale*, not *Michael*. Then he scolded himself for
even thinking about something so stupid and small when
he had so much more important stuff to deal with—like
calling his family.

The phone buzzed again and a new message scrolled
down the screen.

The griffin told me to send you greetings, Mr. Griffin!
Ha! BunBun here. Gather you know who I am.
I think I met some of your siblings the day before
yesterday—Cassie and Paul, is it? They are charming
children, and well. From all I can tell, your entire

family is well. But I am going to go make sure of that again before I go off on my mission. Anyhow, can't dawdle, much to do—hope all is well on your end.

P.S. Here's a picture I took with your brother and sister and their friends. Truly adorable. And smart, too.

The screen filled up with a picture of Cassie and Paul, together with the Tondorf-Schnittman twins, and in the middle, apparently the one taking the selfie, a very large rabbit with antlers on its head. A giant jackalope, basically.

Head spinning, he texted **thanks, good luck** in reply.

Something didn't feel right. Was the photo even real? Even if it wasn't a dream, couldn't somebody have faked an image like that? Couldn't it be that somebody was trying to fool him? Of course using a jackalope wasn't exactly the most believable thing in the world, so if somebody was trying to fool him into going along with something then probably that wasn't the smartest thing to do. But maybe that's what *made* it a smart thing to do.

This was all so confusing. Maybe he should just walk away from it. Go talk to those French police and see what would happen. France was a civilized country, after all, they surely wouldn't throw him in jail or anything.

He looked down at the reply he'd just sent to Agent

BunBun and was struck that it was totally lame. He was not texting a friend about an after-school event here—those two happy kids next to the jackalope were his little brother and sister. And no matter what—even in a dream—he couldn't bear the thought of something bad happening to them. Of Rex happening to them.

PLEASE TAKE CARE OF MY FAMILY, OKAY?! he wrote.

He stared at the screen, half expecting that he was going to be told it was going to be hard to protect them if he stayed around and Rex found out he had come back. But the reply was simply, **Of course I will do everything in my power to protect your family.**

Patrick turned to the van parked in the garage behind him and looked through its streaky back window. The floor was scattered with tools and lumber scraps—it wouldn't be very comfortable, but it would do the trick. He gently tried the handle on the right-side door. It yielded with a rough scraping sound but, fortunately, no alarm. He clambered inside, re-closed the door, and got to work. If there was a chance any of this was really happening, then Rex's killers might soon be here and he'd better be prepared to escape back to Ith. Once he'd taken care of that, *then* he'd call his parents. And say goodbye for a long time, and maybe forever.

CHAPTER 58
Remote Control

BASKING IN THE NEATLY PRODUCED STRAINS OF Creed once again, Rex sipped at his kale smoothie and sat back as he continued to examine the maps displaying inside his head. One was of a small commune in the Aquitaine region of France, the other of the densely built suburbs just north of New York City.

Each map was marked with a single orange dot, stationary on the former, moving slowly east on the latter. On the New York map, three blue dots were converging. On the French map, a single purple dot was racing toward the orange.

It might have seemed out of balance to bring three agents on the one and just the one on the other, but the solo agent—Victor Pierre, the highest-scoring novitiate he'd ever recruited—was probably going to execute (Rex smiled at the double meaning) his mission faster and more efficiently than the other three would.

In fact, the New York scenario made him a tiny bit nervous. The enemy combatant had already gotten the better of one field agent, and now it had fled into such a *very* crowded area. The chances of them taking out their target with complete or even partial silence were now slim to none. Not that there weren't media inoculations, counter-stories, and corporate levers that would enable the situation to be controlled, even made advantageous. But, still, it would cause some mess. And mess would need to be cleaned up. And, rather than worrying about cleaning up little spots like this, really he wanted to get on with cleansing the *entire world*.

CHAPTER 59

Momma Don't Play No Games

WHEN THE CALL CAME, MARY MEYER GRIFFIN, Patrick's mother, was already steeled for action.

Her Patrick was still missing. And, as she had just expressed to her husband—after being wakened by a dream of her missing son, in which he was playing a trumpet atop a huge pyramid—she was done being paralyzed by the situation. She was going to do something (anything, everything she could) about it.

She had managed to not let Lucie's teachers label her an artist so they could rationalize her slipping math grades.

She had not allowed Neil to be labeled as a jock, a boy

who was meant for success on playing fields, and none on standardized tests.

She'd not let the mothers in the neighborhood stigmatize Eva as a mean girl.

She had not allowed Carly to be branded a spoiled brat by her friends.

She had not allowed the Twins to be called "special," at least in that condescending sense in which it was said by certain parents in their day care.

And she was not about to allow her least troublesome, most considerate, sweetest-tempered son, Patrick, to entirely disappear from the face of the Earth.

"I'm simply not going to let him remain lost," she said to Rick.

"No, of course not," her husband groggily replied.

They had barely slept the past two nights, talking to the police, talking to relatives, talking to colleagues (their son officially having been gone more than twenty-four hours, neither was going to the office today), talking to friends, and researching missing child cases on the Internet. So it was understandable that they were just waking up like this. It was nearly nine a.m.

Mary put on her slippers and pulled back her hair with a speed that bordered on frenzy. The day was not getting any younger and there was a child to be found.

"Come on, Rick," she said to her husband, still sitting

on the edge of the bed, trying to blink the fog of strange dreams from his own mind.

There was a buzzing noise, and another.

"My phone!" she said.

Rick sat up and watched as she picked it up from its charging dock on the bedside table.

"E-Y-E-T-H it says. Is that somebody we know?"

"Or maybe it's a *company*," replied Rick, entirely awake now. If a telemarketer had had the poor judgment to call his wife at a time like this—

"Here, let me answer it!" he said.

Mary passed him the device.

He pressed the green Answer icon. "Hello!?" he said distrustfully, prepared to let the person on the other end of the line really have it. "Who is this!?"

CHAPTER 60

Long-Distance Communications

T'S ME, DAD," SAID PATRICK.

Enough silence followed that he looked at the screen to make sure the call hadn't disconnected.

"Patrick!?"

"Hey," said Patrick. "I'm okay, Dad. Look, I don't have much time—I gotta get moving—"

"Patrick, it's you! Buddy! What a scare you've given us—are you really okay—where are you, what's going on, where did—"

"Dad," said Patrick, interrupting his father's emotion-strained voice as he tried to fight back tears himself. There was too little time and already the portable censer was frothing on the van's front seat, tendrils of gray-green transcense emerging from its slotted sides and coming up over the console.

"It's too weird to explain but, really, it's nothing bad. I'm safe. Look, just keep an eye on the news for anything really, umm, abnormal, okay? And get gas masks—really good ones with extra filters—for the family, will you? Probably you won't need them anytime too soon, but—"

"Patrick?" said his dad, the timbre of his voice changing suddenly. "Buddy?! What are you talking about? Are you doing drugs?"

"What?! No. Seriously, Dad, I just kind of got into something, not drugs—I know it sounds insane, but there's some bad stuff going on—it's really for the best that I not come home right now."

"Patrick, you're a twelve-year-old boy, what are you talking about!? Where are you!?"

"I think I'm in France, but that doesn't matter right now."

"France? Patrick, look, if you drank some beer, or smoked some pot, it's totally not a big deal. How old are you now? Twelve? Listen, I never told you, but I was only a year older than you when—"

"Seriously, Dad, do me a favor and ask the Twins if they saw a big talking rabbit the other day. Just do that, okay?

And if they say yes, then please know I'm *not* drinking or doing drugs. And that you've got to watch the news, okay? There's a good chance that a very bad terrorist kinda thing is coming; you've got to protect the family, okay? And don't say you heard from me, all right? You'd be in danger if you did. There's this guy named Rex Abraham—though he may be going by another name—"

There was a shuffling sound, and then his mom's strained, breathless voice was in his ears.

"Patrick, my baby," came his mother's sob-racked voice, "are you okay!?"

Patrick felt the tears forming in his eyes but he didn't have a chance to shed any—something very bad was happening outside.

CHAPTER 61

A Flock of Griffins

THAT'S JUST PLAIN FREAKY," SAID NEIL. HE WAS talking about the transplanted crucifix.

"There's a squirrel under here?" asked Lucie, nudging the loose earth with the toe of her Doc Martens.

"Deer Rabbit put it there."

"A cat killed it," said Cassie.

"It was gray," said Paul.

"The squirrel was gray, or the cat was gray?" asked Neil.

"The squirrel!" laughed Cassie.

Lucie had accepted something very strange was going

on but she was still looking for some evidence, some proof, of whatever it was. And, while there was no doubt in her mind that this apparent grave on a golf course island, a quarter mile from their house, was part of it, it hardly put the matter to rest.

For one thing, she certainly wasn't ready to accept that a giant jackalope was running around Hedgerow Heights. It had to have been a man in a jackalope costume. Her brother had been in a car accident, so he probably hadn't had that good a look. And the Twins . . . the Twins were four years old.

"What are you guys doing!?" came a shrill voice behind them.

The four Griffin kids spun around to see two other Griffin kids, Eva and Carly—having tailed them from the house—emerge from their hiding place in the woods.

Eva was looking disgustedly at her little sister. She'd firmly instructed her to stay quiet.

"Well," said Neil as the two girls came down the hill toward the bridge, "we've got a little situation going on. A very *weird* little situation."

"Does it have to do with Patrick?" asked Eva as she got close.

"We don't know," said Lucie. "But it's definitely weird. Like, can't-talk-to-adults-about-it weird."

"Like what?" asked Carly.

But nobody had to explain anything to Carly because Mr. BunBun broke cover then, too, hopping out of the woods from the direction of the Tondorf-Schnittman residence.

"Oh, hello, young people! Would you possibly all be Griffin children?"

CHAPTER 62

Short-Distance Communications

A **LOUDSPEAKER SQUAWKED. PATRICK TURNED TO** look out the van's dingy rear windows.

His mother's pleading voice was coming through the phone but—though he very much wanted to reassure her—it was clearly not a good time to talk. He muffled the binky against his belly as he took in the sight at the end of the driveway.

A tall man was standing there, looking down at—Patrick's stomach dropped as he recognized the object—a binky. Eyes still on the screen, the man slowly turned toward him, but fortunately, before he could look up and see Patrick's face in the van's window, a little French police car came into view behind the man. Its loudspeaker squawked again: *"Arrêtez! Les mains en l'air!"*

The man regarded the police car and scowled, then took off running in the opposite direction, hopping a wall and crossing the field faster than . . . it was just plain freaky how quickly he ran. He moved like something out of a superhero—or, perhaps, a *horror*—movie.

Well, at least there was *seriously* no question what Patrick had to do now.

He lifted the phone and heard his mom sobbing. "Mom!"

"Patrick!??"

"Mom, it's okay, but I gotta go. Don't worry, okay?"

"Patrick—what's happening?!!"

"Mom, shh, I love you." And then, because it seemed like the kindest thing he could say—both for her and for him—he said, "See you soon."

He closed out the phone application, quietly got down on the van's floor, rolled onto his back, and, shoving his binky in his ninja suit's leg pocket, tried not to freak out so badly that he'd screw up the transubstantiation.

He couldn't get past his mind's image of that man running. This was so bad. It had to be one of Rex's killers, one of the ones My-Chale had told him might be here. Who else would have a binky? And who else would be able to move that fast? And if he was this close already—

"Please hurry please hurry please hurry," he mouthed to himself as he forced himself to concentrate on the first of the preparations. But telling yourself to relax was one thing, actually doing it was obviously quite another, especially when you were lying on lumber scraps in the back of a van in a foreign country with a superhuman assassin trying to track you down and kill you.

The van shook. Somebody was trying the driver's-side handle. There was yelling outside. The words were French but not ones Patrick had been taught in school. Angry words. Then there was a very loud noise, brief as a drum-strike—or a gunshot—and then there was screaming, a woman screaming.

Now the van really began to shake, rocking back and forth like it might tip over. And then there was another bang and a ripping noise and Patrick looked up to see an inch-round of daylight had been punched through the door at the back of the van, right near the handle. There was a new smell in the air now, a smell like electricity and smoke.

The preparations, *the preparations!* he berated himself. He willed his toes to relax—

And then another bang-rip, and a new spear of daylight

pierced the van's interior. Terrified, he said the words aloud,

"Four: Do not struggle—let your impulses run free."

But, he wondered, what if his impulse was to get up and clamber out the front door of the van and try to run away? Or to scream his head off in fear? Oh-God-oh-God-please-hurry-please-hurry!

"Hold fast to your mantra."

And hold fast he did, figuring to himself that if "Song of the Stuntman" had worked the last time—

All right
All set
All fright
No net

He heard another hole get punched through the van. And then a sharp, keening noise, as if a sleigh bell's ring had been caught midpeal and stretched out forever.

And then everything went green.

CHAPTER 63

Fool Me Once

THE ORANGE DOT DISAPPEARED FROM THE MAP, but not in a good way. The three agents had failed to locate the rabbit. The enemy combatant had taken advantage of a loophole in the lamentably imprecise local data infrastructure and tricked the agents into looking in altogether the wrong place—there had been nothing inside the Danbury Public Library but useless books and clueless civilians.

It was fine. The clever beast could have another fruitless, meaningless day on the planet. It was nearly time to thin the novitiates' ranks again anyhow, and there would be no significant staffing deficits to bridge, even after culling three more.

Was it inconvenient and annoying? Yes, definitely. But, was it worrying? Not at all.

The entire situation was so clearly a desperate Hail Mary by his enemies. And, again, so very many precautions, plans, and redundant systems had been put in place. He'd anticipated setbacks far, far larger than this.

He was not going to waste another moment thinking about it. A squad of five agents would go out tomorrow, and seven the day after that, and, if necessary . . .

It would *all* be resolved, and soon.

But, the situation in France? Now *that* was a surprise.

The Griffin boy—the one who had been randomly transubbed by the arriving Anarchist, the rabbit, in the first place—had *come back to Earth*?

And then he had *intentionally transubbed back to Ith*?

It seemed inconceivable, but Victor Pierre had gotten positive visual ID and the database had confirmed his vocal identity on the intercepted calls.

But why? Why would random, unintentional boy X from Earth, inadvertently sent to Ith in the first place, have come back to his home world and then—after less than a single dunt—transubstantiated right back?

Two things were clear. First, the boy was receiving help from those idiotic Commonplacers. There was no way he'd figured out how to get back by himself, and certainly Rex's own people hadn't been behind it.

Second, it was clear that his enemies were *investing heavily* in this Griffin boy. Transcense was one of the hardest-to-come-by substances in the whole universe and he knew it wasn't any easier for them to acquire than it was for him. The fact that they had chosen to blow not one but two entire quantities on the child was, to say the least, unprecedented.

He reviewed Patrick Griffin's records again. It was very, very strange. There was absolutely *nothing* to suggest he was special in *any* way. Not off-the-charts on his tests, no signs of leadership, no unusual skills . . . and yet here this had happened?

Well, maybe one other thing was clear: the Common-placers had served their purpose on Ith. They'd been a good foil, a valuable common enemy to keep the populace in line. But now they were starting to do things as unexpected as *this*, their time had come to an end. It was time to re-move them—and this Griffin boy they'd adopted—from the equation.

He'd attend to it himself. It would be nice to be back on Ith for a while—to see firsthand how his vision was progressing.

And his presence here wasn't necessary. The plans were set, the processes in motion. Earth's purge would soon be initiated, and the boring, painstaking cleanup under way. He'd simply rewrite himself into the history afterward, just as he'd done before on Ith.

"Prepare the transubstantiation chamber," he said to the air and then, with something of a smile, "and hold my messages."

CHAPTER 64
Wakey Wakey

THIS TIME IT WAS THE FORCE OF THE SUN ON HIS face that woke Patrick. They were clenched shut, but still its brightness seared his eyes. He put his hand to his brow like a visor as he picked up his head and tentatively cracked his eyes open.

He was in a meadow, or a stretch of prairie. What looked like a derelict gas station was maybe a hundred yards distant. The slanted stumps of telephone poles indicated where a road once had been.

He guessed the transubstantiation had worked. He guessed he was safe. He guessed he was back on Ith.

A bird—a robin—landed near his feet. Its eyes were huge.

"Yep," he said to himself. "Ith."

It felt good, being here. And, yes, it did feel real. But, even if he was wrong—even if his overactive brain was momentarily fooling him into believing all this—he had at least, at last, figured out something more important.

What *mattered* was caring. If you cared, then when a decision had to be made, you made it—you made sure to *do* something. If you didn't care, you wouldn't. It was that simple. If you don't care about something, you might as well be dreaming it. It might as well not exist.

Like, deciding *not* to stay on Earth just now—what had made up his mind had been his caring about his family. Even the chance that staying there would have caused them harm had made the decision clear. There had simply been no choice but to come back to Ith. What would have been the alternative? Getting killed in the back of a van in order (hopefully) to wake up and prove to himself it was just a dream?

It was like what My-Chale had said. This was the way it worked: you gave a crap, and you were awake to the situation around you. Or you didn't give a crap, and you slept—or at least sleep-walked—through it.

So here he was back on Ith away from his family and having no idea when or even if he'd ever see them again.

But at least he had heard his mom's and dad's voices, and at least had seen a picture of the Twins. They were okay. And he was sure Neil and Carly and Eva and Lucie were fine. That was something, for sure.

And didn't he care about Oma and all the others he'd met in the past two days—the poor people in collars and endangered griffins and giants and even Kempton and the big-eyed kids in the school? And therefore wasn't the only thing now to be aware of—to be awake to—the fact that he *might* be able to do something to help them all?

Whether or not it was a dream, he either cared—and showed it by what he did—or he didn't.

That was the answer. You cared about others—*you gave them credit for being as real as you were*—or you didn't. That was all you could hope to know.

He sneezed just then, the sickly sweet stink of transcense smoke all over him.

Which reminded him that My-Chale and Oma had given him instructions to—what was it? He might at last be certain he was awake, but it sure was a very groggy and tired awake. And the sun was so awfully bright. He racked his brain. On Earth he was supposed to call Uncle Andrew and his parents. When he got back to Ith, assuming he came back to Ith, they'd said to—

The binky buzzed in his pants pocket. He pulled it out and saw Oma's face in its screen.

"Remember, My-Chale told you to call the moment you got back," she said.

"Sorry," he said. "I think I'm a little disoriented from all this, umm, traveling."

"Kind of like you just woke up, huh?" she said. He couldn't see it very well but he could hear the smile in her voice, and it felt brighter than the sun on his face.

ACKNOWLEDGMENTS

I have had the good fortune to have made a career in the book industry for—at the time of my writing this—nearly eleven years. If you ever have the chance to join this ancient, mostly impecunious guild, I heartily recommend doing so. People in the book industry are—with a few exceptions we won't dwell upon here—among the best people on Earth. They are well read. They are articulate. They are funny. They are wise. They are generous. They are self-effacing. In fact, they are SO self-effacing that they have pretty much effaced themselves from the public eye and to this day rarely draw credit to themselves, as is done in movies, plays, musical recordings, or video games. There tends to be but one name associated with a book, the author's. And most of us go a long time (often forever) believing that one person—the author—has done the vast majority of the work. I don't mean to be obnoxious in breaking with this genteel vision, but since I'm an author who's labored behind the curtain and knows that every book in the modern era is a result of at least dozens of people and sometimes thousands of hours—and for what it's worth buried here in the hindquarters of this manuscript—I'd like to give a Hollywood-style credit-roll to the very many people who took this author's compulsive labors and made them into the hopefully readable book you now possess.

Director (editor) Connie Hsu
Producer (finding of editor, publishing house, legal counsel) Cindy Eagan
Executive Producers (our judicious financiers) Jonathan Yaged, Simon Boughton, and the Macmillan Finance Team
Cinematography Jake Parker and Elizabeth Clark
Strategic Adviser Bart Rust
Title Inspirer Anneka Rust
Script Advisers Allison Devlin, Steve Westrum, John Cote, Bill Robinson, Lexi Preiser, Lauren Wohl, Pat Strachan, Maya Packard, Linda Jamison, Fiona Brown, Martha Stillman Otis
Unit Directors Emily Feinberg and Kate Jacobs
Distribution The Mighty Macmillan Sales Force and Your Dedicated, Discriminating Local Bookseller

Location Scouting (finder of exciting places for this book to go) Liz Fithian and the Roaring
Brook Publicity Team
Sound Engineers The Macmillan Audio Team
International & Licensing Holly Hunnicutt
Set Design & Production Jill Freshney,
Karla Reganold, and Production Teams
Birthday-Sharer with Mr. Griffin Dick Van Zile
**Mr. Rust's Hair, Wardrobe, Makeup, &
Emotional State** Ruth Rust
Productivity Adviser to Mr. Rust James Patterson
Caterers Sean Ford, Victoria Stapleton, Craig Young
Special Interpreters for Mr. Rust Jonathan Lyons,
Sean Fodera

Don't miss Book 2,

PATRICK GRIFFIN'S
FIRST
BIRTHDAY on ITH

. . . . .

Coming Summer 2017